MURDER FOR BREAKFAST

I placed a large slice of pancake on each plate. "Last night was truly the stuff of nightmares, especially since it was so close to home." I added bacon to the plates and brought them over to the table.

"Close to home! It was right *in* your home." He shook his head and took a seat. "This murder is affecting me more than I care to admit, Linds. How was it done?" he asked. "How did someone get that body on that tree during the filming of a ghost-hunting show?"

I took a sip of coffee and shrugged. "I'm still struggling with *why*, as in *why* would somebody hang the body from my oak tree? It's positively sinister."

"It is," Rory agreed, and began eating his pancake. Although cooking always helped me relax, I found that I wasn't very hungry after all. "Tuck will be going on duty this morning," Rory offered. "No doubt he'll be looking into it. It's the talk of the town . . ."

Books by Darci Hannah

MURDER AT THE BEACON BAKESHOP

MURDER AT THE CHRISTMAS
COOKIE BAKE-OFF

MURDER AT THE BLUEBERRY FESTIVAL

MURDER AT THE PUMPKIN PAGEANT

Published by Kensington Publishing Corp.

A Beacon Bakeshop Mystery

Murder At The Pumpkin Pageant

Darci Hannah

Kensington Publishing Corp.
www.kensington

KENSINGTON BOOKS are published by

Kensington Publishing Corp.
119 West 40th Street
New York, NY 10018

All Kensington titles, imprints, and distributed lines are available at special quantity discounts for bulk purchases for sales promotion, premiums, fund-raising, educational, or institutional use.

Special book excerpts or customized printings can also be created to fit specific needs. For details, write or phone the office of the Kensington Sales Manager: Attn.: Sales Department. Kensington Publishing Corp., 119 West 40th Street, New York, NY 10018. Phone: 1-800-221-2647.

The K and Teapot logo is a trademark of Kensington Publishing Corp.

First Printing: August 2023
ISBN: 978-1-4967-4172-1

ISBN: 978-1-4967-4173-8 (ebook)

10 9 8 7 6 5 4 3 2

Printed in the United States of America

For Barb and Bob Hannah,
my wonderful in-laws,
in loving memory

ACKNOWLEDGMENTS

It's such a great pleasure to be able to write an-other Beacon Bakeshop mystery, especially one that takes place during Halloween. For me, writing these mysteries is all about the journey that brings me to the end of each book, and the people who inspire and help me along the way. There are too many of you to name you all personally. But I thank you!

At this very moment I'm up to my eyeballs in pumpkin baked goods, having baked and sampled so many of them during the writing of this book. It's one of the hazards of the job. Fortunately for me, I have family and friends who agree (most of the time) to be tasters, and to help me improve the recipes that make it into these books. On that note, I'd like to thank my amazing husband, John, and our brave friends, Debbie and Todd Coy, for sacrificing their sobriety in my quest to find the perfect pumpkin pie martini. All I can say about that festive evening is, "Yay! We did it!" To my dear sons, Jim, Dan, Matt, and my lovely daughter-in-law, Allison, who were treated to several versions of a pumpkin cheesecake during consecutive Sunday dinners in July ("Pumpkin cheesecake again . . . in the summer?"), you four are real troupers. Love you all! And the answer to Matt's burning question as to why I make pumpkin pie for Thanksgiving and not pumpkin cheesecake would be . . . tradition? I may have to rethink that one. To my dear friend and neighbor, Erin Heap, for taste-testing my pumpkin sugar cookies. Erin's enthusiasm inspired me to include them in this book. Thanks, Erin! I must admit, they are rather delicious. And to my wonderful mother, Jan Hilgers, who taught me how to bake and to write. You really are the best mom in the world! I can't tell you how much I cherish our morning coffee chit-chats, and all your fun and creative dessert and entertaining ideas. You're the original domestic diva! Keep the ideas coming, Mom! I write and I bake because of you, and Dad.

These books wouldn't be possible without the amazing team at Kensington Publishing. A huge thanks to my gracious and savvy editor, John Scognamiglio, for his enthusiasm and vision regarding this series. To the lovely and amazing Larissa Ackerman, publicist extraordinaire. You are a pure joy to work with, my dear! A huge thanks to Rebecca Cremonese and her team of editors for making the pages of these books look so good. And to everyone at Kensington who works so hard on my behalf, I truly thank you! And to my dear agent, Sandy Harding. Thank you for your kindness, your great advice, and your friendship.

And to my late in-laws, Barb and Bob Hannah, a loving couple with a truly wonderful family. I believe I told you once before, but I'll say it again: thank you for raising such a wonderful son.

And a heartfelt thank you to you, dear readers, for holding this book in your hands. I hope you enjoy your Halloween visit to the Beacon Bakeshop.

CHAPTER 1

Time to make the donuts! Time to make the donuts! That ridiculous sound bite from the old Dunkin' Donuts ads swirled in my head as I sprang awake in the pitch-black darkness. Although it wasn't the first time this plaguing earworm had struck in the wee hours of the morning, I didn't appreciate the irony and tried to thrust the singsong voice from my head, but to no avail. Was it indeed time to make the donuts? As a baker, I embraced early mornings as a rule, even chilly fall mornings such as these (and it was chilly!), because that was my job. I had left the Wall Street world of finance to become a baker in a small town in Michigan. Purchasing an old lighthouse was my own folly, but I loved it. I truly did, even if it was haunted.

I sat up in bed and stared at the time on my alarm clock. I even squinted to make sure I was reading it correctly. One a.m. Not time to make the donuts (and sweet rolls, and coffee cakes, and pumpkin scones . . .). I still had three hours of blissful sleep left. Feeling confused, I was ready to

plop back on my pillows and fall back to sleep.
Then Welly, my giant Newfoundland dog, barked
again.

"What on earth . . . ?" I stared at the noble head
of my dog silhouetted by moonlight streaming
through the window. Then I heard it too. The jig-
gling of a door handle. It sounded like it was coming from the light tower, and not my front door. I
stiffened at the sound and addressed my dog.
"Someone is trying to break into the light tower!"

Welly barked again. I couldn't imagine that whoever was on my lawn trying to break in couldn't
hear him. Welly had a bark to rival thunder.

I sprang out of bed and threw on my thick night
robe. It wasn't only warm and soft as a cloud; it was
pretty enough for the runway. Bless Mom, it was an
Ellie & Co. original. Dressed for an unpleasant
night encounter, Welly and I left the bedroom. My
dog ran ahead of me down the stairs and to the
front door, barking all the way. Although the
racket was coming from the external light tower
door, which was twenty feet from the main lighthouse door, I thought that springing out the front
door just might scare the would-be intruders away.
I paused long enough to grab a flashlight, then followed Welly.

I flung the front door open, shouting, "Get
away! Get away from there!"

Whoever had been rattling the light tower door
handle must have heard us. The moment I swung
the beam of light at the door in question, all I
caught was a swiftly moving black mass that disappeared behind the curvature of the light tower. I
got the impression that there was more than one
person responsible for the racket. I also distinctly

heard a giggle, followed by a swift shushing sound. Likely not the sound of a deranged murderer. Still, my heart was racing like a spooked herd of deer heading for the safety of the forest.

Holding Welly back by his collar, which was no small feat, I cried again in my most intimidating voice, "Get away! This is private property! And it is not funny!"

I waited a whole minute or two before I could muster the nerve to investigate. When my heart was nearly back to normal, I let go of Welly and followed him into the chilling darkness. It wasn't until I rounded the entire light tower and came into the backyard that I saw it. Welly was already there, barking at it like a demon possessed.

"Oh, no way!" I cried as my heart flipped right back into panic mode. Because there, hanging from the bare branches of the old oak tree, was a body. As it gently swayed into the beam of my flashlight, I realized I was staring up at the hideous face of none other than Freddy Krueger!

CHAPTER 2

Halloween was approaching, and someone was finding it hilarious to target my lighthouse with a host of spooky, disrupting pranks. Finding the life-sized dummy of Freddy Krueger, the *Nightmare on Elm Street* icon, dangling from a noose on my oak tree, had, unfortunately, been the first of many to come. I had awakened to find a handful of wispy ghosts once, then a vampire, followed by a spree of generic ghouls in creepy masks. The worst, in my opinion, had been my predawn discovery of Pennywise, the terrifying clown from Stephen King's *It*, swinging from the gnarled branches of my tree. And on more than a few nights, someone kept trying to break into my light tower. They were obviously trying to make contact with my resident ghost, the first lightkeeper, Captain Willy Riggs, the ghouls! Unfortunately, everyone in the village knew my lighthouse was haunted.

I loved fall. I truly did. I loved everything about it, including Halloween. This year, however, as the town of Beacon Harbor prepared for its annual

Beacon Harbor Halloween Bash, my patience was really being tested. The Halloween Bash was the highlight of October, and the Beacon Bakeshop was embracing the celebration with zeal as well. Our pumpkin-inspired baked goods were a hit! I mean, who could resist a fresh-baked pumpkin scone with a pumpkin-spice latte on a chilly fall morning? Not me. I loved fall baking, and I was looking forward to Halloween as well, but, truthfully, I was on pins and needles. I hated having the daylights spooked out of me every morning as I made my way to my bakery kitchen!

Rory, my boyfriend, wasn't as concerned with the spooky pranks as I was. He marveled at the ingenuity and often commented on the creative flare of the spooksters before helping me take down the creepy ghouls and ghosts from my tree. I think he found them funny. After his morning coffee with me, he'd then head off to his warehouse at the marina with a handful of men from the village who were more than willing to offer their two cents. Rory was in the middle of transforming the old warehouse into the Beacon Harbor Aquatic Adventure Center. It was his passion project, and I was proud of him for embracing his dream. But, as I pointed out, no one was pranking his lakeside warehouse with ghouls.

I took great care to decorate the entrance of the Beacon Bakeshop to be inviting during the fall season. A smattering of plump orange pumpkins and dried cornstalks, bound with fall ribbon, decorated the front steps. It was pretty. It set the mood, and yet even this harmless fall décor had been targeted by a plague of spiderwebs and ghosts! As if fighting a very determined tide, I finally took my

barista Tom's advice and left the prankster's handi-
work. But I was quickly losing my sense of humor!

I had complained about the Halloween harassment to my friend, Betty Vanhoosen. Betty, above
anyone else, had her finger on the pulse of Beacon Harbor. She owned Harbor Reality, was on the
town council, was president of the Chamber of
Commerce, and, best of all, she was my friend. If
anybody could help me find the culprits and stop
the harassment, it would be Betty.

"Ooo," she had remarked as she thought on my
dilemma. Betty, always one to embrace the colors
of the season, had walked into the Beacon Bakeshop
wearing a bright orange angora sweater over black
leggings that were tucked beneath tall brown boots.
Although cute, she resembled a fuzzy pumpkin. A
tad ironic, I mused, as she sipped her pumpkin-
spice latte.

"This sounds like the work of high schoolers,"
she said without hesitation. "I'm going to put you
in touch with Leslie Adams. Have you met Leslie
yet?" Before I could shake my head, she sent me a
text with Leslie's phone number. "Leslie is a history teacher at the high school. Not only has she
won Teacher of the Year over a dozen times, but
she also knows every young person in that school.
She's also the teacher sponsor of the senior class.
If any young person is responsible for the de-
bauchery at your lighthouse, Lindsey, Leslie will
know. Call her. And don't forget my cinnamon
roll, dear." I didn't forget the cinnamon roll, and
Betty carried on with her day.

I called Leslie Adams, as Betty had suggested.
That was why I was now driving Rory's pickup

truck back from the pumpkin farm. Leslie and I had formed a plan over the phone.

"Do you really think this ridiculous plan of yours is going to work?" Kennedy asked, looking up from her phone for the first time since leaving the pumpkin farm. Kennedy had come with me to help pick out pumpkins. At least that was my expectation. But who was I kidding? She'd been as much help as Wellington had. While Welly preferred to lick and drool on the pumpkins, Kennedy had just stood there taking pictures of him and sharing them on her social media. Not the best helpers, but they were good company.

"It is short notice," I admitted. "But why not host an impromptu pumpkin-carving party for the senior class at the lighthouse? Halloween is tomorrow, and we now have plenty of pumpkins to carve. Besides, Leslie told me the kids were very curious about my lighthouse."

"Correction, darling. Those teens are curious about your resident ghost." She cast me a wry grin before returning to her phone and her relentless thumb-typing.

"Well, well, Officer Cutie Pie must be chatty today." I tossed her a grin as I turned down Main Street. "Is he bored?" The officer in question was Officer Tuck McAllister, Beacon Harbor's youngest and hottest man in uniform. For reasons I still couldn't fathom, my fashion-forward friend was in a relationship with the humble, hometown young man. I believe the fact they were still seeing each other surprised even her.

"I'm not texting Tucker, darling. He's on patrol, and therefore, according to scary Sergeant Murdock, unless I'm dying, I am forbidden to bother him." She glanced up at me long enough to deliver a cheeky grin. "What I am doing is promoting the Beacon Harbor Halloween Bash. Correction," she added with a pointed look. "I'm promoting the Pumpkin Pageant that Ellie and Company is hosting during the bash. I also have a few other spooky surprises up my sleeve that I'm certain you're going to love." Although she didn't divulge what those spooky surprises were just yet, the look on her face could only be described as coy.

We were back at the lighthouse, and I was in the process of parking Rory's truck when Kennedy inhaled sharply.

"What is it?" I asked, thinking she might have caught a glimpse of Captain Willy leering at her from the panoramic window of the light tower. Kennedy and the ghostly captain were not on the best of terms. His presence spooked her, and part of me thought he took a little pleasure in reminding her that he was in residence too. Whenever Kennedy was with me in the light tower, the captain showed up early for his watch, often with a gust of wind and a flicker of the decorative Edison lights I'd hung there. However, the look on Kennedy's face was not one of horror, nor was it delight, but something in between.

"You're not going to believe this, but I've finally done it."

Turning off the engine, I ventured, "You've finally cancelled your subscription to Gamer Grub?" Although Kennedy was now financially on track and doing very well (after I'd helped her with her shopping addiction years ago), she did have an awful lot of silly subscriptions that billed her monthly for the privilege. Gamer Grub, essentially junk food for gamers, was, in my opinion, the worst of the lot. Honestly, how much effort did it take to walk to the corner market to buy a bag of Doritos rather than having them shipped to you monthly?

"Don't be silly, Linds. That's for Tucker. Do you remember when I was telling you I wanted to do a podcast on ghosts?"

I vaguely remembered the conversation. In fact, due to her ignorance regarding ghosts and saying things like, *"We're safe outside, because everyone knows ghosts can't come outside,"* and her real fear of them, including the captain, I might have even suggested such a podcast. I gave a little nod.

"Well, you are not going to believe this. The Ghost Guys from the Travel Channel are coming here, to Beacon Harbor, tomorrow night to investigate your lighthouse!"

"Wait. What? On Halloween night?" I was having a hard time comprehending what she was saying.

"Exactly! On Halloween night! And I'm going to be doing a livestream video podcast while they summon the spirit of Captain Willy Riggs. This is my spooky surprise. I wasn't sure I was going to be able to pull this off, but I did. Isn't this amazing?"

With my heart inexplicably pounding in my ears, I asked, "Why? Why would you arrange to have ghosthunters here . . . at my lighthouse?"

"Because it's Halloween night, darling, and everyone knows your lighthouse is haunted."

"That's . . . really not a good reason, Ken," I countered as my stomach gave a painful lurch. "And anyhow, how did you arrange to have real TV ghosthunters come all the way to Beacon Harbor?"

"Lindsey, I'm crushed. You underestimate my vast network of connections." Her smile was too quick and too shallow to be genuine. I knew she was bluffing.

"Okay, I will admit I've watched an episode or two of *The Ghost Guys*," I told her, trying to calm my racing heart. This wasn't a lie. Once I realized I was living in a lighthouse with a ghost, curiosity had compelled me to jump on YouTube and go down a ghost video rabbit hole. I looked Kennedy in the eye. "Although the Guys are undoubtedly up on their ghost tech, I doubt they can spot real fashion if it hit them in the face. They're all baggy jeans, printed tees, ball caps, and hoodies. I specifically remember one of the Guys wearing a T-shirt that said, 'Ghosts were people too.' I sincerely doubt they follow you on Instagram."

"Alright," she confessed with a dramatic eye roll. "You got me. It was Teddy who called them. He has the connection, not me. The text came from him. But I'm still doing the livestream podcast."

"Teddy Pratt?" I questioned, staring at her. "My new assistant baker?" The moment I blurted his name, the man in question sprang out of the bakeshop door, as if he'd heard me. He hadn't, of course, but that didn't stop him from bounding to the truck as he waved excitedly. The smile on his face was not only incandescent, but tinged with a hint of pride. *Assistant bakers*, I mused darkly, responding to Teddy with a half-hearted wave. *I really knew how to pick 'em!*

CHAPTER 3

"Sweet, swirlin' pumpkin pies!" Teddy was grinning at the ridiculous load of pumpkins in the back of Rory's truck. He stopped just long enough to give Welly a two-handed ear rub. Welly loved our new addition to the bakeshop. The moment he was out of the truck, he ran to Teddy and leaned his 150-pound frame against the man's legs. Welly groaned in tail-wagging pleasure. "How many pumpkins did you buy, Lindsey?" Teddy raised an eyebrow at me, then released Welly with a pat on the head.

"Every one of them that wasn't rotten, smooshed, or flat-out ugly," Kennedy offered with a grin. "She's reached *favorite customer* status at the farm."

"I'll bet." Teddy grinned.

"I just wanted to make sure we had enough. These are seniors in high school we're dealing with. I shudder to think what would happen if we ran out of pumpkins to carve. Also, I wanted to have plenty for our helpers too, your kids and the

Jorgensons included. Whatever is left, I'm sure we'll find a use for."

"No doubt, but those aren't the best baking pumpkins, Lindsey." Teddy walked to the bed of the truck to take a better look. "I'm surprised the farmer didn't give you a gift card, or a complimentary fruit basket, for buying all these," he teased.

"No gift card or fruit basket, but we did get a complimentary cup of hot apple cider," I told him. "And speaking of apple cider, are those apple cider donuts I'm smelling?" I knew it must be. Teddy and Wendy had been working on the batter when we'd left for the pumpkin farm. The heavenly scent of fried dough comingling with the spicy-sweet tang of apples and cinnamon-sugar was out of this world. Somehow, the crisp fall air seemed to heighten the mouthwatering smell to greater effect. My stomach growled in anticipation. It nearly wiped the unpleasant thought of the Ghost Guys from my mind. *Nearly.*

"Like your pumpkins, Wendy and I might have overdone it a bit in the kitchen," Teddy remarked with a grin. "Don't think we'll be running out of pumpkins or donuts this afternoon."

"That's a comfort," I remarked. "However, before we start setting up for the party, we need to talk about these ghosthunters that are coming to the lighthouse tomorrow."

"What a stroke of luck!" Teddy remarked with eyes twinkling. "Can you believe it? It was very short notice, but the Guys are a class act. A few of the sites they were about to investigate pulled out at the last minute, leaving a gap in their itinerary. When I contacted them about the Beacon Point

Lighthouse, they pulled some strings and decided to make it happen. I guess the lure of a haunted lighthouse—" Noticing the frown on my face for the first time, Teddy fizzled to a stop, cleared his throat, and corrected, "A *supposedly* haunted lighthouse on Halloween night was too much to resist."

"Yes, Halloween night. And that's the problem." As I spoke, a ripple of anxiety moved though me.

Teddy cast Kennedy a questioning look. She heaved a theatrical sigh. "Forgive me," she said with a hefty dose of sarcasm. "I guess I never got around to talking to Lindsey about it."

"What?" Teddy, to his credit, looked truly aghast. "But . . . you said Lindsey was on board with this!"

With arms crossed and a deep, fortifying breath, Kennedy corrected, "What I said was that I was *sure* she'd be on board with it—once I got around to mentioning it to her. Which I just did. I know," she offered with a look of concern, "I'm shocked by her reluctance too. I mean, who wouldn't be elated by the news?"

I raised my hand and wiggled it like a school kid trying to get the teacher's attention. "The owner of the lighthouse, that's who. And anyhow, how do you have connections with these Ghost Guys, Teddy?"

Teddy, in his early forties and standing a good six-foot-two, was thickly built, which one would expect for a baker. He had short, chocolate brown hair and a clean-shaven face that accentuated his sunny personality. However, there was something about his round blue eyes that reminded me of the best assistant baker I'd ever had. They were clear, guileless, and punctuated by laugh lines.

Therefore, when he looked me in the eyes and re-marked, "Lindsey, did you even bother to read my résumé?" alarm bells went off in my head.

"I . . . I did. Of course, I did. You have an excel-lent résumé with a great list of baking skills, work experience, and glowing references." Dear heav-ens, what had I missed?

Having hired my share of *interesting* assistant bakers, to say the least, I decided I needed to be extra-diligent when looking for a new person to fill the position. Although I loved baking with my dad in the mornings, I knew that he and Mom were snowbirds at heart and would be heading to sunny Florida after the holidays. Knowing that baked goods were always in season, Dad had suggested I hire a new assistant baker. I had no sooner put the word out when my friend and fellow shop owner Felicity Stewart came to the Beacon Bakeshop with a glowing recommendation for Teddy Pratt. Felic-ity owned the Tannenbaum Shoppe, but her hus-band, Stanley, owned a software company in Traverse City that catered to wineries, microbreweries, and local distilleries. Teddy's wife, Jessie, had been a powerhouse marketing consultant to many bur-geoning wineries in Napa Valley, until Stanley offered her a position at Tartan Solutions in Sep-tember. His hope was that Jessie Pratt would work her magic on the wineries in Traverse City and be-yond. Jessie accepted his generous offer, and the couple moved their young family to Beacon Har-bor, Michigan.

Teddy, father of two precocious preteens, and with enviable baking skills, had been aimlessly frol-icking around Beacon Harbor until I met him. One look at Teddy, a witty, talented man with child-like wonder in his eyes and a laugh that was infectious, and I practically begged him to come work for me. It really was the perfect fit. Teddy preferred early mornings so he could leave with plenty of time to pick up Willow and Tanner from school. He had given me his résumé, and I had read it, was impressed by it, and had hired him on the spot. I looked at Teddy for help. Thankfully, he obliged me.

"Before I was a baker, I worked in film and video, Linds. It's what I majored in at California Institute for the Arts. All my work experience in film was on the back of the page."

"There was type on the back of the page?" An inexplicable welling of panic seized me. How had I missed it? "All I saw on the back of your résumé was an impressive graphic of a cupcake." Although I knew he had received a BA from California Institute for the Arts, I was so excited to find a worthy baker that I never took a closer look at the back of his résumé.

"Lindsey," Kennedy snapped at me. "Are you mental? Who in their right mind draws a cupcake on the back of their résumé?" She said this as if I were the crazy one.

"To be fair," Teddy interjected with a look of pure innocence, "there is a graphic of a cupcake on the back of my résumé. My cupcake of irony, I call it. After all, I spent all that money on college, only to become a baker. I'm rather proud of that cupcake. Besides looking awesome, it's actually made of very small type, four-point to be exact. That's where I brag about my former career in film and video editing—like the fact that I've worked for both the Discovery and the Travel Channel, and how I've flown all over the word with a camera in my hand, filming such compelling reality TV shows as *The Loch Ness Papers, Dare You to Eat This, Victorian Sewer Tours, My Sasquatch Summer*—spoiler alert, I've never caught a Squatch on camera—and the first season of *The Ghost Guys.*"

"Wow, that's quite a résumé," I said, truly impressed. "And it was all there—in that cupcake? I'm going to have to take a closer look at it." The thought that I needed glasses did cross my mind. I looked at my surprising assistant baker and asked the obvious question. "After all that adventure, why did you become a baker?"

"Well, I was traveling so much with the different film crews that I hardly got to see Jessie and the kids. Willow and Tanner were babies back then, and Jessie did all the hard work. She knew I loved what I did, but we both wanted me home more." He shrugged. "So, I took a leap of faith and quit my job. I then stayed home with the kids while Jessie pursued her marketing career. I knew she was the brilliant one. It doesn't take a genius to hold a video camera while crawling through sewers. I clearly have a few marbles loose, but not Jessie. Anyhow, that's when I started baking. I realized I had a talent for it and took a job at a local bakery once the kids started school."

"So, you really do know *The Ghost Guys.*" For some reason, I was impressed by this.

"Yep. One of the weirdest yet most rewarding shows I've ever worked on, and this coming from a guy who spent two chilly months in Alaska trying to catch a Sasquatch on film."

"Point taken." Kennedy gave him a thumbs-up. "You're a nutter . . . a well-connected nutter, which is why you fit in so perfectly here."

"Apparently, for better or worse." He crossed his arms and shrugged.

Kennedy directed her attention to me. I could tell she was determined to bring these ghost-hunters to my lighthouse. And as I well knew, once my friend fell in love with an idea, she'd embrace it, for better or worse.

"Remember how I'm always telling you there's no such thing as bad publicity?" I stared at her, un-blinking, as she talked. "We all know the light-house is haunted, Lindsey. Why not give the people what they want and be done with it? When my pod-cast goes viral, you'll be thanking me."

Will I? I sincerely doubted it. Battling a flock of unsettling mental scenarios, none of them good, I attempted to remain calm. "In . . . in a few hours I'm throwing a pumpkin-carving party for forty-six high school seniors. At the moment, I don't know which terrifies me more, your livestream ghost hunt, or my party."

"Undoubtedly the teenagers, darling," Kennedy quipped. "They're the real ghouls here."

"I agree," Teddy piped up. "I was a teen once. I get it. Besides, TV ghost-hunting shows are pure entertainment. What's not to love about a couple of guys with a lot of ghost tech poking through an old, spooky building in the dead of night?"

Against my better judgment, I relented. "Alright, you can have your Ghost Guys and your podcast, but first you're both going to help me with my party. The kids will be carving pumpkins, and things are going to get messy. Maybe we can sniff out these little ghouls before they strike again."

CHAPTER 4

With the entire crew of the Beacon Bakeshop working like demons possessed, my impromptu pumpkin-carving party had come together in record time. I was carrying yet another tray of fresh apple-cider donuts to the boathouse, where Wendy, Elizabeth, and Alaina had outdone themselves setting up the Halloween-themed refreshment table, when Rory appeared.

"Quick, take one!" I said and held out the tray.

I hadn't seen my boyfriend since the morning, when I had picked up his truck from the warehouse. Even through his charming grin, I could tell there was a sense of joy and contentment about him that hadn't been there when I'd met him. That was because Rory had been struggling to find a way forward after leaving a career in the military. It's never easy to make life-altering decisions, but he had finally realized what he could do that would make him happy while having an impact on the community he had grown to love. By opening Beacon Harbor Aquatic Adventures, he could teach scuba diving, lead others on expeditions to study the lake from below the surface, take divers out to one of the thousand or so known shipwrecks in Lake Michigan, and maybe even discover more. Then there was the other side of the business, the fishing charters and boat rentals. And if that wasn't enough, he was a reserve rescue diver. Rory Campbell was a handsome man on a bad day. He was a tall man, standing six-foot-four-inches, with broad shoulders, a trim waist, powerful legs, and hair the color of espresso. His eyes were a color of blue to rival the Caribbean Sea, and his smile made me go weak at the knees. But when he was filled with palpable joy, I felt he had no equal. Yes, I was smitten with Rory Campbell.

"Always glad to take one for the team, Bakewell," he teased, plucking a warm donut from the tray. Another thing I loved about Rory Campbell was the face and sound he made whenever he ate one of my baked goods. Technically, *I* hadn't made the donuts, but there was no need to tell him that.

"Oh, my gaaah!" he exclaimed. His eyes rolled back in ecstasy as he chewed. Then, swallowing, he added, "They're still warm! Delicious! I'm starving. Do you have extras?"

Teddy, you brilliant, bonkers baker, I thought. To Rory, I replied, "We certainly do, but don't spoil your appetite for dinner. Mom's making a haunted Halloween supper surprise for us tonight."

"Hate to ruin the surprise for you, Linds, but your dad came to the warehouse today. He told me that Ellie's making mummy hot dogs and pumpkin pie martinis." He stuffed the rest of the donut into his mouth and chewed. "That's model food," he said a moment later. "Glad you're bringing dessert. By the way, I'm on pumpkins, right?" Tom, my excellent barista, and Teddy were also "*on pumpkins*," as Rory had put it, having moved an entire truckload of them to the backyard. "That, and security." This he punctuated by taking a third donut.

"Yes, everyone's helping. The Jorgensons and their kids are here too, and they've brought Clara." Clara was the Jorgensons' pet goat, who was more like a dog than a goat.

"I saw that," Rory remarked, having spied Welly and Clara playing on the lawn by the pile of pumpkins. "Anders was helping me install the air compressor today," he added. "He told me he and Susan were helping with your party. Great job, by the way. Are you all ready for this, Linds?"

"I hope so, but first I have to tell you something. And before you ask, yes, it involves Kennedy."

With arms crossed and black brows furrowed in displeasure, he replied, "Great. I can't wait to hear this."

I quickly told Rory about Kennedy and the Ghost Guys as I brought the donuts to the boathouse. However, instead of being aghast, as I had anticipated he'd be, Rory blew out the breath he'd been holding and grinned.

"Wow, that's actually kind of cool. Totally self-serving on Ken's part, but interesting all the same."

"You're not concerned by it?"

He shrugged his broad, flannel-covered shoulders. "Look, ghosts and paranormal dealings are way out of my wheelhouse. I deal with the living and always have. Sure, I've seen the ghost lights.

They're a phenomenon. But maybe there's another, more reasonable explanation for them?"

"You don't believe Captain Willy is behind the ghost lights?"

Rory took me by the shoulders and softened his gaze. "Look, I've seen the lights flicker in the lantern room when we're up there. I've heard something that sounds like footsteps on the stairs as well. And maybe a time or two I've even caught the hint of pipe smoke. But I've never seen a ghost."

"You . . . think it's all in my head?" My heart fluttered at the thought. Was he right? Were my paranormal experiences in the lighthouse just a result of rumors and suggestions? I entertained the thought a second until my inner voice screamed a resounding, *No!*

"I didn't say that, Linds. All I'm saying is that maybe these Ghost Guys will have a different take on things here."

They might, I thought, but I didn't have time to dwell on what they might find. The high school bus had arrived.

CHAPTER 5

"Leslie Adams?" I asked as the woman in charge alighted from the bus ahead of the class. Being a tall woman myself, standing five-foot-nine and even taller in heels, I was taken aback by her diminutive size. The voice over the phone, although kind, had a commanding ring to it. I had pictured her taller, beefier, and looking every bit of her fifty-something years. Instead, the woman in the hunter-green barn coat and jeans stood barely over five feet. She was trim, youthful, and petite. Her firm handshake and forthright gaze conveyed confidence, and for some reason (call it a busload of teenagers), it put me at ease. Her eyes reminded me of sun-dappled chestnuts and were the same color as her shoulder-length hair, only her hair had a streak of gray in it that framed the left side of her face. She looked cool, confident, and totally in control.

"Lindsey Bakewell, it's so nice to finally meet you in person. This class outing to your lighthouse was a wonderful idea. Again, as I said over the phone, I'm sorry that it's under less-than-ideal circumstances." Here she paused to wave the kids out of the bus. Teddy and Rory were on the lawn, directing them to the large pile of pumpkins.

"I'm excited to get to know them better," I said truthfully, and waved to a few of the faces I recognized from the bakery. In fact, many of the young adults who were crossing the lawn to the pumpkins were familiar. Why did that surprise me? After all, Beacon Harbor was a small town, and the Beacon Bakeshop was a popular place to hang out.

"Hi, Lindsey!"

I waved back at a group of girls, all fresh-faced and seeming to wear the same long hairstyle and flared skinny jeans beneath their warm, fall coats. They squealed with delight as they spied Wellington and Clara.

"Adorbs! My faaavorite puppy! And a goat! Oooo, it's so cute I can't stand it! Here, Welly!" the tall girl with the amber-colored hair cried. A moment later, Welly and Clara were being showered with hugs and smooches.

The pets were a hit with the boys as well. Most of the small-town, wholesome lot were wearing the familiar uniform of either a letter jacket or a rugged, flannel-lined Carhartt jacket, like Rory favored, and blue jeans. I smiled as Rory and Teddy laughed with the teens and gently brought their focus back to the pumpkins.

"They look like a great group of young adults," I said, then nearly choked on my words as the last group marched out of the bus. Kennedy had chosen that moment to appear by my side and helped me save face by focusing her glorious smile on Leslie as she introduced herself. Tuck McAllister,

in jeans and a coat, had walked over to the pumpkins and was mingling with the teens.

"Are . . . those kids dressed for Halloween?" I
ventured, pointing to the group in question. There
were eight of them, a mixture of both boys and
girls, with the girls being the most flamboyantly
dressed. As they descended the steps, I had the impression of a lot of flowing black robes and black
Victorian lace. Hogwarts sprang to mind, but a
darker, less appealing version of that near-preppy
wizard school. The girls wore black lipstick. The
hair color of choice seemed to be either burgundy
or black, and they wore a lot of dangly jewelry.

My expression caused Leslie to look over her
shoulder. Kennedy, with eyes as large as mine
were, I was sure, swiftly crossed herself in the time-
honored gesture of protection. I was of half a
mind to do the same, but Leslie's focus turned
back on me.

"Are they goth?" I ventured.

Leslie shook her head. "Modern-day witches, or
so they tell me. Thanks to a new craze on the internet called witchtok, the interest in the occult
seems to be growing."

" 'Witchtok'? I've never heard of that."

"It's a subculture on TikTok," Kennedy informed
us, frowning slightly at the teens. "It's growing
more popular than cottagecore, goblincore, and my
personal favorite, grandmacore."

"You're making this up." My lips pursed in
charmed skepticism. Kennedy had a way of saying
ridiculous things and making me believe them. I
was certain she was pulling my leg now.

"Actually," Leslie began, "Kennedy is correct.

Honestly, I can't keep up with it anymore. This generation of young adults has grown up with the world-wide-web at their fingertips. Most parents don't even realize what their kids are looking at, or what latest app is vying for their attention. And how could they? If you try to take away a young person's cell phone these days you risk invoking a near-debilitating form of anxiety, or at least that's been my experience."

What she was saying was undoubtedly true. I knew how I felt at the thought of losing my own cell phone. All my contacts, phone numbers, apps, and even credit cards were on that thing! Uber-convenient, but utterly stupid when you think about how vulnerable it makes you. I looked at Kennedy and couldn't even fathom how she'd function if her phone was taken away.

"Do you think those witchtok kids could be behind the pranks?" I asked, watching as the group ambled over to the pumpkins. They weren't in any hurry to participate.

"It's not out of the question," Leslie admitted. "They are fascinated with the spirit world. However, beneath all the flowing black clothing, beneath all the crystals and the zodiac jewelry, those kids are rather gentle souls. They're more into wearing charms for self-protection, performing dances that honor the sprites and fairies who protect nature, and casting love spells on each other, than vandalizing a lighthouse. Think of it like a club of like-minded individuals. What they're into is mysterious, fascinating, and very counterculture, which undoubtedly makes it attractive."

"Rebelling against 'the man'," Kennedy said, arching an eyebrow. "Same story, different clothing, and a different generation."

"Very," Leslie agreed. "See that group of young people over there, the ones who are petting and caressing their pumpkins as if they were pets?"

I looked to where Leslie pointed. "The girls with the green-tinted hair?" It wasn't an uncommon look these days. Lots of people put bright colors in their hair. It looked fun and modern. Heck, even Clara the goat had sported the look for a while, but that was due to Kennedy and her whims, not the goat's.

"And the woodsy clothing," Leslie added. "They're the ones. Big nature lovers. They are obsessed with the woods. They have a foraging club that meets on Saturday mornings."

"That's really cool," I remarked. "What do they forage for?"

"Mushrooms, mostly," she said. "They really know their fungi."

"Bet they're getting high as well," Kennedy added with a cheeky wink.

"Actually, I don't know that they are," Leslie said. "They're really into making fairy doors that they place on trees deep in the woods—"

"For the fairies, of course," Kennedy finished. "That's on TikTok too, though hardly original. My granny's been talking to the fairies since she was a wee girl."

"Why do I find that interesting?" I quipped, looking at my friend.

"They've started selling the mushrooms they gather," Leslie informed us. "Some of them, like the chaga mushroom that grows on birch trees, are becoming quite popular on the foodie scene, and can fetch quite a good price. There's also the puffball, my favorite."

"You really know a lot about these kids," I remarked, looking at the lively older woman in front of me. "Betty told me you've been teaching at the high school for nearly thirty years. You know kids. You must have some idea who is behind the pranks."

Leslie's forthright eyes held to mine. "In many ways, these kids are like my own children. There are forty-eight this year in the senior class, and I've taught every one of them history since the ninth grade. They are all good kids, even if some of them don't know it yet. Let's just say, they all have their secrets, but unless I have hard evidence of wrongdoing, I would never accuse any of them. So, we'll just try to impart a little empathy by teaching them about what you've been trying to accomplish here, coupled with the history of this fascinating building. Hopefully, that will do the trick."

"That's very wise of you," I told her.

"See this gray hair?" She picked up the lock of white hair that framed her face. "This is wisdom. And I've earned every single strand of it." We smiled with her at the joke. She released the hair and let it fall back into place before changing the subject.

"Betty told me your boyfriend is opening a scuba shop. How exciting. I'm a diver myself. I must talk with him. One of my favorite topics I cover during senior year is the history of the Great Lakes. We don't spend too long on it, but the kids love it. There's a lot of history here, both above and below the water. Your lighthouse is part of that history as well."

It certainly was, I mused, watching as the teacher headed for Rory and the boys. And if all went as planned, I was going to be imparting some of that history very shortly, for better or worse.

CHAPTER 6

"Well, as the saying goes, *The best laid plans o' mice an' men often go awry*," Rory teased, paraphrasing the famous line from a Robert Burns poem. He opened the rear door of the Jeep for Wellington, who promptly jumped in and plopped down on the backseat. Rory shut the door and held me in a pointed look. "In your case, we all know that Kennedy is clearly responsible for *awry*."

"As always." I gave a theatrical eye roll, then placed a foil-covered tray of pumpkin squares behind the backseat next to the bakery boxes containing the pumpkin-spice cupcakes and apple cider donuts. I was loading the desserts for Mom's little Halloween dinner, our second event of the day. I secured the tailgate and headed for the driver's seat. "Ken has a real knack for *awry*. However, until the very last few moments of the party, I'd say it was a success. Did you see all those pumpkins?" This I asked as I got behind the wheel. Rory was already beside me, buckling his seat belt. I continued, "Once the kids settled down and had some refreshments, they really got into the spirit of the party. Say what you will about smartphones and Google searches. I credit the internet with inspiring some of those creative pumpkins."

"Are we, by chance, referring to the *sick* pumpkin?" Rory raised a teasing brow as he asked this.

Unfortunately, I had just started the Jeep when the now-infamous pumpkin sprang into my mind. As one could imagine, throwing a party for seventeen- and eighteen-year-olds had its challenges. For instance, the enthusiasm level for carving pumpkins was met with varying degrees of effort. One young man made two small eyes at the top of his pumpkin and a giant rectangle for the mouth, which took up most of the body of the pumpkin. Another felt a triangle was all his pumpkin deserved. Yet there were also hissing cats, ghosts, monsters, scary faces, cute faces, clever designs, and, yes, one young man had even made his pumpkin look like it was vomiting by his clever use of pumpkin goo and seeds. Even with inspiration coming from the internet, I felt it took talent to pull off some of those designs.

"That one made me laugh," I admitted as we drove down Main Street. "However, my favorite was the young lady who carved the forest scene into her pumpkin, complete with giant mushrooms. I've never seen that before. That girl was an artist. I'm glad most of the pumpkins are being entered in the village jack-o'-lantern contest. Some stand a real chance of winning."

"The vomiting pumpkin has my vote," Rory remarked, then reached into the backseat to give Welly a rub on the head. "However, all your hard work went out the window when Kennedy made her announcement."

I gave a small huff at the memory. And it had been going so well up until that point too!

After my history lesson, where I talked about the lighthouse, some of its keepers, and a few of the heroic rescues that had occurred just off Lighthouse Point, Kennedy stirred the pot, so to speak, by announcing her live podcast on Halloween night. But that wasn't all. Whereas I had downplayed the supposed haunting of my lighthouse, Kennedy, my near-permanent houseguest, had proceeded to tell the kids some hair-raising personal experiences she'd "supposedly" had . . . and lived to tell the tale.

"*One time I was taking a shower when I felt someone touching my hair. I spun around and found all my loofahs on the shower floor!*" she had told them. Could it have been that she had knocked the loofahs off the shower caddy herself and one bounced off her head as it fell? Regardless of a simple explanation, every girl in the class shivered.

"*I was enjoying a glass of wine one night in the light-room when the glass suddenly fell off the sill and crashed to the floor, spilling wine everywhere and ruining my new sandals.*" Heaven forbid! However, could it have been that her foot, propped on the same window-sill next to said wineglass, slipped? Because that really happened.

And my all-time favorite: "*I had put my linen pants on the chair in my room. I popped into the bathroom for only a moment* (half hour if it was a minute!), *and they were gone. I found them later that day on the floor by the fireplace downstairs, crumpled in a heap, and cov-*

ered in slimy ectoplasm." I have never seen ectoplasm (is that even a thing?), but I am an expert on drool. Wellington has a habit of moving laundry and unguarded clothing around the house when I'm in the bakeshop. It keeps him busy.

"It was a captive audience," I told Rory, staring at the darkening sky through the windshield. Shorter days were one of the more depressing aspects of fall. "She was fishing for more subscribers. Heaven help us, but it will be live on her Instagram feed and her YouTube channel."

"Then we can only hope Captain Willy makes a guest appearance." Casting a sideways glance, I caught his devilish grin. "Maybe he'll pop out of a closet . . . or appear at the top of the lighthouse stairs. Something like that would literally unhinge her."

Why did that thought make me giggle? "She'd flip," I agreed. "She'd drop her microphone and run away."

"I'd watch that." Judging from the look on his face, he was relishing the thought.

"Me too," I admitted without hesitation. "She's always telling me there's no such thing as bad publicity. Would that be bad publicity, do you think?"

"It wouldn't be good." He chuckled as I pulled into my parents' crowded driveway. "But it would be entertaining."

Welly, knowing exactly where we were, started to whine.

"Those poor Ghost Guys don't know what they're in for," I remarked, steering around a string of parked cars. "Between Kennedy and the captain, it might be their most memorable investigation ever."

"And this just might be one of our most memorable Ellie Montague Bakewell dinners ever," he remarked as he pointed to the grand front entrance of Mom and Dad's beautiful lakeside home.

Soft lights, from above and below, illuminated Mom's spectacular fall decorations. The wide stone steps were tastefully outlined with large black lanterns aglow with candlelight. There were hay bales, large baskets of mums, and pumpkins in varying sizes and colors flowing down the steps. On the two front porch pillars stood thick sheafs of dried cornstalks tied with festive ribbon, and by the door stood a life-sized witch, complete with pointed hat and a black cape covered in pumpkins. It looked like she was pointing her wand at us. I thought that Mom had outdone herself, until the witch moved.

"Yikes!" The peep escaped my lips as I stepped on the brakes.

"You've finally spied her," Rory remarked. "Is it just me, or are you having a bad Harry Potter flashback as well?"

I looked at the unmistakable platinum-blond bob beneath the tall black witch's hat, and the chubby figure partially hidden by the black cape. "That's Betty Vanhoosen!" I blurted, thinking how perfectly she'd fit in with Mom's decorations. It was then I noticed that Betty was moving her lips as she wiggled her wand at us. "Either Professor McGonagall over there is casting a spell on us, or she's trying to tell us where to park. Wait. No. I'm wrong." At that moment a man-sized scarecrow stepped from the shadow cast by one of the pillars. At first, I thought it must be Doc Riggles, Betty's medical examiner boyfriend. But the scarecrow was taller than Doc, and thinner.

"I'm parking here," I said, pulling under a tree

on the lawn. Welly's whining had escalated into a pitiful, earsplitting moan, and I could hear his giant front paws kneading the backseat in excitement. "I think Betty's talking to that scarecrow."

"Lindsey," Rory uttered, his face pinched with concern, "were we supposed to come in costume?"

CHAPTER 7

"Yoo-hoo, Lindsey, Rory! Over here!" Betty waved her wand as she called to us in the growing darkness. She looked adorable as she bounded down the steps on her sparkly red pumps. I couldn't help myself from smiling. She greeted Welly at the bottom and waited for us to catch up to my giant dog. Welly, always excited to visit Mom and Dad's house, couldn't wait to go inside and play with Mom's little West Highland white terriers, Brinkley and Ireland, collectively known as the models. As he stood at the foot of the steps, patiently waiting for us with swishing tail, I silently wondered if he was supposed to have come in costume too. Mom would be crestfallen.

"I saw your Jeep," Betty explained. "You're the last ones to arrive. Where are your costumes?"

"Ahh . . ." It had been an exhausting day, and I really couldn't remember hearing anything about dressing up for Mom's Halloween dinner. Although I supposed the fact that she'd called it a "*Halloween dinner*" should have tipped me off to the obvious.

"We're saving them for tomorrow," Rory glibly replied. "Can't ruin the surprise." He raised the boxes of cupcakes and donuts he was carrying as we walked up the front steps to where Welly was being greeted by the lanky scarecrow.

"The theme was witches and scarecrows," Betty informed us with a frown. "Ellie figured you'd be so busy that you'd forget. There's an extra hat in the foyer for you," she informed me. "You, Rory dear, are out of luck. Now, there's somebody I'd like you two to meet."

The scarecrow in question, having just met Wellington, stepped forward to greet us.

"What an impressive beast. Jordy Tripp," he said, taking Rory's proffered hand. I shifted my tray of pumpkin squares and shook his hand as well.

Although I was certain I had never met this man before, there was a familiar ring to his name, causing me to wonder if he was an old friend of Dad's. *Not a contemporary*, I mused, noticing that the face under the floppy-brimmed hat had a youthful appearance to it, despite the fine lines around his eyes and mouth. I placed him to be in his late forties or early fifties. He was nearly as tall as Rory and had the body of a long-distance runner. I had to admit, he made a good scarecrow.

"I met Betty a while ago," he continued with a pleasant smile. "I came to Beacon Harbor on a research trip and stumbled upon Betty's Realty office. Ms. Vanhoosen is a font of local knowledge."

Under the dim porch lights, I believe Betty blushed. "Oh, Jordy, you flatter me." Turning to us, she added, "Jordy is a famous fiction writer."

"That's it!" Rory's eyes came alive with recognition. "You write the Matt Malone novels. I've read some of them. They're thrillers, Linds," he said to me, clearing up that little mystery. "I'm a fan. What are you doing here in Beacon Harbor?" Rory asked the author.

"He's doing research for a new book he's writing," Betty answered for him. "Isn't that right, Jordy?" The scarecrow nodded in agreement.

"Another Matt Malone novel?" Rory's voice was tinged with excitement.

"Actually, no," Jordy remarked. "I thought I'd take a break and try a nonfiction book this time. I really think, if the research pans out, it will have all the excitement and drama of a thriller."

Heeding Welly's silent but insistent door-nudging, I was about to open the front door when I stopped and turned to face the author. "And you're doing research here? In this sleepy little village?"

"I think you'll find, Ms. Bakewell, that every sleepy little village has secrets worth killing for."

Although it was nearly Halloween, I found this statement to be utterly chilling. What could Beacon Harbor possibly be hiding that was worth killing for? With an inward shiver, I attempted to push the thought from my mind.

For Welly's sake, I opened the front door. Inside, I could hear the hum of pleasant chatter, the tinkling of laughter, and the smells of delicious food as they wafted my way. I was about to follow my dog inside when Betty chimed in. "Isn't it just intriguing? Oh, and Jordy is particularly interested in your lighthouse, Lindsey."

I stopped so fast that Rory bumped into me. "*My* lighthouse?"

"Yes. It's of particular interest to me."

I noticed the spark of enthusiasm in the author's eyes as he said this. I didn't quite know what to say to that, but Rory did.

"I'm afraid, Mr. Tripp, that you're going to have to take a number. Lindsey's lighthouse is booked through the weekend."

CHAPTER 8

My alarm went off at half-past three. I silently cursed myself for overindulging at Mom's Halloween party and attempted to roll out of bed. Although I knew I was in for an early morning of baking, between Mom's spooky spiked punch and Dad's pumpkin-pie martini, I couldn't help myself. Also, if I was being totally honest, there was a part of me that had been trying to forget about the Ghost Guys and their impending visit to my lighthouse. Kennedy had announced the news at Mom's party. Everyone there had been agog, everyone but me, that was. Even now, like the buzzing of my alarm, the thought was pinging around in my brain like a tiny wrecking ball, hitting me with one terrible thought after another. It was Halloween, I reminded myself. Today was the day, and I was just going to have to trust Kennedy on this one.

As I sat on the edge of my bed, attempting to pull myself together, Welly plopped his big head in my lap. It was dark, but I could tell his soulful eyes were urging me on. I ran my hands over his silky ears, then kissed him on the nose.

"Thanks, buddy. I'm going to need all the encouragement I can get today," I whispered. "And you might need some encouragement too. After all, we're marching in Mom's Pumpkin Pageant." Welly, thankfully, had no idea what I was saying. I cast one last, wistful glance at Rory, curled up in a pile of blankets and sleeping as if he hadn't a care in the world, then headed to the shower. No Halloween costume for me this early in the morning. Welly, if he could understand all my words, would be happy about that too.

Once dressed in comfy baking clothes, Welly and I headed downstairs, where I paused long enough to put on a jacket and grab a flashlight before walking out the back door.

It was a cold, black morning with fog so thick that Wellington disappeared the moment he cleared the back steps. Although I couldn't see him, I could hear his dog tags jingling as he trotted across the yard, heading, no doubt, for the lake. I pulled up the collar of my jacket, turned on the flashlight, and followed.

The fog was so dense that my flashlight was virtually useless. I kept it on, however, because I reasoned that the beam could be seen by Wellington. It also kept me on the trail as I made the familiar trek to the beach.

Early mornings were quiet. It was part of the reason I liked them so much. I could hear myself think. However, walking through a dense fog with only the faint tinkling of dog tags and the gentle lapping of waves to guide me, it felt surreal—like I was walking through both time and space. I then thought about the lightkeepers who had stood on this same spit of land over a hundred years before me and wondered how difficult their lives must have been. Oh, the things they must have seen, I mused, then turned my thoughts to Captain Willy Riggs.

He was still here. I was certain of it. That very thought caused me to turn in the direction of the lightroom. I could only imagine how the great light shining forth from the lighthouse had tried to penetrate such foggy darkness. I had read that for mornings such as these, they rang a fog bell. Everything in the direction of my lighthouse was dark. I couldn't even see the lighthouse through the fog. But I did offer a silent wish for the legendary ghost lights of Beacon Harbor to be permanently extinguished. My belief was that Captain Willy was still on duty. Whenever he sensed danger, the eerie green light would shine from the old lightroom, often resulting in me finding a body. I didn't presume to understand how they worked, and I didn't necessarily want the captain to leave the lighthouse either. But I certainly didn't want to find any more dead bodies.

Welly, finished with his sniff-and-dash morning business, came beside me then, and together we made our way back to the lighthouse.

However, before I went to the bakery kitchen, I walked over to the giant oak tree in my backyard to see if it had sprung any more "ghosts" in the night. The beam of my flashlight hit the bare branches, and I breathed a sigh of relief. Apparently, my little gathering with the teens had worked.

I took a handful of pumpkin Beacon Bites (our dog cookie flavor of the month) and gave them to

Wellington for being such a good boy. And he was a good boy as he plopped himself down between the doorway of the café and the bakery, where he gobbled up his treats. Wellington, being so fluffy and drooly, wasn't allowed in the kitchen while I baked, for sanitary reasons. So, my big fella stayed in the café until we opened. Then he was put back in the house, where he could eat his breakfast in peace.

I turned on some music, then got to work on a large batch of pumpkin scones with cinnamon-maple glaze. Pumpkin was our seasonal scone and had become such a favorite breakfast treat that we couldn't keep them in the bakery cases for long. It being Halloween, I thought I'd make an extra-large batch.

Scones were so easy to make, and they tasted great. Using the industrial mixer, I blended the flour, brown sugar, baking powder, salt, cinnamon, and our premixed pumpkin-pie spice. I then cut in cold butter until it was the size of peas. After that came a gentle mix with the wet ingredients: cream, eggs, and the all-important pumpkin purée. The trick to having a moist scone was not to over-mix the dough. You wanted it a little sticky so that it could be shaped on a flour-covered cutting board before going into the oven. Also, scones didn't need to be baked very long. That was because the oven temperature was hot, ensuring a nice crispy outside while the insides remained moist and fla-vorful. I measured out a pound of dough and formed it into a 9-inch circle that was an inch thick. Then, using my chopping knife, I divided the dough into eight even wedges and placed them on a parchment-lined baking sheet. I repeated the process until all my baking sheets were full, then sent the first batch into the oven. With five trays of scones baking, I then pulled a large metal bowl from the rack and began making the cinnamon-maple glaze.

I'd always felt that a scone without glaze was a missed opportunity. Kennedy could argue that all she wanted to, being English and having grown up on "proper English scones," which, in my opinion, were essentially a crumblier, denser version of a biscuit. My scones were an American interpretation, and I always took the opportunity to add a delicious glaze. The maple extract, cinnamon, and heavy cream added to the simple powdered sugar base not only tasted delicious but also served to enhance the pumpkin flavor of the scone. In short, it was Halloween heaven.

The scones were cooling on the rack, and I was rolling out a batch of our famous cinnamon rolls, when Teddy came through the kitchen door. Welly sat up and barked with excitement.

"Mornin', matey. Are ye ready for our big day? What?" he said, after hanging his long red coat, hat, sword, and hook, on the coatrack, "I was expecting a proper pirate and I get this? Why are you not in costume, Lindsey?"

Teddy had walked through the door wearing an eye-catching Captain Hook costume, complete with a long, flowing black wig and eye patch.

"You look amazing," I said, grinning at him. "Are you going to take off the eye patch, or are you going to bake in character this morning?"

"Why, matey, Captain Teddy Pratt will join ye in the galley, but first I'll take off me eye patch and ruffle the ears of yon cur. Hark, is that coffee I smell?" He put a cupped hand to his nose and took a sniff. It made me laugh.

"Oh, dear heavens, Teddy," I remarked with a grin as the baker sauntered like a drunk pirate to pet my dog. He was in character, and knowing Teddy, he would be in character all day. Welly, of course, loved it. Teddy then took a slight detour to the coffeepot and poured himself a mug of the breakfast blend I had brewed. He turned to me, winked his good eye, then took a sip. The man should have been an actor.

"And does Captain Teddy Pratt remember how to make apple-cider donuts?" I asked.

"Sink me, lassie! Does the crow fly into the wind?"

"I imagine a crow flies wherever it wants to," I answered with a laugh. "I hope that's a yes, or else it's going to be a long morning." I tossed him a red apron, adding, "I'll put on my costume right before we open. I don't want it to get covered in flour."

"Great idea, having the whole crew at the Beacon dress as pirates. Does Ellie know?"

"Not yet," I told him. "And won't she be surprised when she sees this motley crew marching down Waterfront Drive with our pirate dog mascot!"

CHAPTER 9

The Beacon Bakeshop was open for business, and our customers were delighted with our costumes—no one more so than Betty, who, no doubt, would pass the word along to Mom the moment she finished her cinnamon roll. It didn't matter. I was so proud of my staff for embracing our Halloween theme and for keeping it a secret. The girls looked darling as they manned the bakery counter. Wendy was wearing a long peasant skirt, a puffy-sleeved blouse, and a big red sash around her waist. She had a smaller scarf tied around her head. All the girls were wearing them.

Alaina's skirt was a little shorter than Wendy's and had a jagged hemline to give the impression it had been ripped by the wind. She also wore a puffy-sleeved shirt but had worn a fitted black vest over it. Both ladies looked fabulous.

Elizabeth, putting a modern spin on her pirate outfit, wore black yoga pants with knee-high black boots and a fitted red-and-gold vest over her long white shirt. She was making specialty coffee drinks beside pirate Tom, in his red-and-white-striped shirt, red bandanna, and pirate facial hair. Both looked thoroughly disreputable. Ryan, who'd been working in the kitchen with Teddy, par-baking loaves of bread for next week, had dressed like Tom's twin, only his shirt was blue. As for me, I had splurged on a light-blue-and-gold brocade long coat, which I wore over a fancy pirate blouse. I also had on black yoga pants, knee-high black jackboots, and a captain's hat. I had even curled my thick blond hair and worn it long. Most piratical, indeed!

While I was working the register, Leslie Adams came into the bakeshop with four young ladies I recognized from my pumpkin-carving party. They were the girls I'd have termed "popular," and conventionally pretty. Like most of our customers, they were also in costume. In my opinion, the best part about working on Halloween was all the costumes. Some were clever, some were scary, and some were a total mystery to me. But the little kids who came in with their parents were utterly adorable! Our Halloween treat was a free apple-cider donut.

Although I wasn't a fan of clowns as a rule, Leslie's bright, florescent-colored, harlequin-clown costume was very eye-catching. There was nothing sinister about the hot-pink, bright-yellow, vibrant-green, and orange baggie onesie with ruffles. Atop her red wig sat a hot-pink top hat. Her sparkly heels were the same color. Trixie, her little white poodle, wore a matching tutu and top hat. Both Leslie and her pup looked amazing.

"Pirates," Leslie said with a nod of approval as she came to the counter. The girls who accompanied her were dressed like M&M's, each one wearing a different color candy shell. It was very clever. "I love your costumes," Leslie remarked at the counter. "I take it that you and the crew are marching in the Pumpkin Pageant?"

"You betcha!" I answered with a grin. "We are the pirates of the Beacon. We're pretending this is our ship," I told Leslie and the girls as I waved a hand around the crowded bakeshop. "Kennedy and my mom are running the event, so we really had no choice but to dress up. However, I think they are both going to be surprised when they see us."

"To be sure! You'll definitely turn heads," Leslie remarked. "We're all entering the pageant too. But first we came to deliver a little thank-you for that wonderful party you had for us last night." As she spoke, one of the girls handed me a gorgeous bouquet of flowers with a thank-you note. I was touched.

"It was my pleasure," I told them. While Alaina took their orders, I put the bouquet of flowers in a vase on the back counter along with the card. Then I put a complimentary pumpkin scone in a bag for Leslie along with a Beacon Bite for Trixie, who was sitting like a little princess in the crook of Leslie's arm. I then walked with her to the self-serve coffee bar, where I told her how happy I was to find that my lighthouse had survived the night, unscathed.

Leslie looked a bit pale, but she smiled nonetheless. "Lindsey, I'm so glad to hear that. I truly thought that would be the case. Like I said, they're good kids, even if some of them don't know it yet."

"Do you like flavored coffee?" I asked, ready to

fill a mug for her. Although all the specialty coffee drinks were made behind the counter, the Beacon had a coffee bar for those who preferred to make their own hot beverage. Along with hot water for tea, we offered three different coffees, including our Beacon Breakfast Blend, a smooth medium roast that could be enjoyed all day. Then there was Fog Bell, a rich Sumatra dark roast, and for the adventurous coffee drinker, we offered a flavor of the month. This month it was Pumpkin Pie. "We have a delicious pumpkin-flavored coffee that not only goes well with the scone, but in my opinion, is also the perfect Halloween brew."

"It smells delicious, but I'd better not. My stomach was giving me fits last night. I'm taking it easy today. I'll save the scone for later." Leslie lifted the pastry bag in her free arm, while holding her adorable dog in the other. "This morning we took some of the pumpkins from yesterday over to the jack-o'-lantern contest. The young people were very excited about that. I really want to thank you again for last night, Lindsey. I especially enjoyed all the lighthouse history you shared. You're not only knowledgeable, but trustworthy. Which is partially why I'm here this morning. There's something else I'd like to talk with you about..." Whatever the subject was, a troubled look crossed her face. Leslie, although dressed like a clown, was a confident woman. That's why her look set me on edge. However, just as Leslie was about to say something else, Trixie let out a loud yap. Startled, we both turned to the door.

The bakeshop was packed. Another group of teens was coming in, just as the M&M's girls were trying to leave. Greetings were exchanged, along with laughter. Behind the chatty teens came a group of adults, including a tall scarecrow I recognized. It was the novelist, Jordy Tripp. The moment he spied me, he waved.

"You're swamped," Leslie remarked in apology. She shifted Trixie in her arm and adjusted the pastry bag. "Thanks for this, but I've gotta run. We'll see you at the Pumpkin Pageant."

I had just set the empty mug of coffee in the bus tub that rested on the trash can cabinet when the author appeared. "You've actually converted this lighthouse into a bakery!" The way he said it, I could tell it wasn't meant as a compliment.

I turned, smiled, and said, "You were warned."

"I had it pictured differently. In my mind, your bakery was a vendor's cart of baked goods standing beneath the eaves of this historic lighthouse. Pleasant, but not invasive. You've knocked down walls."

I wasn't sure where the scowling scarecrow was going with this, but I didn't have the time to puzzle it out. As Leslie Adams had noted, we were swamped. So I replied, "Guilty as charged. Isn't it gorgeous?"

"But this . . . this lighthouse is a piece of history." It was a patronizing statement, even more so coming from the mouth of a straw-headed scarecrow. It was hard to take the man seriously, but I did.

"Mr. Tripp, this lighthouse was abandoned and severely neglected when I bought it. It *is* a historical building. I'm giving it a second act as a bakery."

I picked up the bus tray and was heading for the kitchen when he stopped me.

"Did you find anything . . . anything hidden in the walls when you knocked them down?"

I thought he was joking, but one look at his face told me he was quite serious. I pretended to think. "Aside from a sack of doubloons and a treasure map, nothing of note that I remember."

I watched as his jaw momentarily dropped. Then, perhaps noticing that I was dressed as a pirate captain, he blew out a breath and smiled. "Forgive me. I'm sorry. It's just that I'm quite passionate about the project I'm working on, and I get very single-minded. As I mentioned at your parents' party, I would love a tour of your lighthouse sometime."

"Lindsey," Wendy called to me from the busy bakery counter. "Just so you know, we're nearly out of donuts, and there's only a half of tray of Danish left. Also, the pumpkin chocolate-chip muffins are running low."

"Okay, thanks," I told her, then checked my watch. We closed at noon on Sunday. It was too late to make more, but I did have a tray of cranberry orange muffins cooling on a rack in the kitchen.

"I'm sorry, this is a bad time," I told Mr. Tripp. "I'll tell you what, come back Monday at one o'clock and I'll give you a tour. Then you can tell me what exactly it is that you're working on."

With the scarecrow appeased, I headed for the kitchen.

"Well, maties, that about wraps it up at the Beacon," Teddy declared, sauntering through the kitchen door the moment the bakery was closed. "The Pumpkin Pageant's about to begin. Isn't that right, Captain Lindsey?"

"That it is, Captain Teddy." I gave a nod and was just about to cross to the door that led to my private half of the lighthouse, when it opened, revealing a stunningly handsome pirate version of Rory Campbell. I was sorry to say, but in that moment, I had tunnel vision. Everything else faded to black but the sexy, swashbuckling pirate before me, carrying a treasure chest. Wellington stood beside him, wearing a pirate hat on his head and a red bandanna tied around his thick neck. He wasn't even trying to shake off the hat, which was a good sign. Welly had the honor of pulling the cart that held our fake treasure chest as we marched in the Pumpkin Pageant.

Shiver me timbers, but there was something compelling about a man in a loose-fitting, linen shirt and old-timey pants. Unlike Teddy in his Captain Hook getup, Rory had more of a rugged Captain Jack Sparrow air to his costume with his dark-gray greatcoat, black pants, and knee-high buccaneer boots. Like Tom and Ryan, Rory was also sporting fake facial hair, an earring, and a red sash. He made a very good pirate. Apparently, from the look he was giving me, he approved of my lady pirate outfit as well.

"Ahoy, Captain Campbell!" Teddy greeted the moment Rory crossed into the café.

"Cap'n." He gave a nod to Teddy. "Cap'n." He grinned, giving a nod to me as well. "I don't mean to pull rank here, but I actually am a captain. Which makes me *the captain*." This was accompanied by a look that could only be termed piratical.

"Maybe, but I own the Beacon," I countered, placing my hands on my hips.

"And I own this sweet Captain Hook costume," Teddy remarked, mimicking my stance.

"But I have the treasure." Rory looked to the amused pirate staff for support.

"Captains," Tom piped up. "No offense, sirs, and ma'am, but I won't be the measuring stick for this spitting contest. We're all pirates of the Beacon. It takes three captains, five crewmembers, and a dog to run her . . ."

"And run we must," Wendy chimed in. "The Pumpkin Pageant is about to begin!"

CHAPTER 10

After hitching Wellington into his treasure cart, our motley crew left the bakeshop and headed down the festively decorated Waterfront Drive. After a foggy start, I was happy to see that blue skies had prevailed, making it another crisp, yet beautiful autumn day in Beacon Harbor.

If the Beacon Bakeshop had been crowded, then the town was a perfect hive of activity as residents and visitors alike celebrated Halloween at the Beacon Harbor Halloween Bash. Nearly everyone we saw was in costume. If they weren't manning one of the many booths that filled the middle of the street, selling fresh fall produce, caramel apples, popcorn, sugared nuts, or some other delicious treat, or they weren't costume judges, it was safe to assume they were entering the costume parade that Mom had cleverly rebranded the Pumpkin Pageant.

As we passed beneath the colorful banner denoting the Halloween celebration, heading to Ellie & Co. to register for the judging, I was so busy eyeing the produce carts that Wendy had to nudge me to get me to notice that people were applauding our group, or, more correctly, Wellington and his treasure chest.

The moment Mom saw us approaching, she beamed with delight. As I had suspected, Mom was wearing the same witch costume from the night before, and just like last night, she was rockin' it! Brinkley and Ireland, who had appeared from under the table to greet Wellington, were wearing identical witches' hats with matching black and purple capes. As always, they looked adorable. Kennedy, sitting beside Mom at the registration table, was clearly a princess, wearing a beautiful medieval gown in pale blue. She was also wearing a beautiful tiara. I was impressed that she'd kept her costume a secret from me. Although she looked great, I had no idea which Disney princess she was supposed to be. Before I had a chance to ask, Mom started gushing over us.

"Lindsey darling, don't you make the most beautiful pirate! I admit that Betty might have slipped and told me about your costumes, but I never imagined how fabulous you all would look. Oh, and Rory!" Here Mom took a step back and theatrically fanned her face, indicating what I already knew: Rory made a smokin' hot pirate. This caused the girls to giggle. Rory, turning beet red, bowed nonetheless at the gesture. Mom then addressed the rest of my crew. "Oh, and Teddy, don't you look marvelous! Tom! Alaina! Elizabeth! Wendy! Ryan! Oh, and Welly! It's a whole pirate crew with a dog and a treasure. I couldn't be more delighted! Kennedy, did you know about this?"

Kennedy shook her head. "No, but I love it. Pirates of the Beacon Bakeshop, I'm putting you in the group competition."

"And which princess are you, Ken?" I just had to ask.

"Buttercup," she said with a gracious smile. "Tucker is Westley."

"The Dread Pirate Roberts, you mean," Pirate Rory corrected with an ironic grin.

"*The Princess Bride*!" Alaina exclaimed. "Oh, I just love that old movie."

"I can't wait to see Officer McAllister," Tom said with a grin.

"He makes an excellent Westley," Kennedy told him with a wink, then gave us our number.

Hearing all the fuss, Dad, wearing his scarecrow costume from the night before, walked out of the boutique carrying a loaded caramel apple. The moment he saw us, he froze, then started laughing.

"This is fantastic! Honey, you look amazing. Ahoy, maties!" He saluted us with his caramel apple. "I'd love to join your crew, but Ellie's made me a judge." He graced Mom with a fake smile. He then lifted the caramel apple again and teased, "For the record, I accept bribes. This delicious beauty came from Ginger Brooks. She's selling them at her ice cream shop. Ginger and Kate are turning heads dressed as Princess Leia and young Rey from the new movies."

Ginger was a good friend of mine and owned Harbor Scoops, the town's famous ice cream shop. Kate was her preteen daughter. I scanned the large group of costumed Pumpkin Pageant contestants and saw Ginger standing in the crowd. Due to the cinnamon bun wig that was iconic Leia, she stood out from the crowd. Of course, the giant coils of hair on either side of Leia's head weren't really cinnamon rolls, but to a baker it was obvious that the giant, scrumptious baked good had provided the inspiration for Princess Leia's unique look. The wiggling lightsaber beside Ginger I assumed belonged to Kate, aka Rey.

"Okay," Mom said, pointing to the huge crowd that had gathered. "You pirates make your way over to that group. The Pumpkin Pageant is about to begin. You'll be marching up Waterfront Street, then across to the town park, where the judging will take place. Good luck, everyone!"

Marching in the parade was a blast. Teddy had taught us a pirate shanty, and we sang it with discordant gusto as we made our way to the park. There, the judging commenced, and I imagined it was a tough decision. However, it was no surprise that Leslie Adams and her little dog, Trixie, won best original costume in the human and animal category. We all cheered when her name was announced. Our category came next. Captain Teddy Pratt was all ready to accept our ribbon when Mayor Jeffers surprised us all by proclaiming the winners of the group costume category to be the Ghostbuster Guys.

"Ghostbuster Guys?" As Rory uttered the name, looking perplexed, a cameraman backed out from the crowd, aiming his lens at three young men who were just emerging from the throng of onlookers. They were dressed in classic Ghostbuster gear with one notable difference to the costume. Under the iconic Ghostbusters logo (a ghost framed in a red circle with a line through it), they had printed the name *Ghostbuster Guys*.

"Ladies and gentlemen . . ." Rod Jeffers, the mayor of Beacon Harbor, was speaking into the microphone as the Ghostbuster Guys ran to the stage amid cheers from the crowd. "These fellas aren't movie Ghostbusters—they're the real thing. Let's give a warm Beacon Harbor welcome to the Ghost Guys from the Travel Channel!" Rod was grinning with delight as he welcomed the young men onstage.

"Why, blow me down, maties," Teddy remarked, staying in character, "those Ghost Guys really know how to make an entrance."

"That they do," I replied, feeling the hair on the back of my neck prickle uncomfortably. "Do you think this was a setup?"

"What I think is that this is the photo op they needed for their show." Rory crossed his arms and shook his head. As the Ghost Guys introduced themselves and waved to their fans in the crowd, Rory continued, "And now the whole town knows how they'll be spending their evening."

"Stirring up the ghost of the Beacon Harbor Lighthouse, that's how," I remarked, staring at the vaguely familiar faces on the stage. "Well, shall we go greet our not-very-discreet guests?"

"Might as well," Captain Rory replied.

CHAPTER 11

After filming some B-roll of the town in the throes of the Halloween Bash, and after a tour of the lighthouse, the gentlemen of *The Ghost Guys* had dinner with us under the Oktoberfest tent on the Tannenbaum grounds. It was the last day of the trendy, pop-up restaurant Stanley and Felicity Stewart had started in August, during the Blueberry Festival. The food, beverages, and atmosphere were so delightful that the Stewarts had decided to keep the tent going through Halloween.

"Again, Lindsey, we want to thank you for this opportunity to investigate your lighthouse," Brett Bloom, the lead paranormal investigator on the team, said. He took another swig of his craft beer, smiled appreciatively, and set it down. "I have a strong affinity for lighthouses. We don't get to investigate them very often, so when we were contacted by Teddy, I was super stoked."

"Honestly, it's hardly haunted," I told them with

a nonchalant wave of my hand. Kennedy nearly choked on her juicy brat when I said this.

"Darling, you're in denial. Your lighthouse *is* haunted." This she declared with a pointed look directed at me. "And these fine gentlemen, with me tagging along, are going to capture the evidence to prove it."

Mike Miller, the other investigator, interlaced his hands and leaned on his elbows. "Kennedy has told us some remarkable stories about your lighthouse. It appears that you have one ghost here, whom you refer to as Captain Willy Riggs. Are there any other ghosts or poltergeists on the premises that we should be aware of?"

"What?" I looked at Mike to see if he was joking. He wasn't. "No, just the one. But like I said, the lighthouse is hardly haunted."

"We like to gather as much information as we can about a location before we investigate," Brett explained.

"Also, we have devices and specially designed tech that help us contact the spirit world," Cody told us. Cody was the guy in charge of monitoring the tech. "Things like footsteps and light orbs are relatively common to catch on night-vision cameras. We have REM pods that react to electromagnetic changes around the device, which can be tripped by spirits when they're present. We have EVP detectors that scan radio frequencies and are used for catching and recording disembodied voices—"

He was about to continue when I cut him off. "I hardly think you're going to need those." I rolled my eyes before eating another French fry.

"There is one thing." Brett leaned on his elbows and held me in a forthright gaze. "Kennedy told us about a strange light that occasionally appears in the lightroom. She called it the 'ghost lights of Beacon Harbor.' That's of particular interest to us. We've never seen anything like that before, and we would love to catch it on film."

"I bet you would," Rory remarked with a smirk. We were all still in costume. The Ghost Guys told us they planned to conduct the entire investigation in costume in the spirit of Halloween. I thought it was a fun twist.

"It has happened," I told them, honestly. "But it's very, very rare."

"Is there a way to provoke it?" Ed, the main cameraman asked. "You know, a trigger object or a word that might make the lights appear?" I could tell he was itching to film the phenomenon.

Rory and I shared a passing look before blurting in unison a resounding, "No!"

"You won't see the lights tonight, gentlemen," I told them. "But you might hear footsteps. That's about as scary as it gets at the lighthouse."

Tuck, dressed as Westley from *The Princess Bride* in black pants and a baggy black shirt, with his lustrous blond hair slicked back, and wearing a fake blond mustache, leaned forward and placed his hand over Kennedy's. "Buttercup, babe, you don't have to go through with this. Seeing a mouse unhinges you. What if . . . what if the captain actually appears?"

"My ratings will go up," she told him with a grin. "Besides, these professionals will protect me."

"And on that note," I remarked, holding out my

keys to Brett, "the lighthouse is yours for the night. Good luck, Kennedy, gentlemen. We'll be watching the investigation live from the comfort of Rory's home."

"That's right," Rory agreed with a nod. "I'm making popcorn."

CHAPTER 12

Teddy had met Kennedy and the Ghost Guys back at the lighthouse to help them set up their cameras and ghost tech for their midnight investigation. Honestly, it was a great relief to have Teddy there at the lighthouse. He fit right in with the team, was familiar with the lighthouse and its legends, and knew the best camera angles for both the lighthouse and Kennedy.

Although Kennedy was a near-permanent guest at the lighthouse, she was too busy prepping for her live podcast to be much help. While Ghost Guy Ed manned the camera for the show, Kennedy would be wearing a GoPro on her head that would live-stream her experience and interview as she accompanied Ghost Guys Brett and Mike during the investigation. Teddy, also manning one of the video cameras, would be following different members of the team, including Kennedy. And Ghost Guy Cody would be in the Beacon's café, monitoring the live video feed as well as the ghost tech placed in various rooms around the lighthouse. It was a mind-boggling setup, but I also found myself highly intrigued by the process. I had to wonder whether Captain Willy Riggs would show himself tonight with so much activity going on around him.

Once I saw that my lighthouse was in good hands, Wellington and I walked through the woods following our private path to Rory's house, which was just across the point from my lighthouse. Although Kennedy and the Ghost Guys would be in costume all night, I had happily abandoned my pirate costume for comfy flannel pajama pants and a sweatshirt. I planned on taking a nap before the podcast was to begin. Welly was also happy to be free from his pirate getup and ran with abandon along his favorite footpath, knowing there'd be a yummy treat for him waiting at the other end.

I awoke from my much-needed nap at quarter to midnight, lured by the smell of fresh-popped popcorn drizzled with butter. It was a mouthwatering smell to be sure, and my mouth was watering with anticipation as I shuffled out of the bedroom and into the great room of the beautiful log home. Rory had already set up the podcast to play on his huge, flat-screen television. Tuck, also having abandoned his costume, was in jeans and a sweatshirt as he lounged on the couch eating popcorn. Wellington was lying between the couch and the coffee table, waiting for rogue pieces to fall his way. And Rory was just coming out of the kitchen with three bottles of soda. I couldn't wait to join them.

"Linds, I was just going to wake you," Rory said upon seeing me. "The show is about to start."

"I know. Is it just me, or are you both as nervous as I am?"

Tuck looked up from his bowl of popcorn. "I'm stress eating. That should tell you something. Kennedy's an excitable woman on a good day. If the captain appears, she going to freak out. It's not going to be pretty."

Rory, who was in the process of filling a bowl of popcorn from the giant bowl on the coffee table, grinned at the young police officer. "That's the whole point of these ghost shows, Tuck. You never really see anything except the investigators freaking out when they hear something, smell something, or they feel cold. Kennedy's going to be a natural at it."

As Rory handed me my bowl, the TV went live, revealing Kennedy in her lovely princess costume standing on the dark front lawn of the lighthouse. She wore a GoPro in lieu of her tiara and was holding a microphone. "That's Kennedy!" I proclaimed, causing Welly to lift his sleepy head. I gave him a buttery kernel of popcorn as I added, "She's live! She's really doing it!"

"That's my little Buttercup," Tuck teased and shoved another handful of popcorn into his mouth. The poor man was definitely more nervous than Kennedy.

As the video camera closed in on Kennedy's beautiful face, she explained to her audience what she was doing on this spooky Halloween night, then introduced the Ghost "Buster" Guys from the Travel Channel, including their cameraman, and Cody in the control center. Because she was my dearest friend and I knew her so well, it never failed to make me proud to see her shine in her element, and Ken was shining.

She explained to her audience that her live

ghost-hunting podcast was unprecedented. We, her audience, were going to experience everything the Ghost Guys were, without the aid of editing. Cody, in the control room, would handle the live feed, switching camera angles as he saw fit. Then Kennedy proceeded to hype up the drama by talking to Brett and Mike about the Beacon Point Lighthouse and its resident ghost, its first lightkeeper, Captain Willy Riggs.

The camera closed in on Brett Bloom. I had to admit, although he was likely younger than even Tuck McAllister, he wasn't hard to look at. There was a reason why Brett Bloom was the lead investigator. He even looked good on the night-vision camera.

"So," Brett began, staring directly into the camera as if he was staring into Kennedy's large brown eyes, "you and the owner of this amazing lighthouse, Lindsey Bakewell, believe the first lightkeeper here has never left? Is that right?" Kennedy nodded. "So cool," he said, then flashed a pointed look at his partner, Mike. That was Mike's cue to ask the next question.

"Maybe you can tell us, Kennedy, what you and Lindsey have experienced here?"

The men listened politely as Kennedy told them some highly embellished stories. She was a good storyteller, I had to give her that. She really got into what she was telling them by using her vast powers of expression, her charming English accent, and her wild hand gestures. Even if Captain Willy refused to play along tonight, I, for one, was glued to the television.

"She's good," I remarked. Tuck nodded in wholehearted agreement as he binged on popcorn. Rory's response was a noncommittal shrug accompanied by a grunt. We then settled in and watched the investigation begin.

It was a surreal feeling to watch a couple of strangers mill about your house in the dead of night with the lights off. Their focus was the paranormal, not baked goods, which I found slightly unsettling as well. Then there was the ghost tech, those odd contraptions that would light up if something crossed an energy field. That was happening a lot, especially in the guest bedroom down the hallway from mine. And every time it happened, Kennedy jumped. The camera feed would then switch from the GoPro on Kennedy's head to the one Teddy was holding so the audience could see her reaction. She was freaking out, but in a good way. Teddy, the consummate professional, never flinched or squealed that I could tell.

"Does anyone else find that unsettling?" I asked, watching what the Guys called the *ghost meter* light up like a Christmas tree. Rory placed his hand over mine.

"Linds, I hate to tell you this, but that's garbage technology. It's an EMF meter—electromagnetic field meter. It's meant to detect changes in the electromagnetic field. Electricians sometimes use them to locate potentially harmful EMF radiation leaking from power lines or household appliances. But they're not that accurate. A cell phone can set that thing off. Probably that GoPro as well." Leave it to Rory to make me feel better.

I was just about to eat a handful of popcorn when my hand stilled before my lips. "Wait. What's going on now?" Apparently, everyone on the big screen was freaking out about something they'd heard. Admittedly, there were a lot of noises that could be heard in the lighthouse. First, there was the constant rolling of waves hitting the shore. Boat horns were also common, as was the wind. Often, I could hear voices coming from the beach, dogs barking, and the cry of seagulls, just to name a few.

"Footsteps," Brett blurted, looking at the bedroom door. "Definitely footsteps. Where are they coming from?"

Mike, with a puzzled look on his face, was staring at the door as well. "I hear them too. They sound like they're coming from out there."

"Relax, boys," Kennedy told them. "That's the captain. He's walking up the light tower stairs. We hear that quite often." She looked so calm, but I knew it was just an act. Although we, the viewers, could not hear these footsteps, I truly believed Kennedy and the Ghost Guys could.

"No way," Brett said as excitement animated his face. "Let's go!"

A moment later, Kennedy and the Guys were at the foot of the circular stairs in the light tower. Ed, working the other camera, pointed his microphone at the stairs as everyone fell silent. Yep. We heard them. It was unmistakable. As I knew from my own experience, it sounded like someone was walking up the circular metal stairs. Hearing it over the television caused the hair on the back of my neck to prickle. Perhaps Captain Willy was going to make an appearance after all.

Mike, halfway up the steps, pulled out another handheld gadget. This one he called an EVP detector. He told the viewers, through Kennedy's GoPro, that with this device scanning different radio frequencies, he could catch and record ghostly voices. The mere thought sent a shiver up my spine.

That shiver turned to a spasm when, a moment later, a shockingly deep voice rose over the static on the digital recorder. The voice said one word, but it was as clear as a bell.

Danger.

"Whoa! Did you hear that?" Mike looked ecstatic, and a little shocked as well. "It clearly said, 'Danger'!"

"I heard it," Brett confirmed. "That's amazing. Can you play it again?" As Mike rewound the recorder, the three of them huddled together on the stairs, entirely forgetting about the footsteps.

"Who are we talking to?" Brett asked the recorder the moment the last word had played again. "Are we talking to Captain Willy Riggs? Captain, are you here with us tonight?"

If the captain heard him, he didn't feel like replying. Instead, the deep voice offered another warning.

Evil afoot.

Not only did Kennedy jump, but Tuck and I jumped as well. Rory, for his part, looked merely skeptical.

Spurred on by this new evidence, the Ghost Guys got brave and ran up the stairs to the night-dark lightroom. Due to the view from Ken's GoPro, I could tell she was right behind them.

"Captain Willy. Are you here with us? We're in the lightroom. Do you remember . . ." If Brett was about to say another word, it died on his lips as another thought hit him. "Do you smell that?"

"Dude, that's crazy," Mike replied, looking totally freaked out by something. "It's like pipe smoke . . . and . . . and something else."

"Kerosene?" Brett offered, walking to the center of the room. He was looking around. "There's no kerosene up here, or a pipe."

Then, suddenly, the entire room burst into a bright, eerie green light. It not only shocked the night-vision cameras, but the ghost hunters as well. I heard Kennedy's bloodcurdling scream. The Ghost Guys screamed as well. Limbs and bodies scrambled for the door. It was a mad dash down the cramped, circular stairs. The bouncing video stream from Ken's forehead camera was making me dizzy.

I was on the edge of my seat as I watched the feed from Kennedy's GoPro. Brett, Mike, Teddy, and Ed had turned toward the front door the moment they were out of the light tower. Kennedy, running in their wake, took another route through my kitchen and out the back door. I believed in that moment she was making a dash for the safety of Rory's home.

Kennedy was looking back at the door as she ran. She must have looked up because the light tower came into view. We all sucked in our breath when we saw the unmistakable ghost lights of Beacon Harbor.

"Oh my," I uttered. My hands were shaking.

"Ahhh!" The cry came over the television as Kennedy screamed. For some reason the feed was still coming from her camera. Then, however, the camera came to an abrupt stop and appeared to drop backward. Ken must have hit something hard that knocked her on her backside, I thought. It was the only thing that made sense. I knew I was correct when the camera focused on the bare branches of my oak tree.

But the branches weren't bare. Someone had hung another gruesome dummy of a clown. The impact from Kennedy colliding with it had sent it swinging. However, the anger that bubbled within me at the prank was swiftly pushed aside by disbelief as the camera moved in for a closer look. The face of the clown came into view. This was live feed, I thought, as terror seized me. Everyone watching was seeing the same thing. And night vision wasn't helping any.

Then, as if aware that her camera was still on, a hand came over the lens and the TV screen turned black. This time I was the one screaming, because the face of the clown was unmistakable. It was Leslie Adams. And she looked very, very dead.

CHAPTER 13

Our hearts were racing as we ran out of the cabin to the lighthouse. Tuck drew his flashlight and had thrown on his utility belt; Rory strapped on his gun, both men not knowing what we were going to find once we broke through the trees. Kennedy was still screaming.

Welly raced ahead of us. The moment we hit the lighthouse grounds, we saw her. Bathed in the eerie green light still coming from the lightroom, we found her kneeling on the ground near the tree with her arms around Wellington. She had thrown off her GoPro and was holding on to my dog as if her life depended on it. My dear, brave friend was beside herself with fear, and I couldn't blame her. The body dangling on the end of the rope was a gruesome sight, belying the bright, happy colors of the handmade clown costume. Seeing the body hanging there with my own eyes caused a welling of both nausea and tears.

Rory went to check to make sure it wasn't a sick prank. But we all knew this time it was very real.

There was no mistaking the petite, bright clownish form of Leslie Adams. She had won a prize in the Pumpkin Pageant for her festive costume.

"Murdock's on her way," Tuck informed us, thrusting his walkie-talkie back onto his utility belt. "She saw the whole thing too." Tuck shook his head, then relieved my dog of his duties by pulling Kennedy to her feet and wrapping her in his arms.

"Babe. It's okay," he said to her, calming her in a gentle tone. "I've got you." In that moment, all I saw was Princess Buttercup embracing her brave Westley. My heart fluttered a bit at the sight of them.

Welly was sitting beneath the body of Leslie Adams, whining pitifully.

"I want to take her down from there," Rory remarked, his intense gaze focusing on the body hanging from my oak tree. My attention shifted back to him. "She deserves better than this."

"I know," Tuck replied. "What a tragedy. But we have to wait for Murdock and the crime scene investigators."

I could see this went against Rory's nature. Although he could do nothing for the body, he did pull Wellington back to where we stood. I took hold of my dog's collar and held Rory's hand.

The sirens that had pierced the night were getting closer. The Ghost Guys and Teddy must have heard them, too, because they all began to appear. They must have made their way to the beach after their frantic flight from the lighthouse, because they were now walking single file up the pathway. Teddy and Ed were still pointing their cameras at the glowing lightroom, no doubt fascinated with the ghost lights of Beacon Harbor. Then, just as suddenly as the light had burst on, it turned off, leaving everything in the lightroom dark once again.

"Whoa!" Ed cried, lowering his camera. "What the heck is going on here?"

It was a good question.

Even in my wildest dreams, I couldn't have imagined Halloween night going so far off the rails. And the worst part of it was that for the past few weeks leading up to Halloween, I had been finding life-sized dummies of ghouls and ghosts hanging from the exact same spot on my oak tree. And now this—the body of Leslie Adams. What on earth had happened? She was a petite woman. There was no indication that she'd hung herself. There was clearly no stool beneath the tree. Someone must have done this to her, but why? I had just met her, but even I could see she was a beloved teacher, a mentor to the senior class, and a good and decent woman. The irony of this bald-faced murder wasn't lost on me. Neither was it lost on Rory, Tucker, or Kennedy.

"Oh, my God!" Brett Bloom cried, spotting the tree for the first time. I recalled then that the Guys hadn't yet seen the tree or the body hanging from it. They had run out the front door with their cameras in hand. The eerie light they had experienced in the lightroom had consumed their focus. Only now did they begin to understand the reason Kennedy had kept screaming.

Teddy, seeing us all there and hearing the sirens, dropped his camera and ran to us. Apparently, he also understood that what he saw wasn't a prank.

"What's this?" he cried.

I stopped him before he got to the tree. "Leslie Adams." There was no need to say more. Teddy gasped in anguish and covered his eyes.

Cody, who until then had been in the control room in the Beacon's café monitoring the cameras, had come around the building from the opposite side. He was running across the parking lot. Everyone could see he was distraught. His face was pinched with fear, and he was sputtering a string of expletives as he jogged across the lawn to where we stood. He pulled up short of the body, as if afraid to come any closer.

"Christ, that went live!" he cried, on the verge of a total freak-out. "*Live*, as in everyone watching saw that!" However, due to the reaction from the Guys, apparently it was news to them.

"What are you talking about, Cody?" Mike said, trying to calm himself. However, the crestfallen look that overcame Brett's handsome face meant he was beginning to understand.

"This!" Cody pointed to the tree. "This nightmare went live!" he explained. "I didn't know what was happening. Everyone freaked out in the lightroom when the lights came on, and before I knew it, camera one, the GoPro, was focusing on the face of a clown! I thought it was a joke," he sputtered, clearly shaken up. "The feed from every camera was terrible. Everything was bouncing around, and I couldn't tell what the hell was going on . . . not until . . ." He stopped talking and squeezed his eyes shut, as if trying to erase what he'd just seen. "We left it too late, fellas. We just filmed the discovery of a dead body!" This he yelled as if the revelation had just hit him. "There's no taking it back! It's out there, and now we're in a heap of trouble. This is a nightmare!"

That was an understatement.

To make matters worse, emergency vehicles had started to arrive in the lighthouse parking lot, including a van from the local news station. The noise, and quite possibly the live podcast, had pulled curious onlookers out of their houses. One chillingly familiar group, recognizable from their macabre clothing, was stumbling over from the public beach, where they must have been watching the podcast on their smartphones. They were just teens, but I found their sudden appearance unsettling. But the teens certainly weren't alone. Curious onlookers stood in the parking lot, with heavy coats thrown over their pajamas. Some were still in costume. Naturally, the commotion on the lighthouse lawn was too much for the townspeople to ignore. Even my own phone began buzzing. It was Dad. I quickly explained what was going on, then ended the call. That was because Sergeant Stacy Murdock had arrived.

"Stay back, people!" she warned, alighting from her police cruiser. "This is a crime scene! Keep off the grass. Stay back behind the emergency vehicles. Let us do our jobs!" With a hand gesture, two Beacon Harbor policemen began cordoning off the area with yellow crime scene tape. Then Murdock and Officer Bain, an officer in his mid-forties, made their way to where we stood.

Pulled from her house in the dead of night, I couldn't imagine that the sergeant was going to be happy. I knew from past experience that scary Sergeant Murdock liked her sleep. Although I admired Sergeant Murdock, and although she admired my baked goods (her uniform had gotten a size or two snugger since the bakeshop had opened), we weren't on the best of terms. I had the feeling this incident wasn't going to help our relationship any.

"Oh, Bakewell," she said, addressing me with a sorry shake of her head, sending her wispy blond bangs fluttering across her eyes. The woman liked to wear her bangs a tad too long. She then looked at Rory and Kennedy, then finally her dark gaze fell on Tuck. "What a sad turn of events this is. I wish I could say I'm surprised to see you here, but I'm not. It looks as if we have another body on our hands. And here I was hoping that suspicious deaths had left our little village. Apparently, it was too much to ask."

"We had nothing to do with this, Sergeant," I protested. "We're just as horrified as you are."

"I imagine so," she said, still clearly upset. "I watched the whole thing on my iPad. For a moment I thought it was all a spooky Halloween setup—you know, a shameless fright to drum up ratings for the Ghost Guys, Kennedy, and your bakery, Lindsey. However—and don't take this the wrong way, Ms. Kapoor—but you're not that good an actress."

"Likely because I'm not an actress, but a podcaster, Sergeant!" Kennedy corrected with a shiver of disgust.

"I realize that." Murdock gave a little nod and crossed over to the body. "When I saw the face of this poor woman, I knew it wasn't an act. This is very real."

"It is, Sarge," Tuck informed her. "The victim is Leslie Adams. She's a teacher at the high school."

"I know who she is, Officer McAllister," Sergeant Stacy informed him. "What I need to know is, were you three on the premises when this happened?"

"We were watching the podcast from Rory's cabin," Tuck explained. He had wrapped his coat around Kennedy and was holding her tightly. "We got here as fast as we could."

"Good. The question is, what is she doing here?" As Murdock spoke, she pointed her flashlight at the tree and walked over for a closer look.

We were all standing in a group, huddling in the middle of the yard. The wind was coming off the lake, rustling the fallen leaves at the base of the tree.

"The body's cold," the sergeant remarked. "And stiff, as if rigor mortis has set in. I realize it's a chilly night, but I don't think this just happened. Tell me, did any of you come into the backyard before the ghost hunt began?"

There were blank looks all around, and Kennedy shook her head.

"We started the podcast at the front of the lighthouse," Kennedy told her. She was still trembling from shock. "It's . . . it's a far better shot of the building from over there."

"Did anybody hear anything or see anything out of the ordinary?" The sergeant's deep-set brown eyes were scanning the Ghost Guys as she asked this.

"No," Brett replied. "All our focus was on the investigation and the live podcast. We had no idea about this until a few minutes ago."

"Three of you had cameras," Sergeant Murdock pointed out. "Maybe one of you caught something while shooting the show?"

"The three cameras you speak of were all focused on the investigation team," Cody pointed out. "However, we have more than those three. We place cameras in other hot rooms, which are places we believe paranormal activity might occur."

"You have more than three cameras?" This, apparently, was news to the sergeant. Teddy, and every Ghost Guy present, nodded. "I'm going to need them all," Sergeant Murdock told them. "Every one of them, gentlemen. Officer Bain will take them. Also, nobody leaves town until I give you the okay. You will all be required to come down to the station tomorrow to give statements, including Ms. Bakewell, Mr. Campbell, and Officer McAllister." That was fair enough, I supposed, since the body was hanging from my tree, and we had been the first to arrive on the scene.

Doc Riggles arrived with his team from the medical examiner's office. The crime scene unit had arrived as well. It was going to be a long night.

Sergeant Murdock had turned to leave, but she stopped suddenly and faced us once again. "You know what the pity of it all is?" she began, looking intently at us. "I was really enjoying your live podcast ghost hunt. We're all fascinated with this lighthouse. We've all heard the stories, and you Ghost Guys were making a good case that this place just might really be haunted. But then you took it a camera angle too far. I suspect none of you realized that there'd be a real person hanging from this tree, dead as a doornail. But you did announce the live podcast. The whole town knew about it. And now, thanks to Ms. Kapoor and her live feed, there won't be a corner of the world that won't know what's happened here. Yes, ladies and gentlemen, it looks like we have another murderer on the loose in Beacon Harbor."

CHAPTER 14

After the police and all the emergency vehicles arrived, the Ghost Guys went back to their rooms at the Harbor Hotel. Tuck, Kennedy, Welly, and I spent the night at Rory's. The fact that my lighthouse was the scene of another heinous crime—the first one having occurred during the grand opening of my bakery—wasn't sitting very well with me. Although we were all exhausted and emotionally traumatized, no one more so than Kennedy, for me sleep was a restless, fitful affair.

Rory had the unique ability to fall asleep practically on command. It was a skill he'd learned during his military days, and I was a bit envious of it. The trick, he told me, was to clear your mind of every thought and concentrate on your breathing until you fell asleep. It was easy for him to say this. Rory had a stronger stomach for ghost stories and dead bodies than I did. Also, it was nearly impossible for me to clear my mind when it was so full of frightful images and spiraling thoughts. I tried Rory's method. I really did, and nearly fell asleep . . .

until a haunting image popped into my head with the speed and intensity of a flash of lightning. Perhaps *haunting* was the wrong word choice. *Suspicious* was more like it. It was so clear, from the strange, modern gothic clothing to the way the cell phones had cast an eerie glow on their faces as they walked across the lighthouse parking lot. I even thought they'd been mumbling something, but I wasn't sure. Also, the fact that this little group had been there so soon after Kennedy had collided with the body of their teacher, had sent the hair on the back of my neck standing on end. True, every nerve in my body had been firing painfully from the shock of discovering the body of Leslie Adams hanging from my oak tree. Still, those witchtok kids had set off alarm bells in my head. They were modern-day witches. They admitted to being fascinated with the paranormal and, perhaps, even death. Could they be responsible for what had occurred on the lighthouse lawn?

Leslie had told me that they were harmless. But Leslie had said a lot of kind things about the young people she'd been chaperoning.

By five in the morning, I'd given up on sleep and made my way to the kitchen. Wellington, who was sleeping peacefully on the thick dog bed Rory had bought him, was more than happy to come with me. Although both Welly and Rory had the same ability to drop off to sleep wherever they were, only Wellington had mastered the ability to wake at the drop of a pin. This, I mused as my dog trotted out of the bedroom door in front of me, was undoubtedly due to Welly's opportunistic belly. He knew that he was about to get a treat.

Welly went directly to the sliding glass door. I

grabbed a blanket off the couch and wrapped it around me before letting him outside. A gust of cold wind hit me as I followed my dog onto the deck. I stayed there, huddled in the blanket, as Welly continued down the steps to the back yard to do his business. Although it was dark, it was a brisk morning, with fast moving clouds that were playing hide-and-seek with the full moon overhead. There was a lot of energy on the lake as well. The waves were high. As I looked out over the dark water, moonlight illuminated the whitecaps moving toward shore, crashing onto the beach with a steady, pounding force. Somehow, I found the roaring of the waves calming. I stared at them a moment longer, breathing in the cold predawn air until Welly came back, ready for his treat.

I was happy to have my pup's company as I rummaged through Rory's kitchen, looking for ingredients that I could use to make breakfast. Since I wasn't sure what I was going to make, the first thing I did was make a pot of coffee. Strong black coffee was a requirement on such a morning. With the pot brewing, and Wellington happily chewing on a rawhide bone under the kitchen table, I then inspected Rory's refrigerator.

Although Rory ate most of his meals at the lighthouse with me, he always kept the basics on hand. I pulled out a carton of eggs, a stick of butter, and milk from the fridge. There was also a pack of thick-cut bacon (a staple for sure!) that I would pull out later. In the fruit bowl, I found some beautiful McIntosh apples. Noting that in one of the cabinets he still had a bottle of the fresh maple syrup we'd gotten at a local orchard, I made my decision. Rory's impressive collection of cast-iron

skillets also helped seal the deal. I was going to
make a Dutch baby . . . or, more correctly, since I
was using apples, I was going to make a classic
German apple pancake. However, calling a large
skillet pancake a "Dutch baby" always made me
smile.

After preheating the oven to 450 , I pulled out
Rory's blender and added four eggs, a cup of milk,
a cup of flour, a half teaspoon of vanilla extract,
and a pinch of salt. I then blended it until a nice,
foamy batter formed. I then stuck the blender
pitcher in the fridge so it could chill while I
prepped the tart apples.

I peeled, cored, and sliced three of the little apples. Then, using a twelve-inch cast-iron skillet, I
melted two tablespoons of butter before adding
the apples to the pan. I also added half a teaspoon
of cinnamon and a large pinch of nutmeg. I then
cooked the apples until they were nice and soft.
Once the apples were done to my liking, I added a
third of a cup of brown sugar to the pan and continued cooking until the tender apple slices cara-
melized in the brown sugar. Once that was done, I
plopped another tablespoon of butter into the pan,
waited until it melted, then poured the chilled batter right on top of the cooked apples. The whole
skillet went into the oven for about fifteen minutes, or until the pancake cooked and puffed up
like a Yorkshire pudding.

While the apple pancake was baking, I pulled
out another cast-iron skillet and began frying
bacon. That's when Welly dropped the bone he'd
been chewing and came over to join me at the
stove. Bacon was his favorite treat, and he begged
shamelessly until I gave him a piece.

"Here you go, good boy." Welly gobbled the piece of cooled bacon so fast that I doubted he'd even tasted it. Knowing he was hungry, and that I didn't feel like walking back to the lighthouse to get his kibble, I decided to spoil him by using the rest of the carton of eggs to make him a heaping plate of scrambled eggs topped with melted cheese and a sprinkling of bacon. Welly, after all, deserved it.

"Wow. Something smells great." Rory appeared in the kitchen just as the giant pancake had been pulled out of the oven. He looked both sleepy and cozy in his plaid flannel lounge pants and a form-fitting waffle knit shirt. I left the pancake on the stove to cool and handed him a mug of coffee with a kiss.

"I couldn't sleep."

"I can see that," he replied, looking longingly at the giant pancake. "That looks amazing." He pulled two plates from the cabinet as he spoke. "I must admit I was having a hard time sleeping as well. You may not believe this, but I had a disturbing dream. That seldom happens."

"I believe it," I told him as I placed a large slice of pancake on each plate. "Last night was truly the stuff of nightmares, especially since it was so close to home." I added bacon to the plates and brought them over to the table.

"Close to home! It was right *in* your home." He shook his head and took a seat. "This murder is affecting me more than I care to admit, Linds. How was it done?" he asked. "How did someone get that body on that tree during the filming of a ghost-hunting show?"

I took a sip of coffee and shrugged. "I'm still struggling with *why*, as in *why* would somebody kill Leslie Adams and hang her from my oak tree? It's positively sinister."

"It is," Rory agreed and began eating his pancake. Although cooking always helped me relax, I found I wasn't very hungry after all. "Tuck will be going on duty this morning," Rory offered. "No doubt he'll be looking into it. It's the talk of the town."

"It is," I agreed and set down my fork. I folded my hands and leaned on my elbows. "But here's what I'm puzzled about. Just about everybody in town knew the Ghost Guys were going to be conducting a live investigation. However, nobody could have predicted that the investigators would freak out in the lightroom due to the ghost lights, or that Kennedy would run out the back door instead of the front door with the rest of the guys."

"Good point," he remarked. "The fact that she ran into the body I have to believe was a total accident. Also, remember that the livestream ghost hunt had just been announced the day before. Therefore, whoever killed Leslie had either planned the murder weeks before by making it seem like your lighthouse was being pranked by kids, or the murderer seized an opportunity by hanging the body on that tree, knowing it would seem like another prank. Maybe the killer was hoping Leslie's murder would go unnoticed until morning."

"Those are two very good points as well," I said, then fell silent a moment as I thought about the murder. "But why on my property? Is this about me? Was I supposed to find the body? Or . . . is it about Leslie? Because you and I both know I've just met the woman. Finding her body like that was beyond disconcerting. What does it mean?"

"God, Linds, I wish I knew," he said, before raking a hand through his mussy morning hair. Rory was flummoxed. "But it *is* a murder, not a suicide. Even Murdock came to that conclusion. And because it's a murder, there must be a motive."

"Are you thinking what I'm thinking?" I asked, looking into his deep-set, vibrant blue eyes. Normally they were as carefree as the summer sky, but today I could tell a storm was brewing behind them.

With a grim set to his lips, Rory nodded. "You know I am, Bakewell."

"Good," I said with a curt nod. "I know I'm just a baker with a lighthouse, but I'll be damned if some sicko thinks they can murder one of our upstanding citizens and make a mockery of it on my property."

"That's the spirit," Rory rallied, then stood up from the table. "I'm going to get a pen and paper, and another slice of that pancake. Then we can start brainstorming ideas. If we're going to find the murderer, we're going to have to learn a bit more about Leslie Adams."

"Whoa!" came a voice from the hallway. Rory and I both spun around to see Tuck walking into the kitchen. "Civilians, stand down," he playfully admonished before grabbing a plate. He cast us a chiding look before helping himself to a slice of German apple pancake. "I know you two are itching to help us find the person who did this, but . . . come on, guys. This is a murder investigation. A woman was hung from your tree, Lindsey." Honestly, he didn't need to remind me of it. "Whoever did this is dangerous. Leave this one to the Beacon Harbor Police," he advised, joining us at the table.

A shuffling noise coming from down the hall alerted us to the fact that Kennedy was awake. Well, *awake* might have been a generous term, I thought, looking at her. She shuffled into the kitchen wearing silk pajamas with white fur trim. The fluffy bunny slippers on her feet broke the illusion of elegance. And although her feet were sort of moving, as they shuffled to the counter, Ken's eyes were red and puffy, and she was yawning as if she hadn't slept a wink. Rory, who was in the middle of a sip of coffee, nearly spat it out at the sight of her. Apparently, Ken's pj's didn't live up to Rory's vision of rugged cabin apparel.

Oblivious to Rory and his sputtering coffee, Kennedy said, "I've had enough frights for one lifetime." She proclaimed with her usual hint of drama, "Darlings, I literally discovered that body! I ran straight into it. I had nightmares! So, forgive me if I don't jump at the chance to find her murderer. At the moment, I'm just trying to forget the whole thing!" Kennedy paused to pour a mug of coffee, added a splash of whole milk to her mug, and leaned against the kitchen counter.

"Although I've been traumatized, you two obviously feel differently about digging in to this one." Her sleepy brown eyes looked at Rory and me.

"Ken, we're all shaken by what happened last night. But how can we not get involved?" I reasoned. "Leslie's body was found on my property! We don't know if she was murdered there or not, but I think we owe it to ourselves to figure that out."

Rory looked at Tuck. "I'm with Lindsey on this one."

Young Officer McAllister, who'd been eating his German apple pancake with quiet relish, set down his busy fork and addressed us. "Okay, look, I know I can't stop any of you from snooping around. Also, I must admit that you three have been very helpful in the past. So here are my rules. Stay out of trouble. Be discreet. And the moment you find anything of interest, let me know immediately." He raised his gold-dusted brows at us before picking up his fork again.

"Of course," I assured him. "Discreet is our middle name."

Rory, liking the sound of this, raised his mug to Tuck in agreement. "Thanks, bro."

Kennedy, not liking the sound of this, shuffled over to the table and plopped down her coffee mug with force. "Weren't any of you listening to me? I've been traumatized!" She stomped a fluffy bunny slipper to make her point. The trouble was, it was a fluffy bunny slipper.

"Welcome to the club, sweetheart. We watched the whole thing unfold. You've traumatized us too, and whoever else was watching that trainwreck last night." Rory gave the table a coffee-mug salute as he added, "To livestream ghost hunts and unexpected dead bodies. May the two never cross our paths again."

CHAPTER 15

"Well, I've done it! My podcast has gone viral." As Kennedy said this, she clicked off her phone and lowered her head, pinching the bridge of her nose as if she had a raging headache.

I glanced at my friend, sitting in the passenger seat, unsure of what to say. Of course, a viral video was every vlogger's dream. Wasn't it? Yet the nature of the video in question was too gruesome to contemplate. It just went to prove the ghoulish nature of internet voyeurs. I turned into the police station parking lot, found a space, and turned off the Jeep. Rory had accompanied me to the boathouse this morning, but I just couldn't muster the nerve to go inside my lighthouse yet—not after last night's ghost-hunting debacle. Also, there was the matter of my backyard being cordoned off with a web of ghoulishly bright yellow crime scene tape.

"I'm sorry," I said at last. "What are you going to do about it?"

"I watched it before we left Rory's house," she

explained. That shocked me. Kennedy had been so upset last night that I doubted she'd ever look at the video footage again. I guess I'd been wrong. She continued, "Out of respect for Leslie Adams and her family, that video needs to be taken down. Currently, all it has is a warning slapped across it for viewers." She made air quotes and mimicked, "'Content may be disturbing for viewers.'" She shook her head in dismay. "Content gets taken down all the time for lesser evils. I stumble into a real crime scene, and all they do is paste on a pop-up warning for viewers! Where's the logic in that? I've already contacted my lawyer. Although unlikely, there is a possibility I could be slapped with a lawsuit for this."

"I'm sorry, Ken. However, in your defense, how were you to know that your podcast would have such an unexpected and horrific ending? Also, do we know if Leslie's family has been notified yet?"

"Well, that's the thing. Rory asked Tucker the same question this morning before he left for his *warehouse of warriors.*" That was the pet name Kennedy had given to Rory's new business venture. Rory was meeting a group of his *boys* there this morning. The men had left earlier while I waited for Kennedy. "I honestly don't know what is going on, or who's been notified, Linds. Like you, I don't know much about poor Leslie Adams at all. Maybe we can find out more when we give our statements."

Kennedy was just about to open the door when I stopped her. "I know you've been traumatized by last night, but I have to tell you something. Remember those witchtok kids from my pumpkin-carving party?"

"They are not the sort of youth one easily forgets. Why?" Yet just as the word slipped past Kennedy's lips, her large eyes flew even wider with understanding. "Don't tell me you saw them last night?" This she uttered with a hint of dark intrigue.

"I did," I told her. "Honestly, I was unsettled by their untimely appearance. A small group of those kids appeared in the lighthouse parking lot at nearly the same time as the emergency vehicles. You were in shock and still crying. Sergeant Murdock and Officer Bain had just arrived. That's when I noticed the witchtok group walking over from the public beach. The thing that struck me was that they all had their cell phones out. Some were recording the unfolding event, while others were staring at their glowing phones, walking like zombies across the parking lot."

"It was Halloween night," she reasoned.

I nodded in agreement.

"Nearly everyone in town knew about the live podcast," she added. "And those teens are just the sort to have gobbled up my spooky investigation."

"That's very true," I conceded. "But unlike everyone else in town, a certain group of high school seniors were thought to have been harassing my lighthouse weeks before last night's terrible incident. Those kids were the reason I had that party to begin with. I hate to admit this, but the moment we saw that dark and gloomy group saunter off the bus, we both believed they were the ones responsible for the ghoulish pranks, including trying to break into the light tower in the dead of night to see the captain."

"Too soon!" Kennedy snapped, holding up a

hand. "Can we not talk about him right now? He . . . he gave me the fright of my life in that tower!" She paused a moment, then corrected, "Well, actually, the fright of my life came a moment later, when I bumped into that neon clown hanging from the tree in your backyard and . . . that turned out to be A DEAD BODY!" This last part she screamed, causing Welly to spring up like a rocket from the back seat.

"*Woof!*" he barked, swiveling his fluffy black head to all points around the car, as if there was something awesome to look at.

"It's okay. It's okay," I soothed, trying to settle them both down. I pulled a Beacon Bite from the glove box and gave it to Welly. It worked like magic. Unfortunately, I didn't have such an easy fix for Kennedy. Instead, I said, "What I'm suggesting is that maybe it wasn't such a coincidence finding those spooky teens there, after all."

Kennedy pondered this a moment. "You might be right. But with Leslie gone, how do we contact them? They're minors."

"Who put us in touch with Leslie?" I cast her a knowing look as I asked this.

"Betty Vanhoosen!" Her eyes lit up as she said this.

"Righto! The Beacon Harbor Police might have fancy computers with access to classified databases, but they don't have Betty's legendary Rolodex . . . Wait." I looked at her through narrowed eyes. "Are you saying you want to help me do some snooping around?"

"While this whole incident has me quite literally quaking in my boots," she admitted with a wave of her hand, "it was your woodsy boyfriend who not-so-subtly reminded me this morning that this whole thing was my doing. That horrific video is proof of that. I . . . um . . . hate to admit this, but I really screwed up this time, Lindsey, darling. You were right. I wasn't ready to investigate ghosts. I don't even like the paranormal, and I perfectly loathe bodies and clowns hanging in trees. But do you know what I detest even more? Murderers. Also, you're my best friend, and I can't let you do this alone."

"Oh, Ken." I softened my gaze as I placed a hand over my heart. I was truly touched by her sentiment. However, I was also worried about her as well. Therefore, I reminded her that Rory was helping me.

"That cotton-headed deerstalker?" She flung the insult with a grin. "He's okay, but we both know I'm better. And I have an alter ego that commands cooperation." She was, no doubt, referring to Lillian Finch, her fake reporter's name. That made me smile.

"Now, let's get in there and give scary Sergeant Stacy our statements. Warning: Mine is going to take a lot longer than yours. Then we'll head over to your parents' house, where half the town has gone to gather. Let's see if we can't dig something up on these teenage witches."

"Sounds like a plan," I said, opening my door. I let Welly out and attached his leash. "I'm glad you're on board," I told her. "You had me worried for a moment."

"I had *me* worried for a moment," my indomitable friend confessed. "But I'm back! However, best not tell scary Sergeant Stacy."

* * *

"Lindsey! Kennedy! And my favorite pal, Welly!"
Teddy stood from his chair in the police station
waiting room to better ruffle Welly's ears in greeting. He was awaiting his turn to give his statement
from last night. "I'm so happy to see you two," he
said to us, taking his seat again. "What a night!
Ken, how ya holding up, girl? I was able to watch
the footage from your GoPro. What a nightmare."

"Teddy, my dear, that's an understatement."
Kennedy shook her head in dismay and plopped
herself down on the seat beside him. I sat on my
assistant baker's other side. And Welly, after a
proper ear rub, stretched out on the floor by our
feet.

"Did you watch the footage from the other cameras?" I asked, knowing the Ghost Guys had placed
video cameras in other rooms around my lighthouse.

He glanced at the woman working behind the
protective glass window of the police station's
front office. Noting that she was busy typing on
her keyboard and that Murdock wasn't in view,
Teddy lowered his voice. "Lindsey, I'm sorry to tell
you, but your lighthouse is most definitely haunted."
He grinned in response to my shocked expression.

"I think everybody already knows that, Teddy," I
gently rebuked. "What I mean is, did you catch
anything out of the ordinary?"

With an amused look on his face, he offered, "It
was a paranormal investigation. We caught a lot of
weird schnitzel on camera last night." I was about
to say something else when he held up a hand.
"However, footage from the camera that was set up
in your dining room caught my interest. Both your

private kitchen and the dining room have windows overlooking the backyard. The camera was turned on at ten forty-five p.m. It had been placed in the cased opening between the kitchen and the living room, facing the back wall of the dining room. From that angle, most of the kitchen and dining room could be seen, including the back door. The investigation began at eleven p.m. At exactly eleven thirty-seven, a light orb appeared on camera."

"What's . . . a light orb?" I tentatively asked, not sure I wanted to know.

Teddy shrugged. "Nobody knows for sure, but it's thought to be visible light energy from a spirit or departed loved one. Anyhow, we thought it was a light orb until a few frames later, when the whole room burst out in dancing orbs. Then they disappeared."

"Holy mother," Kennedy uttered and crossed herself. "And I eat in that kitchen!"

Teddy cast her an admonishing look. "Not to worry. They weren't light orbs at all. Cody instantly debunked them. We went back into that room last night to be certain. The orbs we caught on camera were caused by a sudden flash of light—"

"From the light room?" Kennedy ventured. "The ghost lights?"

Teddy shook his head. "No. We didn't go up to the light room to investigate until midnight. This occurred before that. What I'm trying to tell you is that the light we saw in that room came from a flashlight shining through the dining room window."

"From the person or persons who hung Leslie's body from my tree!" It was a revelation and perhaps even a piece of key evidence. "Is there anything else on the footage?" I asked. "Did you catch any sound, like a voice or voices?"

"No," he remarked. "Just the sound of the waves. They were loud last night. Oh, and then around midnight, a lot of screaming. We also have a good shot of Princess Buttercup here racing across the room and out the back door. Didn't know you could move so fast, Kennedy."

"If I recall, you four were running just as fast. I had to use the back door because the front door was blocked by large, manly bodies and cameras."

"Fair enough." He laughed. "Mike, Cody, and Ed are back there with one of the officers going through all the footage. We're hoping they can prove that what we caught on camera was a flashlight coming from the backyard. That would give them a timeline."

"Good work," I told him, genuinely impressed. I was stroking Welly's head when I thought of something else. "Do we know if Leslie had any next of kin?" Teddy shook his head. "What about Trixie, her dog? Has anyone seen her dog?"

Teddy's eyes lit up at that. "The dog! Goodness, Lindsey. You're the first person to mention anything about that dog."

CHAPTER 16

"Hey, Linds," Tuck greeted us as Welly and I came through the door of the room where I was to give my statement. Welly, seeing his friend there, ran with excitement around the table and put his giant paws on Tuck's lap to better give him a slobbery kiss on the face. Tuck, used to such greetings, handled the situation like a professional. "Happy to see you, too, Welly. Although it's only been a little over an hour."

"So, you're the lucky one taking my statement?" Why did that surprise me?

"Murdock, for reasons I don't need to explain to you, is taking Kennedy's." With a grin and a shrug, Tuck shook his head. "She'll be grilled, but Ken can handle it. Besides, there was a camera on her all night. She has a very solid alibi."

"Nobody in their right mind would believe she had anything to do with this murder," I remarked, noting that he looked tired. I then took the seat across from him. Welly chose a spot under the table.

"It's procedure," he said before a frown took over his handsome face. "What a terrible thing to have happened."

"Agreed," I replied, not sure if he meant the murder or Kennedy finding the body on camera. Either way, my heart went out to him. Tuck might have been young, but he was a good cop. However, it didn't take a genius to see he was doubly troubled by this latest murder. Not wishing to cause him more work, I leaned across the table.

"So," I began, "since we were together the whole night, watching the live podcast from the comfort of Rory's couch, why don't you just make a copy of your statement and put my name on it too."

He quirked a golden brow at this plan, then shook his head. "Doesn't work like that, I'm afraid." He picked up his pen and softened his gaze as he looked at me. "Since the victim was found on your property, Lindsey, I have to ask, what was your relationship to the victim?"

Although he already knew what it was, I told him anyhow. He then asked me to walk him through the evening from the time I'd turned the lighthouse over to the Ghost Guys, to the time the sergeant arrived on the scene, including anything else that might have jumped out at me. I told him everything, except for the group of witchtok kids I had seen walking up from the beach. It was only a hunch, but one Kennedy and I were going to check out first. The truth was, they were just teens, and I was uncomfortable by how they dressed and the fact that they were into darker matters. Their presence last night was likely nothing, I reasoned as I gave my statement. Then, as swiftly as the thought came, another popped up, pushing the spooky teens aside.

"Trixie!" Much to Tuck's surprise, the name of the dog burst from my lips. Tuck set down his pen and looked puzzled.

"That's the name of Leslie's miniature poodle. She's a cute little thing. Trixie was with Leslie all day at the Halloween Bash. They won first place in the Pumpkin Pageant, as well, in the human and dog category."

"No one's mentioned a dog."

"I'm sort of dialed in to dogs," I told him, gesturing to Welly. "Trixie was in my café that morning. Tuck, if Leslie was abducted during the Halloween Bash or murdered on my property, there's a good chance her dog would have been there too. I've talked with Teddy. As far as he knows, not one camera caught the sound of a dog barking."

"What are you saying?" His bright blue eyes narrowed in question as he looked at me. Obviously, he had no idea where I was going with this. But it made sense to me.

"There wasn't a dog at the lighthouse last night," I told him. "Also, we watched the whole thing unfold on TV. Dogs are very loyal creatures, Tuck."

"Okay." He tilted his head, urging me to continue.

"They're pack animals, and Trixie loved her human. Leslie was still wearing her Halloween costume when we found her, which might suggest she didn't have time to go home and change. So, if Leslie was abducted during the Halloween Bash, then Trixie would have been with her. At the very least, the dog would have barked, drawing attention to the situation. If Leslie was on the lighthouse grounds when she died, Trixie would have barked, and we would have heard it. Trixie would have been under that tree, scared, whining, barking, but she wouldn't have left Leslie's side. Not voluntarily"

"This is conjecture," he remarked, thinking.

"It's dog behavior, Tuck. Do you think that dog under the table at your feet would let somebody abduct me without putting up a fight?"

Tuck glanced under the table at my giant dog, then shook his head. "I imagine your dog would tear them limb from limb if they tried. However, you've just told me that Leslie's dog wasn't very big."

"Maybe not, but poodles are one of the smartest dog breeds. They also have a stellar sense of smell. If Leslie was anywhere around town when she was abducted by the murderer, I'd be willing to bet Trixie would have made her way to the lighthouse, and we would have heard her."

Tuck, thinking on this, mindlessly drummed the tip of his pen on his notepad. He then stopped and said, "Unless Leslie's murderer was after the dog in the first place?"

"That's an unsettling thought, Tuck. Why would somebody have wanted her dog?"

"I don't know, Linds? You're the one focused on the dog. I'm just spitballing here."

I frowned, thinking a moment. "What about Leslie's house?" I asked him. "Did anyone mention finding Trixie there? That's probably where the dog is. Look, last night when Sergeant Murdock checked the body, she didn't believe Leslie was murdered on my property. Rigor mortis was beginning to set in, indicating that Leslie had been dead for—"

"At least two hours," he added in a knowing way. "We're way ahead of you. The hanging was a statement, we believe. It didn't kill her, so we're now looking for the cause of her death. There are officers and a crime scene unit at her house as we speak."

"Then Trixie is probably still there. That would make sense. Why don't you check?" I asked and crossed my arms. I wasn't going to lie; the thought of a missing dog on top of everything else was very upsetting.

With a new look of concern, Tuck nodded and picked up his cell phone. Before he made the call, he explained, "Officers Bain and Gunner are there now. Also, we learned that the deceased was a widow, her husband having passed away nine months ago in an ice-fishing accident. Leslie lived alone. Her next of kin is a daughter named Cali. We've learned that she's a grad student at U of M in Ann Arbor. We've contacted her this morning. As you can imagine, the news is devastating to her. She'll be driving up from Ann Arbor sometime either today or tomorrow."

"The poor girl," I said, instinctively placing a hand over my heart.

"I'll make the call," Tuck said and pressed a number. A moment later, he was talking to one of the officers on the scene. After a short exchange, he hung up the phone.

"I'm sorry, Lindsey, but there doesn't appear to be a dog on-site." This troubling statement caused him to rake a hand through his short blond hair. "Also, it appears that specific rooms in the home have been ransacked. That's all I know at the moment." He scribbled something on a piece of paper, folded it in half, then handed it across the desk to me.

"Sign your statement," he instructed as he stood from his chair. He grabbed his hat from the coat hook and placed it on his head. "Then wait for Kennedy. I'm not sure it's the crime scene, Lindsey, but you've got me thinking about that dog. Maybe Wellington can help us out."

I waited until he left the room before I looked at the paper in my hand. To my surprise, it contained the address to Leslie Adams's house. It wasn't exactly an invitation to snoop, but more of an acknowledgment that I had struck a nerve. *Leslie,* I thought, staring at her address, *what secrets were you hiding? And where, oh where, has your little dog gone?* I knew in that moment that I wouldn't rest until I had discovered the answers to both.

CHAPTER 17

"I can't believe he just gave you this?" Kennedy looked at the address on the piece of paper, then at me. "Tucker is usually not happy when we stick our noses in his business."

"It's not an invitation to snoop, if that's what you're thinking." I flashed her a pointed look before turning down a country lane that led to a high, forested bluff. Realizing what I'd just said, I corrected, "Well, of course, we're going to snoop. But I didn't say as much to Tuck. He still thinks you're too traumatized to get involved in this investigation. No, Ken, we have this address and this invitation because I was pressing him about Trixie." From the look on Kennedy's face, she apparently had no idea what I was talking about. "Leslie's dog?" I offered. "You know, the cute, little white poodle dressed up as a clown?"

"Right, the dog."

Having given our statements to the police, we were now following the directions to Leslie's house. It was a moment before I realized that Kennedy was staring at me.

"What?" I asked.

"The dog," she remarked with impatience. "What about the dog? Forget for a moment that I just sat with scary Sergeant Stacy for over an hour, trying to explain why I had a camera strapped to my head last night instead of a tiara, as my costume dictated, and why I was holding a microphone. At one point, losing patience, I looked her in the eyes, and told her, 'You know why, you cheeky woman. You watched the whole podcast on YouTube!' Which was true. Murdock wanted me to admit I was trying to scare the viewers. I couldn't deny it. That's the whole point of a ghost hunt! But what I emphatically denied was her suggestion that I had staged the ending. She thought I had planned to run out of the lighthouse and bump into a dummy hanging from the tree all along, suggesting that somebody in the know had changed the dummy out for a dead body. Can you believe it?"

I pulled my eyes from the road long enough to cast her a grin. "That's actually a good theory. Very cinematic. You didn't do that, did you?"

"Of course not, you numpty! Now, tell me why Tucker gave you an invite to the crime scene because of some dog?"

For the rest of the drive to Leslie's house, I explained to Kennedy my concerns about Trixie. By the time we'd pulled up the long drive that bisected the colorful autumn forest, she was as anxious to find the poor puppy as I was.

Leslie's house wasn't anything close to what I had pictured. Being a popular lakeside vacation area, the homes of Beacon Harbor ranged from the quaint, turn-of-the-century wood-framed cottage to the large, modern, luxury vacation home, and everything in between. Leslie's home, however, surprised me, not only for its grand size, but also for its modern rustic construction that fit so beautifully into the stunning landscape that surrounded it. With dark wood siding, large picture windows, green metal roof, and dramatic fieldstone accents, it was truly one of the most beautiful homes I had seen. However, as we walked up the lovely, stamped cement driveway, all the emergency lights from the many vehicles on the scene detracted from the experience.

With Wellington beside us, Kennedy and I walked up the front steps and knocked on the glass storm door. The heavy oak front door was open, and I was desperately trying to peek inside when Tuck suddenly appeared, blocking my view.

"Hello, Officer," Kennedy chimed in, oozing attitude and a gorgeous smile. "I'm Lillian Finch from *Cherry Capital News*. Perhaps you've heard of me? I'd like to come inside and ask you a few questions about the troubling murder of a high school teacher, although I highly doubt any teacher could afford this stunner."

"It's alright, Ken," Tuck admonished in a near whisper. "You're not here to snoop around. I asked Lindsey to come and help us locate the victim's dog. As you can see, it's a big house surrounded by acres of woodland."

"You haven't found the dog yet?" I asked, craning my neck around him to get a peek inside. I caught glimpses of the tiled entryway and a huge crystal chandelier hanging from a wood-paneled, vaulted ceiling. Not bad, I thought and silently wondered which financial firm had managed her money.

"No," he said, pulling me from my silent musings about the lovely house. "No dog, and now I'm worried. I've checked every room in the house, and I can assure you there are a lot of rooms."

"I can imagine," I said. "What does it look like in there?" I was so curious to get a look inside Leslie's house that I was afraid I might do something stupid, like shove Tuck aside and bolt through the door. But in the name of professionalism, I refrained.

"Bain said the door was unlocked when they got here early this morning," he informed us from his perch in the doorway. "That's not too unusual out here. What is unusual is that the office, den, great room, and master bedroom have been turned over. Someone was in here looking for something."

"How about décor?" I asked again. "Is it tasteful? Gaudy? Meh?"

"Why does that matter?" He furrowed his gold-dusted brows at me in question.

"It doesn't," I told him. "It's just that this house is such an enigma, like its owner. I had no idea it was even out here. I want to see what it looks like inside, especially that messed-up office." Lilian, aka Kennedy, nodded in agreement.

"Again, ladies, this is a crime scene. You can't come in here because you are civilians. And, if you must know, this house is stunning. It's both rustic and luxurious . . . if that makes sense. The person who designed it not only had great taste, but also money. Don't forget," he said, challenging our puzzled expressions, "up until nine months ago, Leslie was married."

"We need to figure out what Mr. Adams did for a living," Kennedy remarked with a look of appreciation. Then, noticing the slightly deprecating expression coming from Tuck, she added. "What, darling? Maybe it's relevant to this murder?"

"Can you tell if anything was taken?" I thought to ask.

"Hard to tell, since we don't know what was in here before the ransacking. Maybe her daughter can help us with that once she gets here. Other than the obvious fact that someone was here, we don't how many people entered the home or what they were looking for. The crime scene folks are scouring the place for evidence, hoping to figure that out, but it takes time." He looked over his shoulder, then lowered his voice. "I'll tell you what I'll do. I'll see if I can take some pictures. Don't think it would hurt to have an extra set of eyes or two on this one. Now, as for the reason I wanted you here in the first place. There's a small dog door in the mudroom that leads to a series of multilevel decks across the back of the house. If the crime happened here, and if Trixie witnessed it, she could have easily run out the dog door."

"And, if she wanted to, I imagine she could have returned through the dog door as well." This Kennedy remarked with a challenging stare at her boyfriend.

Unfortunately, neither Tuck nor I found that fact comforting. Yes, Trixie should have returned home, unless she was taken, injured, or really spooked. With a new wave of urgency, I said to

Tuck, "I'm going to need you to bring me Trixie's blanket. I already have a leash and plenty of dog cookies. If she's in these woods, Welly will find her."

I had high hopes that Trixie would be close to the house. With the dog's blanket in hand, Welly took a good sniff. My pup wasn't a trained search-and-rescue dog by any means, but he had an amazing sense of smell and a strong desire to play with friends. Newfoundlands are known for their search-and-rescue ability and are especially adept at finding drowning victims, possessing the ability to smell underwater. Admittedly, such skills take a lot of training, which Welly didn't have. I was hoping some of these traits were instinctive. Yet I was having my doubts when I brought Welly to the doggie door on the middle deck in the back—the long deck that ran the length of the whole first floor—and watched him try to shove his giant head through the small opening.

"Maybe this was a mistake." Kennedy voiced her concern, standing on the deck beside me with her arms crossed. "We all love Welly, but does he actually think he can fit through that?"

Lord, I hoped not. "It's the novelty of the door," I answered, pretending it was the case. "I don't think he's ever seen one of those before. Welly!" I said, grabbing his attention. With a little tug and a wiggle, he pulled his big, fluffy head back out, nearly getting it stuck under the sturdy door flap. He then looked at me with doleful eyes and two strings of drool dripping from his jowls. Welly had obviously smelled something alluring inside, most likely Trixie's food. It made me wonder if the poodle had eaten. With a new sense of urgency, I gave

Welly a treat and offered him another sniff of the blanket. "Find Trixie," I told him again. "She's out here." I pointed to the yard and the dense forest beyond, hoping he'd get the picture. But Welly did something even more surprising. He lowered his nose to the deck and began walking in circles.

"Maybe the dog we're after is wearing an invisibility cloak?" Kennedy offered unhelpfully. She'd been standing in front of a sliding-glass wall, with hands cupping her eyes and her face pressed against the window. She looked at Welly, gave a shrug, then went back to her peeping.

"You know what I think? I think Trixie came out here and was walking in circles, nervous about what had happened inside."

Kennedy stepped back from the window and looked at me. "Oh? So, you've gone from banker to baker and now to a pet intuitive? Getting into the mind of a poodle, are we?"

She deserved the loving sneer I cast her. "He's following her scent!" I said, pointing at Welly, whose nose was singularly focused on the deck. I really hoped that was what he was doing, and not casting a wide, nosy net for food, which was also one of his favorite hobbies. Just as Kennedy pulled her focus from the window, Welly bounded down the steps to the beautiful patio, where he continued to sniff the bricks. Just as we made it down the wooden steps, he trotted to the far end of the patio and continued along a brick walkway. He was going so fast that he rounded the corner before we made it to the walkway.

"Quick," I told Kennedy as I ran after him, holding his leash and a much-loved quilted blanket. Following the walkway, I ran up a series of stone steps and rounded the corner. That's when I nearly crashed into a man.

"Whoa!" the man said, holding up his hands and bracing for impact. I leapt aside, narrowly missing him. Kennedy, having had more warning, stopped a mere four feet away. The poor guy was as surprised to see us as we were to see him.

"I'm sorry," I apologized, then chanced a look behind him at Wellington. My pup was trotting down the long, winding driveway with his nose to the ground and his tail in the air.

The man, with a curious look, followed my gaze. Then, with recognition blazing behind his light-brown eyes, he said, "You're the woman who owns that lighthouse bakery! I've been in that place. It's wonderful."

"Thank you," I remarked, blushing a little. Although I didn't know this man's name, on second look, he did seem familiar. "Lindsey Bakewell," I told him, holding out my hand. "And this is my dear friend, Kennedy Kapoor."

"Mark Whitcomb," he introduced himself. Then, as a troubled look crossed his face, he addressed Kennedy. "I know who *you* are. You hosted that live podcast last night. I must be the only person in this town who didn't watch that ridiculous ghost hunt. But I did hear about it. That's why I'm here now. Oh, God," he uttered in a pained breath. "I can't believe she's gone."

"I'm so sorry," I replied, understanding that he must have had a personal connection to the deceased. I then ventured, "How did you know Leslie?"

Welly, I noticed, had disappeared from my view.

"I worked with her. We've worked together for a

long time. I'm also a teacher at the high school. I came here to see if there was anything I can do."

"We're here for much the same reason." I held up the leash and Trixie's blanket to illustrate.

"What's . . . this?" His thick brown eyebrows nearly touched on his forehead as he frowned.

"When we learned that Leslie's dog wasn't in the house, we thought we could help find her. That's why we're here."

"Trixie?" Mark was a trim man of medium height, medium build, and with a head of thick brown hair that was a tad too long. He was the sort of man that was unremarkable, until you looked into his eyes. They were a shade of light brown that rivaled a jar of golden honey. And they were expressive. "She's not here? Where else would she be?" I could tell he was as troubled by this news as we were. "Leslie loved that dog."

"I only just met Leslie the other day," I told him, "when she came with the senior class to my lighthouse. She brought Trixie with her to the bakeshop on Halloween. I could tell how much her dog meant to her. That's why we're here. It's not much, but it's something we can do to help."

He pointed down the driveway where all the emergency vehicles were parked. "What's your big dog doing?"

"We think Trixie might have left the house through the dog door. My dog is following her scent—"

"We think," Kennedy reiterated with a hint of skepticism. "Or he's chasing a squirrel. With Wellington, one never knows."

"Dog door?" Mark's troubled gaze shot to the large house. "I didn't know Leslie had a dog door.

The poor creature could be anywhere. And why are the police in the house? I thought Leslie was murdered at your lighthouse?"

"What?" Kennedy and I were both gobsmacked by this. However, anyone who watched the live ghost hunt last night would be inclined to think so. I was quick to tell him differently.

"No-no!" I told him in no uncertain terms. "The police are rather certain she wasn't murdered there. This," I said, indicating the many police vehicles, "is part of the investigation. They're still trying to figure out what happened to her. Until they do, nobody's allowed inside. And unless you're her next of kin, it's doubtful you'll have any reason to be inside this lovely home again. You have been inside this house, Mark, haven't you?"

"Ya . . . yes, I have. We were friends. I was friends with her late husband, Doug, as well. I'm sorry," he said as blotchy red patches appeared on his face. I thought he might have been close to tears. "This is so terrible. So troubling. Listen, if there's anything I can do to help, let me know."

He was about to go when I suddenly stopped him. "I do have something to ask you. You said you're a teacher at the high school, right? Are you familiar with the kids Leslie referred to as 'witchtok'?"

"I am," he replied. He tilted his head, holding me in his golden-honey gaze. "It's a small school. I believe you're referring to the kids who identify as modern witches? Witchtok is a niche section of a social-media platform they follow, participate in, and are influenced by."

"Interesting," Kennedy said with a lack of enthusiasm. "Lindsey's asking because we'd like to know how to get in touch with the leader of that group. You know, darling, the head of the coven?"

"Unfortunately, I do." Mark pursed his lips as he stared at Kennedy for a moment. He then asked, "Why are these kids of interest to you?"

"We met them," Kennedy was quick to remark. "They came to the lighthouse and were particularly interested in its haunted history. We'd like to see if they know anything about their recently deceased teacher."

"You're planning on asking them questions?" His unique eyes gave us a hard look. "You two aren't police. What business do you have snooping around here and harassing high school students? Although it's only Sunday, school's already been canceled for next week due to Leslie's murder. Everyone's just sick about it. Even though school's been canceled, tomorrow the district is bringing in social workers and therapists for both the students and the staff who've been affected. This is a tragedy, a very public one at that." This last bit he directed at my friend. As if she needed any more reminders.

Kennedy was the type of woman who always rose to a challenge, usually with a snappy reply, but I could see she was starting to crumble under the heated gaze of this teacher.

"Actually," I said, pulling his attention back to me, "we're trying to find Leslie's dog. Her students might know where Trixie is, or at the very least they might want to help us out by joining the search and making posters. Now, can you please give us a name?"

After a moment's thought, Mark Whitcomb caved. "Kiley Henderson," he said. "She was close to Leslie. She'd want to help." He pulled out his phone and pulled up the student directory. Once he found her address, he sent it to me via text.

"Thank you."

Mark didn't reply. Instead, he took one more look at the house. Crime scene workers in their white coveralls were bringing out bags of what looked to be Leslie's clothing. Others had black boxes or carried large cameras. Barriers had been put up by the door and walkway. Tuck, carrying a roll of yellow crime scene tape, was coming toward us. The teacher lowered his head and quickly walked back to his car.

"Who was that?" Tuck asked, walking our way.

"His name is Mark Whitcomb. He's a teacher at the high school. He didn't realize this was a crime scene," Kennedy told him.

Tuck nodded, then lowered his voice. "There's some evidence to suggest that Leslie was taken from this house, either by force, or after she was murdered. There are scuff marks from the heels of Leslie's shoes that lead from the kitchen all the way to the front door, as if she was pulled. God only knows why she was transported to the lighthouse from here." He looked both sad and troubled as he said this. Then, thinking of something else, he asked, "Any sign of the dog?"

"Not yet," I told him. "Welly was following a scent down the driveway."

"Which just might make sense," Kennedy added with a new look of appreciation for my dog and his antics. She glanced at the driveway in question, now busy with police activity. "If Leslie was removed from the house, and the dog was locked inside, Trixie, being loyal, might have gone through the doggy door and followed the killer down the driveway . . . which means that Wellington might actually be on to something?"

"Or Trixie was taken as well," I said, dreading the thought. The truth was, we had no clue who had killed Leslie, why she was murdered, or what had happened to Trixie. It was a very depressing situation.

"Alright, ladies," Tuck began, resuming his role of police officer. "I'm going to have to ask you to leave. Keep searching for the dog. We'll touch base later."

CHAPTER 18

Mark Whitcomb had driven back down the driveway, and the house had been declared a crime scene. It was only ten thirty in the morning, and already my head was spinning. Kennedy, from the look of her, was possibly feeling even worse, having been the unfortunate one who had found the body of the beloved teacher. From my own experience, it wasn't something she was soon to forget, if ever.

We walked down the driveway past my Jeep, searching for Wellington. My poor dog had been sent on an important mission, and I had gotten distracted. A moment of panic seized me when we got to the end of the driveway and there was no sign of him.

"Oh, my God! He's lost. What have I done?" My emotions had gone from calm to full freak-out panic mode in half a second. It wasn't pretty.

"Relax, Linds," Kennedy advised in the calm tone of one who had never been a mother or a pet owner. Had Wellington been a baby, I was sure I would have passed out from anxiety. "Call him," she said, staring at me with a look that suggested I was quickly becoming unhinged. I took her advice and did just that.

"He must have gotten tired of waiting for us and decided to chase squirrels," I said, trying to think rationally. But all I could think was that somebody in a car, either driving by or leaving the driveway, had taken him—perhaps just like Trixie. I had no proof, but fear was escalating inside me at an unreasonable pace. Kennedy and I called out to Welly again, with Kennedy standing on the left side of the driveway and I on the right. Although most of the trees were bare and the forest floor was covered in a carpet of exquisite fall colors, I couldn't see my dog.

"He wouldn't leave willingly," I told Kennedy. "Not with me still here."

"He was following Trixie's scent," she reminded me. I could tell she was growing a bit nervous as well. "Maybe Trixie took off through the woods. Which way is your lighthouse from here?"

I thought for a moment, looked at the sun in the sky, then pointed across the street. "As the crow flies, that way is the most direct route, but it's a long way to the lighthouse from here. However, getting here in the Jeep, we came from that direction." I pointed up the gravel road to the left. I looked at Kennedy, and we both ran across the road.

"Wellington!" I shouted to the dense forest. A moment later, we heard rustling and the crunching of leaves. It was coming from a spot deep in the woods along the road. The sound grew louder as we continued calling to my dog.

"There he is!" I shouted. Relief hit me as I caught a glimpse of fluffy black fur moving at high speed through the tree trunks. A minute later, Welly was trotting toward us. My jaw dropped when I saw what he was carrying in his mouth. It was the little neon-colored clown hat Trixie had been wearing at the Pumpkin Pageant.

"Are you seeing this?" Kennedy asked, knowing full well that I was. Wellington, with the dog-sized clown hat in his mouth, came to a stop before me and sat at my feet. He was very reluctant to give up his treasure.

"Good boy," I said and gave him a treat in exchange for the hat. That always did the trick. I then gave him a big hug. "Such a good boy," I told him again, relieved he was safe. I then asked the obvious question, "Where did you find this?"

Wellington was a fairly intelligent dog, but he didn't have a good grasp of the human language. Sure, words such as *cookie, treat, kibble,* and *Rory* were at the top of his list of recognizable words. He was also good with *sit, stay, come,* and *get fish* (which essentially meant getting a treat at Rory's house). However, I knew my question was beyond him, but the fact that he was proud of his find was unmistakable. Panting happily, he gave me his paw and licked my face as I held it. It was enough of an answer for me. Kennedy and I then began walking through the woods along the road with Wellington guiding us, hoping he'd take us to the place where he'd found Trixie's hat. And maybe he had, and we just didn't know it. However, it was obvious that this time Welly was more interested in chasing squirrels. In my eyes, he deserved that much. After fifteen minutes of searching, we decided to head

back to the Jeep. There was no sign of the little
dog, and nothing to indicate she'd been taken.
Although I was still very concerned for the miniature poodle, my best guess was that Trixie had left
the house to try to save her human. I found the
thought both touching and heartbreaking in turns.

To say Mom was happy to see me was an understatement. The moment we came through her
door, we were given big hugs. Mom was especially
attentive to Kennedy, having watched her whole
podcast last night to its abrupt and gruesome end.
Welly paused just long enough for his mom-hug,
then trotted off to play with Mom's two West
Highland white terriers, Brinkley and Ireland, collectively known as "the models." With the dogs off
playing, Kennedy and I were ushered to the dining
room table, where a pot of tea sat waiting for us,
along with Betty Vanhoosen, Ginger Brooks, Felicity Stewart, Ali Johnson, and Christy Parks. Not
only were they friends, but other women shop
owners of the village. It was a cozy setting, with tea
served in dainty China cups and a plate of pumpkin scones from the Beacon Bakeshop. In that moment, I understood that nothing soothed the
nerves quite like a cup of hot tea with dear friends.

"What a tragic night!" Betty Vanhoosen exclaimed
the moment we sat down. Her round blue eyes,
reminiscent of an owl's, relayed both sympathy
and intrigue. I didn't think such a look was possible, but Betty, bless her, pulled it off. Just after her
remark, she tried to take a sip of tea. I say "tried"
because a tremor shook her hand at the worst possible moment, sending a wave of hot Darjeeling

over the rim. It missed her lips and dribbled on her pretty autumn sweater. The perturbed Realtor uttered a little curse word, the likes of which was a surprise coming from her lips, then gently daubed at the stain with her napkin. "I'm afraid my nerves are still on edge after you found poor Leslie Adams last night swinging from that tree. Ooo, it gives me nightmares just thinking about it! Do you have any idea who did the evil deed?"

"Not a clue," Kennedy admitted. "And it's white-hot pokers to the nerves for me, Betty. And nightmares too. You all saw me. I ran right into her very dead body. Why did I think running out the back door would be safer?"

"You weren't thinking safe," I remarked in a soothing tone. "You were thinking fast. Everyone else took the front door."

"It's undoubtedly the worst and most public moment of my life," Ken admitted with a sorry look. "When I had the '*brilliant*' idea to livestream a ghost hunt, the thought of crashing into a dead body never crossed my mind. And why would it? What I want to know is what sicko could have done such a thing?" As she asked this, Kennedy picked up the teapot. With an expert's touch, she filled her cup, then mine. She set the pot back on the table and shook her head.

"Whoever did it is still on the loose, and now it's all over the internet," Felicity Stewart said with sympathy. After a quick flip of her long, thick red hair, she nervously tapped her bright red nails on the tablecloth. Felicity looked good in both red and green. I liked to tease that Christmas was her color, for it was clearly her passion. Felicity was the owner of the town's year-round Christmas store,

Tannenbaum. "Another murder in our little village," she declared and pursed her red lips in frustration. "Not only is this terrible, but people are going to get the wrong impression of our friendly little village of Beacon Harbor." She was obviously thinking about the fallout of yet another murder in our idyllic town. I dare say, I couldn't blame her.

"Do you think this brazen murderer wanted the gruesome deed to be discovered like that—on a livestream podcast?" It was Ginger Brooks who asked this question. Ginger owned Harbor Scoops, the town's famous ice cream shop. She took a bite of her pumpkin scone, then added, "I mean, we all knew about the live ghost hunt. We all watched it."

"I really don't see how the murderer could have known the entire ghost-hunting crew would get spooked by the ghost lights and flee the light-house." I looked at Ginger as I spoke, then took a sip of the hot, delicious tea. Darjeeling was often referred to as the champagne of teas for its musky-sweet notes and the hint of citrus flavors. No wonder it was Mom's favorite.

Betty, forgetting about her tea and scone, leaned on her elbows, locking eyes with Kennedy. "By the way, what was it like in the lightroom when the ghost lights came on?"

"It was very odd," Kennedy admitted softly. We all leaned in, each of us wanting to hear what she had to say. "The entire night was very odd," she added with a somber expression. "Look, I'm going to admit something to you all that I don't want any of you to repeat. But all the ghost shenanigans that I claim to have experienced in Lindsey's light-house are mostly made up. Sure, I've seen the lights flicker a wee bit, but that could have been faulty wiring. I might have even smelled the faint scent of pipe smoke once, but it's an old building. That smell could be stuck in the walls for all I know. I've heard the wind, but not footsteps. Lindsey hears those."

"I do," I admitted and wondered where she was going with this.

"What I'm trying to say is that I'm more frightened of the idea of there being a ghost in the lighthouse than I am of the actual ghost. Captain Willy doesn't give me the time of day, and I'm just fine with that. But I wanted to drum up a little mystique and excitement because it was Halloween . . . and, you know, because of all the rumors about the lighthouse being haunted."

"Because it *is* haunted," Ginger remarked with a knowing look. "What?" she bristled as all eyes shot to her. "Everybody knows it!"

"What are you saying, dear?" Mom pressed, ignoring Ginger's remark and casting Kennedy a look of concern.

"What can I say?" Kennedy, glancing around the table, gave a little shrug. "I love a bit of drama. And last night, for the first half hour of the investigation, I was bringing down the house with drama."

"I'll say," Ali Johnson remarked. Ali and her husband, Jack, owned the Book Nook, Beacon Harbor's much-loved independent bookstore. "We couldn't take our eyes off you during the ghost hunt. It was deliciously spooky . . . until, you know." All enthusiasm left her voice.

"There was a whole crew of people with me," Kennedy continued. "There was Teddy, and all the Ghost Guys. It's hardly an intimate setting when one wants to wrangle up a ghost. Honestly, I thought it was all a bit of a hoax. I mean, all that ridiculous technology. '*If it lights up,*'" Ken mimicked in her best male American impersonation, "'*that means there's a ghost nearby.*' It was all fun, harmless stuff. But then, after a half hour of investigating, I felt a shift in the atmosphere of the lighthouse."

"Whoa!" I was about to take a sip of tea, but I set the cup back on the saucer. I didn't want to pull a Betty and shake it all over me. "What do you mean by that?"

Kennedy shrugged. "It's hard to explain, but for no reason at all, the hair on my arms was standing on end—as if there was a slight electric charge in the air. That's when things really started to get wonky. That's when we heard the footsteps in the light tower."

"Oh, I remember that!" Christy Parks exclaimed, looking frightened at the memory. Christy owned Bayside Boutiques, a charming home décor store that sold furniture, artwork, and all manner of local, handmade treasures. "It was super spooky," she added. I couldn't blame her. I found the incident unsettling as well. And if I was being honest, I was a little afraid of going back to my lighthouse.

"It was," Kennedy admitted. "But what I'm trying to say is that up until that point, the entire investigation was a bit of an act. There was nothing there. Then, around eleven thirty, things went a little crazy. We heard footsteps. Brett Bloom, the head Ghost Guy, caught a disembodied voice on his ghost-box thingy, spouting gibberish about danger. And then, in the lightroom, the feeling was positively electric. It's hard to explain, but it was like stepping into another dimension up there. Lindsey and I go up there all the time, ladies. It's our favorite gal-pal hangout. It's fabulous up there, but it wasn't last night. No, it smelled weird! It totally freaked me out. But it was only for a minute. Then an eerie green light burst into the room—from nowhere! The suddenness of it . . . the prickling of the skin! No one was expecting that."

"It's the legendary ghost lights of Beacon Harbor, dear," Betty uttered in a prophetic whisper, sending a chill down my spine. "We all saw it, didn't we? It's a portent of danger. The ghost in your lighthouse knew Leslie was murdered!"

"Ladies, Lindsey," Kennedy said, holding me in her intense, dark gaze. "Last night, Leslie Adams was murdered, and we learned that Lindsey's lighthouse really is haunted."

I knew my lighthouse was haunted. I'd been trying to tell Kennedy that for over a year now. I was sorry she'd had to learn it the hard way. However, there was still a murderer on the loose, and for whatever reason the sicko felt my lighthouse was the perfect place to display the body. I needed answers.

"Who would do such a thing?" Ginger looked as ill as I felt as she asked this. "Leslie was one of the state's best teachers. I was hoping Kate would have her when she got to high school." The thought made her glum.

"I knew her late husband," Christy Parks told the table. "They were such a nice family, the Adamses, and one of the older names in this town."

I perked up at that. "What did Leslie's husband do for a living?"

Christy smiled. "He was a developer and a quality builder. Doug built homes all over the county, including homes as far north as Petosky. I was very sad when he died. Doug's company purchased a lot of furnishing through my store."

Betty, flashing a smile at Christy, expounded on that fact. "He built some lovely homes in this town."

"Tell me about it," Kennedy remarked. "We were just at his home. It's a stunner."

"You were at Leslie's house?" Although Betty asked this, it was clear that everyone at the table had assumed we'd come from the police station.

"We were," I told them. "We were allowed to go out there when I asked Tuck, I mean, Officer McAllister, if Leslie's dog had been found."

"Her dog!" Mom exclaimed, as a look of concern crossed her pretty face. "That cute little poodle? Was she at the house?"

"No," I told the ladies. "We have a missing dog, and Leslie's house is now a crime scene."

CHAPTER 19

After a somber conversation over hot tea and scones, the lady merchants of Beacon Harbor had left Mom's house, each one promising to spread the word about the missing dog, Trixie. Feeling helpless and out of our league regarding the murder, searching for Leslie's dog gave us a sense of purpose. It was something.

Mom, Betty, Kennedy, and I were in the kitchen straightening up after the impromptu gathering, when Betty, sitting at the kitchen counter, set down the pumpkin scone she'd been eating. One of the things I loved about Betty was that she was a huge fan of my baking. She came into the Beacon nearly every morning, and she never missed an opportunity to spread the word about my bakeshop. It was her second pumpkin scone of the morning, God bless her.

"I didn't want to say anything with the ladies around, but, as you know, Bob is conducting the autopsy today." Betty hit us with a knowing look.

After all, she was dating the county medical examiner, Dr. Bob Riggles.

"I know," I replied and set down the dainty flowered teacup I had just dried on the counter. "He came to the lighthouse last night to examine the body. Doc Riggles and Sergeant Murdock both knew Leslie had died before being hung in my tree." Just saying that gave me a sick feeling in the pit of my stomach. From the looks on their faces, it apparently wasn't sitting too well with them either. Seeing the poor woman hanging there in that brightly colored clown costume was certain to give me, and the rest of them, nightmares. Also, whenever Doc Riggles showed up in his professional capacity, it was never a good thing. However, the doc was good at his job, which was a small comfort. He would discover how Leslie had died, which just might lead us to the bigger question of who had done the deed, and why.

"Betty?" Kennedy addressed the Realtor with an arched brow. "We know that Bob is working on this. What are you suggesting?"

Mom was at the kitchen sink rinsing out a teapot when she turned to face us. "You know very well what she's suggesting. We have insider knowledge, thanks to Bob. The victim was found at your lighthouse, dear. I think that gives us the right to get involved."

"It's time to put on our sleuthing hats, ladies!" Betty, the busiest busybody in Beacon Harbor, flashed a wily grin as she said this. No one could resist returning the gesture.

"I knew it!" I flashed Mom and Betty a conspiratorial look. "I, for one, am glad you two are not shying away from this one, although I wouldn't blame you if you did. However, Kennedy and I are going to need some help."

"Very true." Kennedy gave a nod. "I detest murderers as a rule, but this one, when we find the person responsible for that despicable stunt, will feel my wrath." As if to make her point, she gave a little snarl.

It was discussed that when Doc Riggles discovered the cause of death, Betty would pass it along to us. She'd done it before, and we were happy to learn she'd do it again. Mom and Betty would do what they did best: crank the handle on the gossip mill and see if they could piece together Leslie's movements after she'd won first place at the Pumpkin Pageant. It had been a busy day, and no one seemed to remember where she'd gone after winning first place for her brightly colored clown costume that matched her dog's. However, somebody must have seen something. It wasn't like she was just going to blend into the crowd with a costume like that. Whom was Leslie with? Whom did she talk to? What time did she leave to go back home? We prayed someone would have an answer for us.

While Mom and Betty were working their magic in town, Kennedy and I would investigate the lead we'd been given by Leslie's coworker, Mark Whitcomb. The group of teens who referred to themselves as modern-day witches, or witchtok kids, had been on the cold, dark beach during the paranormal investigation. Had Leslie and her dog been with them when the investigation began? I hoped not. But that group of kids had been acting suspicious, and I had the feeling they were hiding something.

I was just about to call Rory at the warehouse to see how he was doing (I was sure the retired men of the town had gathered there to discuss the horrific murder of Leslie Adams), when a knock came at Mom's door. The dogs started barking. Brinkley and Ireland ran through the kitchen, followed closely by Welly, who was carrying Dad's tennis shoe in his mouth. Unfortunately, the bright white leather shoe was now covered in drool.

"I'll get it!" I assured Mom and followed the barking dogs. I calmed them down (they were always so excited to greet newcomers!), gingerly removed the tennis shoe from Welly's mouth, and answered the door.

I was hoping for Rory, or Tuck, but to my surprise, it was Jordy Tripp, the writer. He was with another man, perhaps a friend of his. This other man was smaller, a decade younger, wore black glasses, and had his long, mousy brown hair tied back in a ponytail. He gave off the air of a geek but was trying to disguise it with the trendy brown hiking pants and the black, puffy Patagonia jacket he wore. I thought he might be another writer, or a tech genius, or perhaps an academic. However, one look at Jordy, and I suddenly remembered I had offered to give him a tour of my lighthouse today at one o'clock. Awkward. It was after one, and I wasn't at my lighthouse. In my defense, I was still a little unsettled by the Halloween ghost hunt, not to mention my backyard was still roped off with bright yellow crime scene tape.

"I'm so sorry," I apologized. "With all that's

been going on, I forgot all about the lighthouse tour I promised you."

Jordy grimaced and held up a hand to stop my apology. "We've just come from the aquatic adventure center Mr. Campbell is building. Your father and a group of other gentlemen of the village were there as well. We were told we might find you here today after last night's public calamity. Yes, I watched it. What a terrible turn of events. I'm, ah . . . very shaken by it all, as you can imagine." To his credit, he did look troubled and a tad haggard as well. Whether it was from the murder, or the fact that it had occurred at my lighthouse, I couldn't tell.

Jordy, having looked me in the eyes, dropped his gaze to his shoes. "I came here to tell you that I'd like a rain check on that tour. I have no wish to disturb a crime scene." He took a deep breath, looked at me again, and continued. "I would also like to apologize for my behavior yesterday at your bakery. I realize I came off as a bit of a cad. My only excuse is that I was shocked by the grandeur of your bakery renovation. Whenever I'm working on a project, I get tunnel vision."

"To say the least," replied the smaller man with a smug grin. He then offered his hand to me. "Grant Fairfield. I'm Jordy's research assistant on this project. I can also personally attest to the fact that he can be quite the taskmaster when he's working."

"Research assistant?" For some reason that impressed me. It also piqued my interest to an even greater degree, causing me to wonder about the project the famous Jordy Tripp was working on that involved my lighthouse. I silently hoped this wasn't about Captain Willy Riggs and his untimely death. Ignoring the hundreds of questions popping into my head, I took the man's proffered hand. "Very nice to meet you. Won't you come inside?"

As I brought the men to the sunroom, and after shooing the dogs to the yard, Jordy continued, "I'm afraid nothing else matters but the book I'm working on. An author is only as good as his latest book, Lindsey, and I'm afraid my last Matt Malone novel fell short of the mark. I'm hoping to redeem myself with this nonfiction project that I'm writing. I'm quite passionate about it. But my personal obsession with my work isn't a good excuse for bad manners."

"Thank you for the apology," I told him sincerely. "I know a little something about passion and drive myself. You saw my lighthouse. That renovation was a work of passion. I look forward to giving you a tour when I'm able."

My parents' sunroom, with its curved wall of windows, offered a spectacular view of both the lake and the forested hillsides of the bay on which the house had been built. Jordy took a seat and soaked up the view before offering, "I'm glad you understand, Lindsey. I've been reading historical documents regarding your lighthouse. In my mind I had it pictured exactly as it had been back in its heyday. I hadn't been expecting that thorough and modern renovation."

"Isn't it just wonderful!" Mom beamed proudly as she came into the room, followed closely by Betty and Kennedy. "Now, what can I get you gentlemen to drink?"

Jordy had met my mom, but the younger man, Grant, was staring at her as if he'd never seen a beautiful, older woman before. The bug-eyed look behind the black glasses was not only unsettling, but a bit comical as well. He asked for coffee with cream and sugar, swallowed loudly, and said, "Has anyone told you that you look a little bit like Ellie Montague, the old supermodel?"

"The '*old supermodel*'?" Mom narrowed her eyes at him. "Honey, I *am* Ellie Montague Bakewell! And age isn't going to stop me!" She flipped her long, tawny-blond hair over her shoulder and cast him her cover girl smile. "I'll be right back with that coffee."

Grant Fairfield turned an unhealthy shade of red and looked as if he was about to bolt out the door. Jordy laughed, and Betty exclaimed, "Welcome to Beacon Harbor, Mr. Fairfield."

"It's a town full of surprises," Kennedy added with a narrow-eyed gaze aimed at our visitors.

"Right." Now that the gentlemen were sufficiently thrown off guard, I hit them with the one burning question I just had to ask. "Now, what is so compelling about my lighthouse that lured a famous writer and his research assistant to our little village? And don't say the mini pumpkin Bundt cakes. We all know they're delicious, just as we know that writers need them and black coffee to keep churning out pages. All joking aside, gentlemen, why are you here?"

The gentlemen exchanged a glance, heavy with question. Then Jordy, coming to some conclusion, leaned forward and confessed, "A fabled shipwreck, my dear, and the deathbed confession of a lightkeeper from the Beacon Point Lighthouse. Your lighthouse is at the center of this mystery, Lindsey. And yes, the missing piece to this puzzle just might be worth killing for."

My jaw dropped. "'Missing piece'? 'Worth kill-ing for'?" My head was spinning. "What the devil are you talking about, Jordy? And what exactly are you looking for?"

"We're not exactly sure," Grant confessed with a shrug. "But we believe that somewhere in your lighthouse, there just might be evidence that will help us verify the story we're investigating. We'd like you to help us find it."

CHAPTER 20

"Is it just me? Or did this day just swerve from terrible to outlandishly weird?" Kennedy closed her eyes and shook her head, as if to wake up from a bad dream.

"Amazing, but yes. It did. I'm so confused right now I don't even know what to think. I'm calling Rory." Kennedy, Welly, and I were back in the Jeep again, this time heading out of town to the house of the head witchtok girl. Part of me wanted to drive back home, but part of me was scared to do that. It was ridiculous. I'd been living in the lighthouse for over a year and a half now and had never been afraid of being there. However, a ghost hunt and a terrible murder had changed everything. And to top it off, Sergeant Murdock wasn't returning my calls. I didn't know if I would even be allowed to return home, or not.

While Welly napped in the back seat and Kennedy managed her social media accounts on her phone, I put in my earbuds and called Rory.

"Babe!" he answered on the first ring. "I was just

going to call you. It's been hectic here. How's your day going? Did you have any trouble this morning with Sergeant Murdock?"

I briefly told him about our morning, including my conversation with Tuck, and our little excursion to Leslie's house to find her missing dog.

"Did you and Kennedy get inside the house?" After learning that Trixie was still missing, I could tell he was just as anxious to get a look inside Leslie's home as I was. I hated to disappoint him.

"No. We couldn't get past the door. It's now a crime scene. Tuck told us they believe Leslie was murdered in the house before being taken . . ." I didn't need to finish that sentence. "Anyhow," I continued, "Tuck told us somebody was inside the house looking for something. The obvious guess would be it was the murderer. Anyhow, it appears that some rooms in the house were ransacked."

"Very interesting," he said, and I could just picture his dark brows furrowed in contemplation as he thought on what I was telling him. "Did Tuck hint at what it was the murderer was looking for?"

"They didn't have a clue. They just saw that everything was turned over."

"Terrible as it may be, the Ghost Guys will be relieved to hear that the cops believe the deed was done off-site. Murdock was very hard on them, or so they tell me. They're here with me at the warehouse, as are half the gentlemen of the village, your dad included. Hope you don't mind that I've invited the Ghost Guys over for dinner tonight."

"Not at all," I said. The truth was, the moment he mentioned dinner, I was already planning the menu in my head. The meal I could handle. My one concern I voiced to him. "Just a warning, but

I'm not sure we're allowed back in the lighthouse yet. I'm still trying to get the okay from Murdock."

"Not to worry. We can always have it at the cabin. By the way, did Jordy Tripp find you?"

"He did. He came over to Mom's house."

"What did he want? He and his friend paid me a visit earlier, asking some very curious questions."

"Like what?"

"Lars and I are just building the main counter, and Jordy came in inquiring about chartering a boat and renting diving equipment. They wouldn't tell me what for, only that it was important to the project they are working on. It's the first of November, Linds, and my compressor has just been installed. Also, the lake temperatures are plummeting, and the conditions are far from ideal. They hardly look capable of a leisurely snorkel, let alone a dive in freezing, choppy waters with dangerous currents. I told them to come back next summer and enroll in my Intro to Scuba class. I'd be happy to take them out once I know they have the basics under their belts."

"Wow. That's a little disturbing," I admitted, thinking of the very guarded conversation I'd had with Jordy and his assistant, Grant. They were after some piece of information to verify the story they were working on. They wouldn't tell me any more than that. "However, I think I might know why they're asking after a boat. Jordy wanted to reschedule a tour of the lighthouse. He believes there's information in the lighthouse that might help them find an old shipwreck they've been researching."

Rory exhaled sharply into the phone. "A shipwreck? That's what they're after? What a couple of idiots! There's something like fifteen hundred shipwrecks in Lake Michigan alone, Linds, and most of them have been documented and dated, very likely including the one they're looking for. If they're looking for a map or a description of the wreck site of some undiscovered shipwreck, first, the accuracy of the information would be in question. Old-timey mariners had nothing close to GPS back in the day. Secondly, it's doubtful the ship would be in the same place it went down, due to the intervening storms and currents. Did they tell you the name of the wreck and why it's so important?"

"Ironically, that's the one thing they did not wish to reveal."

Rory found that just as interesting as I did. However, we'd talk about that later. I was nearly at the house of Kiley Henderson, Leslie's student, and told him how we'd gotten her name.

"Excellent work, Bakewell. Keep me posted. And let me know what Murdock says regarding the lighthouse."

"Will do. Miss you."

"Miss you too, babe." I was about to add a bit more when Kennedy chimed in from the passenger seat.

"Will you please put an end to it already!" Kennedy cast me a look of mild disgust. I had been so busy talking with Rory while following directions to Kiley's house that I hadn't realized she'd put her phone away. "It's not like you won't be seeing Hunts-a-Lot in a couple of hours. Pray tell, he wasn't talking you into a romantic dinner at the lighthouse, was he? That man has some nerve."

"I'm not sure where dinner will be tonight.

However, he's invited your buddies, the Ghost Guys, to dine with us wherever we're eating." Her face paled a little at this news.

"I misjudged the conversation. That's the danger of only hearing one side of it, Lindsey darling. I'm not sure I'm ready to see those gung-ho ghost lads just yet."

"Ken, don't worry. We'll all be there this time. Besides, maybe one of them will remember something about last night that might help us find Leslie's killer."

"Perhaps," she said, giving the Ghost Guys the benefit of the doubt. Then, like the sudden shifting of the wind, her dark-brown eyes shot to the windshield. She gave a sudden shiver. "Unbelievable. Tell me this isn't the place."

"This is the place."

Panic seized her. "It's a dead end. We're on Gravesend Road. This has to be some kind of a joke." She gave the house another look before crossing herself.

I stared out the window at the ancient-looking redbrick farmhouse. It stood at the end of the dirt driveway and had obviously seen better days. Behind the house was a barn that looked to be newer, with chickens strutting around the bushes and a horse grazing in the paddock. I brought my gaze back to the house. The wood trim around the long, narrow windows was chipped and rotting. The front porch wasn't any better. Lopsided and with wobbly railings, it looked as if it was ready to fall off at any moment. I hoped, for our sakes, that it wouldn't. Also, the fact that there weren't any shrubs around the square, two-story house gave it a forlorn, haunted look. I had to agree with Kennedy. There were far more inviting homes in Beacon Harbor than this one. However, the address checked out.

I cracked the back windows for Welly, then turned to Kennedy. "Ready?"

Kennedy narrowed her eyes at the old house once again. "I might live to regret this, but let's go see what the little witch has to say."

CHAPTER 21

"Hello." A dark-haired woman, somewhere in her mid-forties, opened the door just enough to get a good look at us. Her light-green eyes, heavy with skepticism, scanned us from head to toe. I wasn't sure she liked what she saw.

"Have ya come for a reading?" she asked, narrowing her eyes at us. "Didn't think I had one scheduled for today. In fact, I know I don't. If you want one, make an appointment online." She made to shut the door.

"No. No reading," I assured her, stepping closer so she wouldn't shut the door in our faces. "Your daughter came to a party at my lighthouse with Mrs. Adams to carve pumpkins. I'm sure you've heard what happened to the poor woman."

"You're the baker at the lighthouse," the woman said as recognition blazed behind her pale eyes. She opened the door a little wider and turned to Kennedy. Her face darkened. "And you're the one from the podcast, trying to drum up a ghost. You went about it all wrong, ya know." She wrinkled her nose at my friend as she shook her head.

"Kennedy Kapoor. Very nice to meet you. And I wasn't trying to drum up anything but a little entertainment. This reading you speak of, are you a medium?"

"Crystal Henderson," the woman introduced herself. "Yes, I am." Her pale green eyes were back on me.

"Lindsey Bakewell." I extended my hand. "So sorry to stop by unannounced, but I'd like to ask your daughter a few questions, if it's alright with you." I wouldn't lie. Her pale green eyes were unnerving as they stared right at me without blinking. It reminded me of standing in the full-body scanner at airport security. I prayed I hadn't left anything incriminating in my pockets.

"You've got good energy," she finally said with a nod. She then looked at Kennedy and frowned. "And you, Ms. Kapoor, are in desperate need of a chakra cleansing. They are out of alignment. Death and trauma will do that. I don't have time today, but we can talk about that later."

Kennedy looked affronted. "There's nothing wrong with my chakras, whatever they are, thank you very much." Crystal ignored her as she ushered us through the front door.

Entering the house was like stepping back in time, I thought, admiring the heavy crown molding and all the fine woodwork. Although in need of good lighting and a fresh coat of paint, the interior of the house was clean and tidy, and in much better shape than the exterior.

"As you can imagine, Kiley is very upset by the

death of her teacher. Mrs. Adams was not only her
favorite teacher, but a mentor to her. She understood that Kiley had the gift."

"And what gift might we be talking of here?"
Kennedy asked.

"Clairvoyance," Crystal said, leading us to the
parlor. "It runs in the family, females mostly. I realized Kiley had it when she was seven. That's when
she asked me one day if she could see my pin. I
had no idea what she was talking about. She went
on to explain that the pin she had in mind had the
head of a lion on it. That shocked me. My grandmother had given me a similar brooch when I was
ten, but I hadn't seen it in ages. I didn't think Kiley
was talking about that particular pin, but I asked
her anyway. She insisted it was the one, and that
she not only knew about it, but she also knew
where she could find it. Curious, I followed her to
the barn and watched as she climbed into the
hayloft, then disappeared behind a wall of hay. A
few minutes later she returned with a little wooden
box. It was a box my grandfather had made for
me. Sure enough, when Kylie opened it, that beautiful lionhead brooch was in there. Of course, I
was flabbergasted. Tears sprang to my eyes at the
sight of it. I asked her how she knew where to find
it, and she replied that Grandma had told her
where it was."

"What a lovely story." Kennedy offered a smile
that didn't quite reach her eyes. She took a seat on
the antique upholstered chair and crossed her
legs. "She found an old box in the hayloft with an
even older piece of jewelry in it. Have you considered that she might have placed it there herself?"

"She wasn't allowed in the hayloft without supervision," Crystal informed us. "And Kiley's grand-mother died the year before she was born."

A shiver with the impact of a bowling ball traveled up my spine as all the hair on my body stood on end. I was sorry to think I was nervous to speak to this girl. Kennedy, I noticed, had lost control of her jaw. It wasn't her best look.

Crystal excused herself to get Kiley. A moment later, the witchtok teen I had seen in the lighthouse parking lot the night before shuffled into the room. She was wearing a baggy cable-knit sweater in rusty orange over black leggings. Her long dark hair was pulled back into a ponytail, and her face, except for the heavy-handed black eyeliner, was void of all makeup. She looked younger now, and vulnerable, and not at all spooky.

"You wanted to see me?" the girl questioned. "Why?"

"You're the clairvoyant one," Ken quipped. Before she could add another snarky comment, I shot her a look to zip it.

A frightened look crossed the girl's face as she looked at Kennedy. "It . . . it doesn't work like that."

"Kiley, we're very sorry about Mrs. Adams," I said, shifting her focus to me. Kennedy's presence appeared to be making the girl uncomfortable. "I came here today because I saw you last night by the lighthouse. You and some of your friends were coming up from the beach, right after Ms. Kapoor found Mrs. Adams's body. Were you watching the podcast?"

The girl nodded. "Yes. On our phones. Why?"

"Was Mrs. Adams with you at any point during the night?"

"No." She shook her head, causing her thick, black ponytail to swing like a pendulum across her thin back. "We hadn't seen her since the Pumpkin Pageant."

Kennedy leaned forward. I hoped she was going to be civil and not snarky. "Kiley, it must have been cold on the beach. Why were you out there at that time of night, and not in some place warm to watch the ghost hunt?" It was a good question. I gave Ken a nod for the effort.

Kiley wrung her hands before answering. "I . . . wanted to be there. I asked the others to come with me because it was important. We were performing a protection spell."

I was sorry to think that the word *spell* caused another shiver to crawl up my spine. I blew out a breath, steeled my nerves, and asked, "Um, so you were on the beach casting a spell?" I tried to keep my voice light and conversational—as if it was a normal thing teens did on the beach these days. I wanted to stop myself from asking the next question, but couldn't. I was here to get answers. I smiled at Kylie, adding, "Did this spell happen to involve Mrs. Adams?"

Kylie studied her feet a moment before answering. When she did, I could see she was upset. "No," she said. "It had nothing to do with Mrs. Adams, and that's the problem!" Her chin quivered as she said this, and then she burst into tears. Her mother gave her a big hug.

"It's alright, dear," she soothed. "You don't have to tell them anything more if you don't want to."

Kiley sniffled and dried her eyes. "It's alright, Mom. I just . . . I can't believe I missed it. She didn't deserve to die!"

"Kiley, what do you know?" I asked softly. It was obvious the girl was troubled, and I couldn't blame her. "What did you miss?"

She crossed her arms, hugging herself, and raised her shoulders. "All day long I had the feeling that something bad was going to happen at the lighthouse. I get feelings, sometimes. You know? It was strong, and I was certain that something bad was going to happen, but not to Mrs. Adams. She never crossed my mind. Don't you see? I failed her. I cast the spell on the wrong person!"

Although this didn't sound healthy at all to me—casting a spell on the wrong person—I had to admit I was curious. Admittedly, I knew next to nothing about clairvoyance, and I was slightly confused by her very real feelings of guilt. For guilt it was. The girl wasn't faking it. And for that reason, I was strongly getting the feeling that my suspicions about her, and her spooky little friends, were all wrong. "Kylie, who did you think was going to get hurt? Whom were you casting your spell on?"

Kylie wiped her tears, and then she pointed at Kennedy. "Her!" she said. "Ms. Kapoor. I kept seeing her in my head all day. Doom. It was the feeling of doom that came to me, and I thought . . . I thought I could help. I was wrong."

For the second time in the space of ten minutes, Kennedy Kapoor had lost all control of her jaw.

CHAPTER 22

"Well, she wasn't *that* wrong," Kennedy remarked, tucking in her new amulet before adjusting her scarf in the visor mirror. She flipped the visor back in place and looked at me. "I *did* feel a sense of doom. I did get hurt. I ran headlong into a dead body and landed on my bum. Not fun, that. Wee Kiley's spell of protection didn't do a thing. It's all rubbish anyhow, this hocus-pocus witchcraft stuff." She waved the thought off with her hand.

"And yet you were happy enough to take the crystal Crystal offered you." I cast her a lopsided grin as I drove.

"I took it simply because I didn't want to offend her. It would never do to make an enemy of a witch."

"A 'witch'? Do we know she's a witch?" I questioned with a sideways glance her way. "Crystal told us she was a medium and a clairvoyant. I don't remember her saying anything about being a witch.

That's her daughter's thing. And even if she is one, I thought you didn't believe in witches?"

"I don't. But I believe that they believe in themselves, so who am I to rock that boat? Anyhow, crystals are all the rage right now, so I thought I'd give it a try. It's obsidian, you know," she added, patting her chest where she had just thrust the dangling crystal beneath her shirt, coat, and scarf. "Black and shiny. I don't have anything like it. Besides, she said it was a protecting stone, one that's supposed to ward off negative energy and bad juju. Bumping into a dead body hanging from a tree is very bad juju."

"I'll say. Hope it works."

Hearing the word *juju*, Welly sprang up from the back seat and thrust his big, fluffy head between us. He obviously thought juju was some kind of treat. He'd been a good boy, and very patient as well. Also, his pleading eyes undid me. I opened the glove compartment and pulled out a pumpkin Beacon Bite for him. He gobbled it up with minimum drool.

"And what about that sage stick she gave *you?*" Kennedy remarked with an arched brow. "Are you going to *smudge* the lighthouse when we get back?" The way she said "*smudge*" made me laugh.

"Like you, I'm desperate. I'll try anything if it will help me forget what occurred in my home last night. However, smudge stick aside, the real takeaway today was the name Kiley gave us. She's a good kid. I'm sorry I misjudged her."

Our visit to the Henderson house had not only been fascinating, but rather productive as well. While it was clear that Kiley was very fond of her deceased teacher, she did have some keen insight on other things. She clearly didn't want to be a snitch, but once she realized we were trying to help the police find Leslie's killer, she did offer up a name when I asked her about the harassing of my lighthouse. She told me it was the work of a few of the boys on the football team. It was the quarterback I needed to talk to, a boy by the name of Jake Van Andel. As she explained to me, my lighthouse was low-hanging fruit, so to speak, and the boys couldn't resist pulling a few spooky pranks on me. I was a newcomer to the town, my lighthouse was haunted, and they thought I was jumpy. Jumpy? I'd been called many things, but never jumpy before. Yet the fact that their ghoulish pranks were affecting me only served to encourage them. However, Kylie was quick to defend the boys regarding the murder of Mrs. Adams.

"The boys were out for a bit of spooky fun, Lindsey," she had told me. "They're not murderers. Everyone loved Mrs. Adams." The thought of her beloved teacher caused another wave of tears, causing me to drop the subject. Leslie's students had been through enough, I thought.

There was one more thing that struck me as we were about to leave the Henderson house. Kennedy had brushed it off as nonsense, but for some reason I felt it was worth keeping in mind. Kiley, having had a close connection to the teacher, told me she had a feeling that whoever killed Leslie knew her. To her way of thinking, that feeling of trust helped explain why she hadn't picked up on Leslie's death.

"I don't think Mrs. Adams was frightened by her killer," she had explained to us. "But I felt a lot of conflicting emotions coming from *her*"—she had pointed to Kennedy—"fear and doom being the most powerful. I just knew something bad was going to happen to her. That's why we cast that spell on her."

At this, Kennedy thrust out her hand in the universal gesture of a hard stop. "Darling, in the future, I'll thank you not to cast any more spells on me. The thought is touching, and I thank you for your efforts on the beach, but I prefer to move through this world unmolested by spells and whatnot." Kennedy offered a smile that was more forced than genuine.

"I was only trying to help," Kylie told her, and I believed her. Kylie Henderson was a teenager who dressed different, dabbled in making potions, wore crystals, and practiced casting spells on herself and the people around her. Her mother supported it. Maybe Kylie did have a gift of some sort, but I didn't think her hunch regarding Leslie would stand up in a court of law. There was an evil murderer out there who had taken the life of her teacher, and I was determined to find the culprit the old-fashioned way, sniffing out clues and connecting the dots.

After a quick stop at the grocery store to pick up ingredients for dinner, we headed back to the lighthouse. Sergeant Murdock had finally returned my call. The poor woman had sounded exhausted over the phone. However, she'd given me the okay to return to my lighthouse, thank goodness. The bakery could be opened as well. Knowing what life was like in our small village, she advised me to prepare for a busy Tuesday morning. I smiled at that and vowed to make sure we had plenty of warm cinnamon rolls on hand. It was the sergeant's favorite breakfast treat. It also meant I had to conquer my fear and return home.

"Alright, ready?" I asked Kennedy, handing her a ramekin filled with sand from the beach. Wellington was sniffing around the backyard, and the groceries were still in the Jeep. I thought it best to get the smudging done, then head to the kitchen to start dinner.

"You're really going to do this?" she asked, wrinkling her nose at the sand.

"You're wearing your crystal. This is all I have. That sand is for extinguishing this sage stick when we're done. Crystal wrote down the directions for smudging here." I held up the little piece of paper. We were standing by the back door when I lit the stick of white sage. I stared at it for a minute.

"Now what?"

"We walk around the house with this smoking herb stick, only thinking good, positive, happy thoughts. No bad thoughts, Ken. Okay?" I began walking through the kitchen and dining room, holding the smoldering herb before me like a flashlight. I glanced at the instructions to make sure I was doing it correctly.

"Clarify 'bad thoughts' for me, Linds." Kennedy was following me, holding the bowl of sand.

"Seriously? Just don't think about—"

"Murder?" she blurted. "It's hard not to when that tree is right out there." She pointed out the dining room window, as if I didn't already know where the tree was.

"Dammit, Ken! Now we have to start again!" I retraced my steps and began walking clockwise around the house once more. "It's not hard. Just think happy, sunny, cheerful—okay?" Although those exact words weren't on the list, I thought it best to improvise.

"What if we say something in the kitchen like, 'delicious foods'?" she asked.

"I don't see the problem there. Let's do it," I told her, and together we said, "*Delicious foods.*"

"Good company," she said, following me into the living room. "We only want good company in here. Am I right?" Yes, she was!

I cast her a grin. "You're really getting the hang of this, Ken," I told her, and together we said, "*Good company,*" as I circulated the smoke through the room. Oddly enough, I felt good. I actually felt the horrors of yesterday melt away in the smoke. In short, I felt it was working. We continued the process throughout the house, moving up the stairs as we called out happy thoughts and fond wishes. When we got to Kennedy's room, she stopped.

"I'll take it from here, if you don't mind," she said and took the smudge stick from me. In return, she gave me the ramekin of sand. "Don't think it'll hurt to smudge up a little magic in the bedroom." She winked and shut the door. A moment later she appeared with a grin. "I gave it, as you Yanks say, the old college try. Let's hope it works. I'm doing yours too. You can thank me later." Before I could stop her, she was gone.

Dumbstruck, I found myself standing in the hallway alone, holding a little bowl of sand while surrounded by the scent of sage. That's when I heard the distinct sound of footsteps coming up

the stairs. I froze as frightening images of last
night came flooding back to me. Dear heavens, we
were smudging the house! It was supposed to shoo
away all negativity and bad juju. In that moment I
felt like the biggest fool for believing in such hog-
wash. I closed my eyes, hoping the sound would
fade away. But it didn't.

Kennedy opened the door and screamed.

I dropped the sand.

Startled, I spun around and came face-to-face
with Rory. My careening heart slowed a measure,
but it sped back up when he brushed past me and
began stomping on the hallway runner like a mad
bull.

"What the devil are you two doing?" he demanded, looking both upset and confused. It was
then that I saw the burn marks on the carpet and
what remained of the sage stick reduced to a
smudge beside it. My ramekin had also broken.
Sand was everywhere. That little faux pas was on
me. Kennedy was responsible for the rest. Honestly, I didn't even know what to tell Rory. Unfortunately, Kennedy did.

"Just putting a little spell on your virility, darling, but in a good way. It's called smudging. We
learned it when we talked to the witches."

"Good Lord," he uttered and looked at us as if
we'd lost our minds.

CHAPTER 23

In my opinion, oven-roasted chicken was under-rated. It was a savory, fortifying, comforting dish, and when combined with apple stuffing, roasted root vegetables, and a side of cranberry sauce, it was as close to perfection as a meal could get. I was going to raise the stakes even further by serving it with a three-layered pumpkin-spiced cake with cream cheese frosting and a scoop of butter-pecan ice cream from Harbor Scoops for dessert. It would be the perfect meal to amend the process of clearing bad juju that Kennedy and I had started earlier but had failed to complete. My lighthouse would be filled once again with the welcoming scent of good food. There'd be laughter, as well, and good conversation. It was the best way I knew how to restore order to the lighthouse, and hope-fully dispel a little bad juju in the process. Really, that was enough for me. Also, I was certain that Rory, Tuck, and the Ghost Guys would appreciate a good meal after the trying couple of days we'd had. As for Kennedy, her penance for dropping the smudge stick and starting a fire in the lighthouse was helping me in the kitchen. Although, whom was I kidding? That was my penance too.

"Why do you have so many chickens?" she asked, watching me clean, dry, and stuff each of the three chickens with half a lemon, a few sprigs of sage, a few sprigs of thyme, and half of a garlic bulb cut lengthwise. If you wanted flavorful, juicy roast chicken, that was the secret. On the outside, each bird was liberally brushed with melted butter (the milk solids in butter create that crispy, brown skin, so don't skimp on the butter!) and seasoned with kosher salt and pepper. That was it for the birds.

I finished trussing the legs of the birds with twine, tucked in the wings, and turned to Kennedy. "We're feeding eight people tonight, and six of them are big guys. *Really big guys* with hearty appetites. When entertaining, Ken, it's always best to make more and have leftovers. But I'm not counting on having leftovers with that crew."

"Astonishing," she breathed and continued cutting the bread for the stuffing. "How many gallons of stuffing are we making?"

"Enough to go with the chickens. Believe me, nothing will go to waste. If we do have leftovers, Wellington will see that they're disposed of properly."

Hearing his name, Welly popped up from under my modest kitchen table and came beside me. He'd already eaten his dinner but was homing in on the three chickens poking above my giant roasting pan. It was nearly ready to go into the oven. The only thing that excited Welly more than the smell of roasting chicken was frying bacon. Thankfully, there was no bacon in this meal. "If you're a good boy, your next meal might be chicken leftovers with carrots and potatoes." He liked the sound of that. Seizing the opportunity, I slipped him a nub of raw carrot. Welly took it, then immediately dropped it on the floor as if it was poisonous. Once he realized it was all he was getting, he'd circle back around to the carrot and make another attempt. But for now, it remained like a forgotten castaway in the sea of my kitchen floor.

"I'm a good boy!" Rory appeared in the kitchen with six bottles of wine and a wily grin. "I put up with you two, and I put out a fire outside your bedroom door. Chicken leftovers sound good. I'm starving."

"We're two hours out. But you can help yourself to the cheese and meat tray in the fridge." Rory set down the six bottles of wine and headed for the back door. "Where are you going?" I asked.

"To get the rest of the drinks. Those are for Kennedy." He was teasing, of course, but he made us both laugh.

Kennedy left her station at the stuffing counter to pick up a bottle of wine. She held it aloft in a half-hearted salute to him. "Three whole chickens for you and six bottles of wine for me, and they think we don't understand one another. *Tsk-tsk.*"

"I don't pretend to understand either of you ladies—especially after finding you two purposely filling the house with smoke. But I endeavor to make you happy." He grinned and pulled Welly out the door with him to retrieve the beer.

* * *

"That was truly delicious," Brett Bloom declared, setting his napkin beside his plate, signal-
ing an end to the meal. I was just brewing coffee
for dessert. It wasn't over yet. "Haven't had a meal
that good since I was back home in Cherry Cove,
and it's been quite a while. My Grandma Jenn can
really lay out a spread."

"She sounds like my kind of grandma," I remarked.

The other Guys agreed. My meal had gone off
even better than I had planned. Brett, Mike, Cody,
and Ed had eaten to their hearts' content, leaving
just enough for Welly's breakfast. It made me wonder if they had eaten anything at all since yesterday. Tuck and Rory were used to such dinners, yet
the look of sated contentment on their faces never
failed to cause a bubble of pride to well within me.
Food was my love language, and I was happy to
share it with the man I loved, as well as family,
friends, and whoever came through my bakeshop
doors. And yes, the lighthouse had been filled with
good conversation as well. Laughter would come
in due time.

"Like I said, we've largely been cleared of any
wrongdoing by the police, but we have been asked
to stick around awhile longer," Brett continued.
Tuck gave a nod in agreement. "And while we're
here, we'd love to have another look in the old
lantern room if it's okay with you. We've gone over
the footage several times today. It's uncanny. We've
never experienced anything like that before."

"Right," Mike concurred. "We got the fright of
our lives up there. I'm sorry to think we all looked

like a bunch of scaredy-cats on the live feed. We just want to see if we can find anything that might account for what we experienced."

"You experienced the ghost lights of Beacon Harbor," I told them as I poured coffee. "Every one of us in this room has experienced them at one time or another, but not up close." I placed a mug in front of Brett. "You three, Teddy, and Kennedy have the honors there."

Cody, working all the technology, had been in the café monitoring the investigation through the video feed on Ed's, Teddy's, and Kennedy's cameras. He hadn't been up in the lantern room yet and was eager to have a look around.

Ed took a sip of coffee, then set it back down, keeping his hands on the mug for warmth. "I've been thinking. What if that light was set off remotely? It came on with a blinding flash. We had little warning. What if the murderer decided to spook us by rigging some type of remote control to set off that light, knowing we'd freak out and then discover the body on our live video feed?"

"Fellas"—Rory leaned in—"it's a good thought. But to do that this person would need to have had access to the lantern room. Lindsey has the only key, and she keeps the lighthouse locked when she's in the bakeshop."

"True," I said. "I really don't think someone could have rigged that light, but you're welcome to have a look around."

The men continued to discuss the probability of rigging a remote-control light in the lantern room while Kennedy helped me in the kitchen. We were plating up the pumpkin–spice layer cake with a scoop of butter-pecan ice cream. The men might be stuffed, but there was always room for a piece of delicious cake with a side of ice cream!

We had just sat back down to start dessert when Brett told us something interesting.

"While Mike, Cody, and Ed were at the police station this morning, going over the video footage with the sergeant, I decided to go to the library and do a little digging around to see what I could come up with regarding your lighthouse. It's part of our procedure," he explained. "We like to have a little background on the building we're investigating, its history, and the people who lived there that might possibly have a connection to the paranormal happenings that are reported."

"Brett, dear, I could have saved you the trouble," I told him with a kind smile. "I did a good deal of that when I moved in here. The ghost lights, we believe, are connected to the first lightkeeper, Captain Willy Riggs. The records say he was shot on the beach and made his way to the lantern room, where he valiantly kept the light going until he died. Only now we know he was fatally shot that day on the beach. His murderers brought his body back to the lightroom and filled the lantern with more kerosene to buy more time. Captain Willy is still there. He's the lighthouse ghost."

"Right," Brett agreed. "You've told us something about him. However, it was the keeper who took up the job after him that caught my eye. His name was Arthur Adams."

"*Adams?*" Tuck questioned, staring intently at the other man. "I know it's a common enough last name, but could there be any connection to the murder victim, Leslie Adams?"

We were all thinking the same thing. Was it just coincidence? Thankfully, Brett had delved a little deeper into the matter.

"Captain Riggs is reported to have died on May eighteenth, 1892. In June of that same year, Arthur Adams and his wife move into the lighthouse to take over his duty. Arthur had worked at other lighthouses in the area since he was sixteen. Before he was moved to the Beacon Point Lighthouse, he was the assistant keeper at a lighthouse in Marquette, Michigan. Now, here's the interesting part. Mr. Adams only serves at the Beacon Point Lighthouse for eight years. In 1900, he makes a rather substantial land purchase just to the north of town. He moves there with his family, and that's the last we hear of him. He never returned to light-keeping as far as we know. However, when I went to look up the land records, I found that most of the land Arthur purchased has been handed down through the Adams family for generations. Over the years, it's been subdivided, of course, and parcels have been sold off to developers, but a large chunk of the original land purchase remains. Two things jumped out at me when I saw this. The first is that lightkeepers don't generally make good money. Back in the late eighteen hundreds, Arthur Adams would have made roughly seven hundred dollars a year to live here in this lighthouse with his family. Unless he inherited a great deal of money, that's not enough to purchase the amount of land that came into his possession when he left his post. The second thing that jumped out at me is that all the remaining Adams land has very recently been put in the name of Leslie Adams, the woman whose body was hanging from the lighthouse tree."

I inhaled sharply at this. Kennedy did too. Our eyes met and held as Brett added, "I checked. Leslie's house is built on that land. So, I believe there *is* a connection."

"And her husband was a builder," Kennedy remarked with a touch of sarcasm. "Free land, free labor, teacher's salary—mystery of the stunning home in the woods, solved."

Rory scowled at her. I did too. But Kennedy's moonstruck boyfriend, oddly immune to her snarky comments, smiled at her as if she was the only person in the room.

Prying his gaze from Kennedy, Tuck looked at the Ghost Guy. "Excellent work, Brett. You're the first person to connect Leslie Adams to this lighthouse. But what does it mean? Why was her body placed in that oak tree?"

"Good question," I concurred. "But remember, Adams was Leslie's married name. Her husband, Doug, is the one who has the blood connection to the family."

"And Doug Adams died nine months ago in a tragic ice-fishing accident," Tuck reminded us with a grave expression. "I now have the unsettling feeling that somehow there's far more going on here than we realize."

CHAPTER 24

"Alright, gentlemen . . . and Kennedy." This I added as Kennedy plopped down in her favorite wicker chair in the lightroom. "We have one bottle of wine left and a slew of empty pages in my fake lighthouse logbook. Let's make good use of them."

"I hate to involve my friends in another investigation," Tuck began as he took the seat next to Kennedy, "or my girlfriend." He turned to Kennedy with such a private, tender look in his eyes that I had to look away. "However, I'm desperate, and I could really use your help on this one. Now, before you all get carried away and go headlong into your amateur sleuthing routine, I must insist that you stay out of harm's way. Don't go being a hero, okay? And keep me informed on all your findings so I can follow up on any leads you might uncover. Most importantly, don't let Murdock know that you're helping me. My head will roll if she hears about any of this."

"Mum's the word, darling." Kenney leaned over

and gave him a kiss on the cheek before handing him a glass of pinot grigio. "There's a murderer on the loose in Beacon Harbor, and I have no wish to run into any more dead bodies. As we've learned before, when we put our heads together, we get results. Now, did you remember to bring those pictures you promised us—the ones from Leslie's house?"

Rory cast me a quizzical look. "You asked to see the inside of Leslie's house?"

"The outside was stunning. We were curious," Kennedy told him.

"The inside was, too, if that helps any." Tuck shrugged and pulled out his phone.

Noting the look on Rory's face, I put a hand on his arm. "Although we're all curious to get a look inside that house, Tuck mentioned that a few rooms were ransacked. Since it's believed that the murder happened there, we thought it would be helpful to look at some of the pictures Tuck took."

"'Ransacked'?" Rory narrowed his eyes at Tuck in question.

Tuck nodded and handed his phone to Rory. "Although the kitchen is also a focus of this investigation," he informed us, "Leslie's office and her bedroom are of particular interest. Both were turned inside out. Unfortunately, we don't have a clue as to why, or what was taken. It could be anything from money, to drugs, to a flash drive containing sensitive information." Tuck shrugged. "Leslie was a high school teacher. We don't know much more about her than that. Also, whoever was inside that house—and we're not even sure if it was one person, two people, or more—they were

careful to cover their tracks. That leads us to believe this was a premeditated act. Yet one of the
theories Murdock is entertaining is that Leslie's
murder might have been accidental. Leslie might
have come home from the Halloween Bash earlier
than expected and caught an intruder in the act.
There weren't any signs of blood at the crime
scene, but there were marks around the victim's
neck from the hanging. They could be covering
earlier signs of strangulation. We'll know more
when Doc Riggles sends us his autopsy report."

Rory was still studying the pictures on Tuck's
phone when I thought to ask, "If Leslie's murder
wasn't premeditated, why would the killer go
through the trouble of hanging her from my oak
tree?"

"Good question," Kennedy remarked and turned
the full heat of her gaze on Tuck.

"It could be as simple as to throw suspicion off
the killer's trail. After all, the ghost hunt at the
lighthouse was public knowledge."

"Or . . ." Rory began, looking up from Tuck's
phone, "it could be as Brett Bloom has suggested.
Leslie's family has old ties to this lighthouse. Look
at this picture from her office. The place is a mess.
There's no way to tell what's been taken, but this
frame on the wall . . . this caught my eye." Rory en-
larged the picture on Tuck's phone to illustrate
what he was talking about. "Leslie and this other
man, whom I take to be her husband, are both in
wetsuits. They're happy, smiling, and on some large
body of water."

"Leslie was a scuba diver!" I exclaimed, recalling
what she'd told me at the pumpkin-carving party.

"She was interested in your aquatic adventure center."

Rory nodded. "She came over to talk with me about diving and to tell me how excited she was that I was going to offer scuba-diving classes. Leslie was an experienced diver. This picture illustrates that. What a pity," he remarked with a sad shake of his head. "She told me she was interested in getting involved in my center."

"Interesting, Hunts-a-Lot, but how is scuba diving related to her murder?" Kennedy raised a perfectly shaped brow at him in challenge. Rory shrugged.

"Not sure yet, but this picture jumped out at me."

As we took turns looking at the pictures from the crime scene on Tuck's phone, we filled the guys in on what we had learned from Kiley Henderson, the witchy girl in Leslie's class.

"Those witchtok kids were down at the beach near the lighthouse during the investigation," I explained. "We thought they might have been involved in some way regarding Leslie's murder. However, we were wrong. Sure, the kids were all fascinated by the thought of a Halloween ghost hunt, but Kiley told me she had another reason for meeting down at the beach last night. She told us she had a bad feeling that something terrible was going to happen at the lighthouse."

"To Leslie?" Rory's interest was piqued. I shook my head, while Kennedy answered for me.

"No, silly, to me. Can you believe it? That witchy teen thought some terrible tragedy was going to befall me, and she was right. Only I do find it interesting that if she was so close to her teacher, which she claimed to be, why didn't she get her spooky premonition about Leslie's death rather than me bumping into her very dead body?"

"Interesting point," Rory agreed. "And here's another one. Whenever we see the ghost lights, they usually happen as a warning, a portent of danger, which in most cases has meant death. However, the night of the ghost hunt, the ghost lights clearly went off after Leslie's death. We know this because of what you told me earlier, Lindsey, about the video footage the Ghost Guys caught from your dining room window. They saw what they thought was a light orb, which they were able to debunk as a reflection from an outside light source. That happened twenty minutes to a half hour before the ghost lights went off in this lightroom. Does anyone else find that strange?"

I was about to add my two cents to this question when Kennedy wiggled her fingers in the air. "Let me take this one, darling." She graced me with a smile before stating very matter-of-factly, "That's easy. Captain Willy had been distracted by the investigation. For heaven's sake, every two minutes that pesky Brett Bloom would ask him to make a light flicker or demand him to talk into that voice thingy he was holding. Those boys came with gadgets to spare, and every one of them designed to capture a ghost. I don't profess to know by what means that poor dead captain gets his information, but he was clearly trying to make it up to this very room all night. By the time he got through their ghost-gadget gauntlet, the poor thing was likely disoriented. But he got up here ... right after we did. You saw the rest."

I didn't even know what to say to that, but for some strange reason it did make sense. As for Tuck and Rory, after mulling over Kennedy's wildly speculative explanation a moment longer, they both came to the same conclusion. After all, who were we to question the intentions of a ghost?

"Alright," I began, opening my logbook. It was the book we had used before when murder had reared its ugly head in Beacon Harbor, and we would use it now to help us make sense of what we had learned. "If we're going to help Officer McAllister find the killer, we'd best start making a list of our suspects."

"'Suspects'?" Tuck questioned. "We don't even have suspects yet. That's the problem."

"Good point," Rory agreed. "Then perhaps Lindsey should just write down what we know so far. We have some facts and some strange coincidences. Let's hope they lead us somewhere soon."

"I'll toast to that." Kennedy raised her glass as I began writing.

"*The Mysterious Murder of a High School Teacher,*" I said, writing the heading in my logbook. I glanced at Kennedy to see if she okay with my title. She gave me a regal nod, and I began scribbling down the facts as we knew them, hoping to find some small nugget in the mire to cling to. Yet soon it became clear that although we had made some interesting discoveries—the flash of light from the lawn possibly indicating the exact moment Leslie's body had been hung in the tree, Leslie's husband's ancestor having been a lightkeeper at my lighthouse, and the fact that her house had been ransacked earlier—the holy trinity of all murder investigations—means, motive, and opportunity—

were not there. There was no name or logical explanation that jumped out at me. All I knew for certain was that Leslie Adams had been murdered, and her dog, Trixie, was missing. For all our sakes, I prayed that tomorrow would bring us closer to the truth about what had really occurred on that dreadful Halloween night.

CHAPTER 25

My alarm went off at the usual ungodly hour, indicating it was time for me to wake up and start baking. It was a cold Tuesday morning. There was a chill in the air of my bedroom, and the voice of the powerful wind as it whipped off the lake gave me a shiver. I reached across to the bedside table and was about to turn my alarm off when Rory threw his strong arm around me and pulled me against his warm body.

"Hit the snooze," he whispered. "Stay with me a moment longer." Dear heavens, it was tempting . . .

"I have to take Welly out and give him his cookies before I head to the bakeshop. I'll be late."

"I'll be up in three hours." His voice was husky with sleep. "I'll take Wellington out and feed him. I'll even take him on a field trip to the warehouse with me. Hit the snooze, Bakewell. Stay with me awhile longer."

Thinking . . . thinking . . . and sold! I didn't need any more convincing than that. I hit the snooze button, pulled up the comforter, and rolled back into the cocoon of his strong arms.

"You're the best," I whispered, snuggling against him.

"I know," was his sleepy reply.

Twenty minutes later, I sat up in bed once again, this time turning off my alarm. I looked at the time and uttered a small curse. I wished I could say I felt refreshed from the extra twenty minutes. Sure, it was twenty minutes of pure, delightful snuggle heaven, but I was still tired, and it was still cold outside. Rory, oblivious to the time and the wind, looked to be in a blissful state of slumber. I placed a kiss on his cheek and headed to the shower.

Dressed and ready to leave the bedroom, I met Wellington by the door. The room was still dark, but I could tell his tail was wagging in anticipation.

"You get to stay here with Rory this morning."

I believed that my dog was processing this. Going with me meant a romp through the darkness, and cookies. Staying meant being allowed on the bed and snuggling with his second-favorite human. It was a tough choice. Welly loved his cookies. However, if the tables were turned, I knew which one I would choose. After I patted the bed and invited him up, Welly made the right decision. I kissed him on the nose, then slipped out the door.

I normally entered the bakeshop kitchen through the outside door at the back of the lighthouse. However, this morning I was happy to avoid the biting wind by using my private entry to the café. It was one of the luxuries of owning the lighthouse.

I was hard-pressed to say whether the smudging ceremony Kennedy and I had attempted had worked, but it felt oddly still and quiet in the lighthouse since coming back after the tragedy on Halloween night. Maybe Captain Willy had been traumatized too? Maybe he needed a vacation. Or maybe, just maybe, we had pushed him over to the other side against his will. Whatever the case, I felt a pang of regret.

I turned on the kitchen lights and started brewing a pot of coffee. I needed to jump back into my morning routine and claim some normalcy. Yesterday, after learning we could reopen the bakeshop on schedule, I had called all my employees to check up on them. Of course, they had all watched the live ghost investigation podcast on Sunday night, and every one of them had been freaked out by it. Elizabeth, pragmatic to a fault, stated that she was anxious to get back to work. She hadn't required any changes to her schedule, and for that I was grateful. Tom was the same; he would be here as well. Same with Alaina and Ryan, although they were more up front with their motivation. Both had wanted to be at the bakeshop purely because they didn't want to miss a beat or the latest gossip. They knew that Rory, Kennedy, and I would be, in Ryan's own words, 'matching wits against the Beacon Harbor Police in a race to find the killer.' I didn't have the heart to tell him there was no race involved. We'd do everything we could to help the police on this one.

It was dear Wendy who would be taking a few days off. She was an empathetic soul who also suffered from a rare disease that caused her to faint when confronted with gross or stressful situations.

Watching Kennedy run into a dead body dangling from the lighthouse tree had been both gross and stressful. We learned that poor Wendy had passed out cold after watching that. Thank goodness she had been at home with her parents. I told her to take all the time she needed.

Truthfully, I was grateful to be back in the kitchen. Baking relaxed me and allowed me to think while I worked. As I prepared our signature sweet-roll dough, my mind turned over everything that had happened since finding Leslie's body. I was still struggling to make sense of the fact that she was a beloved teacher with lots of friends in this town. Who would want her dead, and why? What was the point of her murder? Why had her body been hung from my oak tree on Halloween night? Did this have something to do with Halloween? The ghost hunt, perhaps? Was this related to her husband's recent death, or the fact that he had a connection to this lighthouse? Did she upset one of the teens, or a group of teens, whom she taught? Was this about another teacher at the high school? And, just as heart-wrenching, where was Trixie?

I proverbially threw my hands in the air and started on the batter for our giant pumpkin chocolate-chip muffins, a yummy fall favorite. My head hurt from trying to puzzle out what had happened to poor Leslie Adams. I turned instead to my muffins. I added the wet ingredients to the industrial mixer—eggs, sugar, melted butter, and pumpkin purée. Once blended and smooth, I added the flour, baking soda, baking powder, a little salt, and a nice, spicy amount of my premixed pumpkin-pie spice. I liked our muffins to fill the senses with the best of fall flavors. Once all the ingredients were mixed up to my satisfaction, I added the appropriate amount of semi-sweet chocolate chips. I was just about to give them a gentle stir when Teddy burst through the bakeshop door, looking as if he'd just seen a ghost.

"There's . . . there's something moving out there," he said, pointing to the door he'd just wrangled shut. The wind was fierce this morning!

"Where?" I asked, concern filling my voice. I stepped back from the mixer and wiped my hands on my apron.

"By the oak tree. Do you have a flashlight?"

"The oak tree? Oh, God! Tell me it's not another body."

"I don't know what to tell you, Lindsey." He grimaced as he said this. "Heavens knows, I'd love to tell you that it's not a body, but I can't. Not yet. But I'd like it if you'd throw on your coat and come with me."

Teddy was spooked. The poor man had certainly experienced the worst of my lighthouse in the past few days. I didn't really want to go with him to the oak tree, but I also didn't want to lose this talented assistant baker so soon after finding him. I had a real peppered history regarding assistant bakers. It was because of this, and Teddy, that I grabbed my coat, and a flashlight and followed him out the bakery door.

I kept an iron grip on his arm, and together we battled our way through the biting wind to the oak tree. I aimed the strong beam of light into the branches as we walked, searching for any trace of a rope. Although all the branches were now stripped of leaves, I was slightly relieved to see there appeared to be no sign of a rope.

"Not up there," Teddy chided. "Aim it at the base of the tree!"

I took a deep breath and dropped the beam to the base of the tree. That's when I caught sight of the shadow Teddy had seen. It was a small, dark, slinking form that had dashed behind the tree. My heart thumped painfully in my chest as I tried to understand what I had just seen.

"I . . . think it's an animal," I told him, hoping I was correct. With caution, I walked toward the tree, aiming the beam of light at the base of the trunk. I was just about to walk around the tree when a little white face poked its head out, looking at me. I gasped. Teddy did too. The little face disappeared again, causing a welling of panic.

"Oh, my God! It's Trixie," I cried above the wind, recognizing the little poodle. I motioned for Teddy to walk around the other side of the tree in case the little dog got spooked. The poor thing had to be cold, scared, and likely starving as well. I came around the tree and shined my light on the dog. Teddy took a step toward her, but I motioned for him to step back. Trixie could easily slip away in the darkness, and we'd be hard-pressed to find her again. I had another idea.

"She knows Wellington. They're friends. I think it's best if we send him out first." Teddy agreed, and I went to fetch my dog.

The moment I let Wellington out the back door, I believed he knew she was there. The nose of a dog is a remarkable thing. It never ceased to amaze me what my dog could discern from a good sniff. As the poodle crouched and the wind howled, Wellington tempered his urge to leap off the steps and dash over to his friend. Instead, Welly padded down the back steps with a gentleness that belied his great size and then walked to the oak tree. There he met the little poodle nose-to-nose. Trixie began to whine, and then she lay down in the fallen leaves. Wellington lay beside her. That was my cue. I walked over to the dogs, picked up Trixie, and held her shivering body close to mine.

"It's alright, Trixie," I cooed, gently stroking the dog's head. "You're safe now. We've got you." To Wellington, I said, "Good boy, Welly. You not only get cookies, but you and Trixie get to share a yummy chicken dinner." He liked the sound of that and bounded into the darkness to do his business. Trixie, although still trembling with fright, rested her head on my arm.

"You found her," Teddy remarked. "Oh, Lindsey! Thank goodness."

"No. *You* found her," I told him, staring out into the dark yard. I could hear Welly, but I couldn't see him. "I didn't go outside this morning. I don't know how long this poor pup has been out here. I'm so happy you came along when you did."

"I was humming a tune, heading for the bakery door when I saw something move. I have to be honest, Linds, I was totally freaked out by it."

"Well, Teddy Pratt, you might be a scaredy-cat, but you did good."

Once Welly trotted back, we all went inside. I briefly brought Teddy up to speed on the baking, then left him in the kitchen to work his magic. I then made good on my promise to the dogs. They were fawned over and fed. Once I was satisfied that Trixie had eaten her fill, and after a quick assessment in which I learned that she was hopelessly matted and covered in dirt, but healthy, I then brought her upstairs to Kennedy's room.

I gave a series of knocks before offering my warning of, "Cover yourselves. I'm coming in!" I loved Ken and Tuck, but I only ever wished to see the PG version of their relationship, and nothing more. I waited until the rustling subsided, then opened the door and flipped on the lights. "Sorry for the intrusion, kids, but you'll be happy to know that Trixie has been found." I lifted the little dog Simba-style to illustrate my discovery.

Tuck stared with alarmingly wide eyes. I wasn't certain if he was spooked by my sudden appearance, or the fact that I had the dog. Kennedy sat up and struggled to remove her sleep mask. The moment she did, she let out a little utter of surprise.

"You found Trixie!" Her large brown eyes focused on the dog. "Where was she?"

"Under the oak tree. Yesterday, when we couldn't find her, I had the feeling she was following Leslie's scent. Dogs are very loyal creatures."

"Indeed, they are. What a miracle. But . . . oh, what a mess she is! Your lighthouse, darling, is turning into a beacon for dirty strays." I couldn't help it, but for some reason my eyes shot to Tuck as she said this. "Leave her with me. I know what to do."

"Thanks." I flashed her a smile. "I thought so. But please, this time, how about you and Peggy limit the bedazzlement to nail polish and a bow. I think that would be acceptable. Right, Tuck?"

"Right," he croaked. He cleared his throat, then added, "Good work, Linds." The poor man had been sound asleep until I barged in. However, any guilt I might have felt for the untimely intrusion was quickly pushed aside by the fact that Leslie's dog was now safe. Also, it wasn't that early. It was nearly six o'clock, and Tuck's alarm would go off in a few minutes. After all, he was a cop appointed to this case.

"Missing dog found," I proudly proclaimed. "Now all we need is a suspect, a motive, and a murder weapon. I'll leave that to you, dear Tuck. Sorry I can't stay and chat a little longer," I told my sleepy friends. "I have a bakery to open."

CHAPTER 26

If I had thought opening the Beacon Bakeshop after a murder had taken place on the lighthouse lawn would mean a slow day at in the bakery, I'd have been wrong. This was Beacon Harbor. The residents were as friendly as they were nosy, and everyone loved a good bit of gossip, none more so than our own dear Betty Vanhoosen. Add to that a bit of gore nearly the entire town (and beyond) had witnessed on Halloween night, and you had an unholy trinity of curiosity, rumors, and wild speculation. After all, a beloved teacher had been murdered, and the mystery of her death was alive and buzzing around the café. And there was no better pairing to juicy gossip than a cup of hot coffee and a warm, gooey cinnamon roll. Pecan rolls were good too. Giant pumpkin muffins bursting with melted chocolate chips also hit the spot. Donuts? Why, they were the best kind of fuel for jaw-waggling. In fact, every item in our bakery cases seemed to cater to those who loved a good bit of gossip.

Elizabeth and I were working the bakery counter as Tom made the specialty coffee drinks. Alaina and Ryan had the later schedule today, lucky kids. It got so busy around nine o'clock that I had to sweet-talk Rory into assisting Tom for an hour, which he was happy to do. Although he hated to admit it, Rory knew his way around an espresso machine. I was sorry to think that watching him pull a perfect shot of espresso in his form-fitting, off-white waffle shirt and blue jeans sent a ripple of longing through me that drew heat to my face and made me blush. Thank goodness we were busy.

Every chair at every table was occupied. Even Rory's fan club, lovingly known as the League of Extraordinary Gentlemen, was holding court at my biggest table. The original five were always there in the morning: Mayor Rod Jeffers; Book Nook owner Jack Johnson; retiree Bill Morgan; medical examiner Doc Riggles, when he wasn't working on a case; and my dad, James Bakewell. And their numbers were growing. Anders Jorgenson, who was working with Rory on the buildout of his business, had joined them. Anders had brought Clara with him this morning so she could play with Welly; both were in the boathouse getting into mischief, no doubt. Both would be heading over to the warehouse at the marina once the men were on the move. Rick Bingham, librarian Margaret's husband, was there, as well, this morning. Then when Sergeant Murdock came in for her morning cinnamon roll fix, her longtime boyfriend, Brian Brigalow, abandoned her for a seat at the Gentlemen's table. In all fairness, Murdock was on the job.

Since the tables were full, all newcomers took to gathering around the coffee bar, scanning the café for the next available table. The buzz, the noise, the wild theories that circulated the café typhoon-style were a bit much. Teddy, who was a crowd favorite, was one of the biggest pot-stirrers in the café, and he delighted in it. He'd come from the kitchen with a tray of fresh-out-of-the-oven baked goods (a feat that always drew ooos and ahhs) and would pause for a chat with whoever happened to be standing at the counter. He'd start with, "Did you hear what we found under the oak tree this morning?" That got 'em talking. Thanks to Teddy, everyone in town now knew the story of how Leslie's little dog, Trixie, had traveled all the way from her home deep in the woods, miles south of town, to my oak tree by the lake, the very same oak tree that her owner had been hanging from.

One would think such a macabre story would dampen the spirits, but it had quite the opposite effect. The dog story spurred the gossip. Then Rory did, too, when he told the Gentlemen a rather embellished tale about the smudging ceremony Kennedy and I had attempted at the lighthouse. Talk about embarrassing! Yet maybe that was his plan. Once our smudging story began circulating, I couldn't get Rory out of the bakeshop fast enough. I packed up a dozen muffins and a dozen apple-cider donuts, added some Beacon Bites for Welly and Clara, then handed the bakery boxes to Rory with a kiss.

"You've done a great job, but we can manage from here. Thanks for helping out."

"My pleasure," he said with a grin. "And these are much appreciated. I feel a bit like a reverse

Pied Piper. Instead of leading the children of the town away with the sweet sound of pipes, I'm luring the geriatric gentlemen to the docks with baked goods. It's all one and the same to me." He grinned so deeply that his crystalline eyes were mere slits of blue.

I laughed. "Don't call them geriatric. They'll rebel."

"Good point. Elderly?" he questioned with a pointed look and took off his apron.

"Don't say anything at all. And before I forget, remember that I told you last night about the football player, Jake Van Andel? Well, Kennedy and I are going to speak to him today after work. Kiley, the modern-day witch from Leslie's class, felt he might be one of the boys who was hanging those scary dummies in my tree. If he was, he might know something about why Leslie was found hanging there as well."

"You think those boys had something to do with Leslie's murder?" Rory had been helping those boys carve their pumpkins. He knew the kid I was talking about. The look on his face reflected what he felt, which was skepticism.

"I honestly don't know what to think. That's why we need to talk with him."

"Okay, but wait for me, Linds. I'd like to come too."

I assured him that I would, then headed back to the bakery counter. Rory left and the large café table was suddenly made available for other customers. Sure enough, the Gentlemen were following Rory to the warehouse. I looked out the window and saw Anders bringing up the rear with a little white goat and a large, fluffy black dog trotting happily behind them. Pied Piper, indeed!

I was making the usual small talk with my customers when Mom, Betty, and Christy Parks came through the door. Mom saw me and waved. She looked stunning in her long, hooded, form-fitting sheepskin coat of caramel brown with white fur trim. One of the perks about living in the north during the colder months was that you got to wear all your fashionable coats. Mom could never pull off this look in Florida, I mused with an inward smile. She'd be sweating so much that her expertly applied, age-defying makeup would be melting off her face in rivulets like a spring thaw. Not a good look. But here, in Beacon Harbor, Mom was glowing.

Betty, just as excited to see me, rushed the bakery counter, pulling Christy along with her.

"We heard you found Leslie's dog!" Betty looked both relieved and excited. "Good work, dear. I knew you'd do it."

"Teddy's the one who technically found her," I corrected. Betty waved the thought away with a hand.

"Well, she was under your oak tree. Kennedy told us all about it. She dropped the poor, raggedy little thing off at Peggy's Pet Shop and Pooch Salon this morning for an emergency grooming. Said Tuck explicitly told her no bedazzlements, but we all know he doesn't wear the pants in that relationship." Here Betty winked at me, reminding me of a blue-eyed owl with a nervous eye twitch. "Our Kennedy certainly has a flair for bedazzlement! And it's a little poodle, for goodness' sake!

People have been primping up poodles since the invention of poodles. Oh, and I hear that Leslie's daughter has finally come to town, the poor dear. I spoke with Stacy Murdock this morning. She said Leslie's daughter was coming into the station some time before noon."

"Murdock told you that?" For some reason, I was slightly hurt. Sergeant Murdock and I had our moments, but I was really beginning to think that she and I were becoming, well, nearly friends. All Murdock had said to me this morning was, "*Cinnamon roll, Bakewell, and a latte. Oh, and nice job finding the pooch.*"

"Well, I might have pried a little bit," Betty admitted, feigning innocence. "I might have used our friendship and the fact that we're in a book club together. Anyhow, Stacy told me they've put Cali, the daughter, up at the Harbor Hotel because she can't go home. Not yet. Not that she would want to either. I hear that house is where the *real crime* happened." She had the decency to lower her voice a tad as she said this. Not that it mattered. Thanks to Betty, everyone in town knew Leslie's house was now the crime scene.

"Has Doc told you the cause of death yet?" I asked. I knew these things took time, but I was growing anxious. Betty shook her head, causing her blond bob to jiggle about her pleasant, round face like a golden halo.

"Not yet, dear. He has his suspicions, but they might be wrong. All I can tell you is that he is nearly certain that Leslie was poisoned . . . nearly. He'll know soon enough."

"Poison? Betty, that's huge. How was she poisoned?"

"Well, that's just it, dear. He's not quite sure. He's waiting for the labs to come back. Also, Cali is going to the morgue today to identify the body. I certainly don't envy that poor child. Now, before I forget, I'll have one of your yummy pumpkin scones, and a latte, Tom." This last request she called out to my barista, wiggling her chubby, beringed fingers in the air at him as she did so.

Tom, you patient soul, I thought. To Betty, I said, "Got it. And you, Mom?"

"It's definitely a pumpkin chocolate-chip muffin kinda morning for me, dear. Yet before you plate my beautiful muffin, I must tell you, we've heard about your smudging yesterday." She gave me her stern, *What were you thinking?* look, and crossed her arms. Unfortunately, that was my mother's second-favorite look in her facial expression arsenal, next to her cover girl smile. I honestly wasn't sure which one irked me more.

"That's part of the reason why I'm here," Christy Parks said. She was quick to add, "And, of course, because of the baked goods. I'll have exactly what Betty's having, including the latte, Tom, only make mine a caramel . . . with almond milk."

"That's not *exactly* the same thing, Christy," Tom gently admonished with a grin.

As Tom and I worked to fill their orders, Elizabeth, having heard the word *smudging,* leaned an elbow on the counter and stared at me.

"What?" I said to her. "It wasn't exactly my idea."

Mom leaned in, as well, oozing disappointment. "Honestly. And I tried so hard to give her a normal childhood! Yet here's my daughter, living in a haunted lighthouse and smudging up a storm. I heard they almost burned the lighthouse down . . . from all the smudging."

"What?" Elizabeth's large blue eyes were twinkling with intrigue and a touch of mischief as well. "And I thought this day couldn't get any better. Throwing down on a murder investigation, finding a missing poodle, and smudging the lighthouse? Lindsey Bakewell, who are you?" She tried not to smile as her large eyes locked on mine. I grinned at her, waved her mocking eyes away, and then addressed my mother.

"Mom! Smudging isn't like smoking. You can't *smudge up a storm.* It's a sacred cleansing ceremony. And we didn't burn down the lighthouse. Kennedy just lost her grip on the smudge stick, and it fell on the carpet. Yes, it might have caught on fire, but we stomped it out in a hurry." That was a lie. Rory was the one who had come to the rescue, but I didn't want to appear like the idiot I felt in front of both Mom and Elizabeth. Betty, honestly, was taking it all in with a look of wonder. "Anyhow, it wasn't our idea," I continued. "It was a woman named Crystal Henderson who convinced us that smudging the lighthouse would erase all the bad juju from the Halloween fiasco."

"Crystal Henderson?" Christy Parks piped up. "You met with her?"

"Yes. Do you know her?"

"I do. That woman is so interesting, and a little spooky, if I'm being honest." Her warm brown eyes held a look of caution as she said this. "Crystal is not only a psychic, a mystic, and a Reiki practitioner, but she also makes hand soaps with an interesting concoction of herbs and oils, and a line of jewelry that focuses on healing crystals and mystic symbols. That woman is a new age industry unto herself! She was at a garden club luncheon I went to a few years back and told our fortunes. She said I'd run a successful business and have a successful second marriage. Oddly enough, shortly after that I found out that my husband was having an affair. I'm still waiting for Prince Charming number two to arrive," she teased with a grin.

"What's Reiki?" Elizabeth asked, stuck on that word.

"Did it work?" Betty asked. Her round blue eyes were boring into mine.

"Did what work?" I asked, not sure whether the question was for Christy or me.

"The smudging, dear. Is *you-know-who* gone? Is, as they say, the air cleared?"

"The captain?" I ventured. Betty nodded. At the mention of my lighthouse ghost, all eyes turned to me, including Elizabeth's and Tom's. "I'm going to say . . . maybe? It's really too early to tell."

"Pity," Tom said. "I wouldn't have done it. Shouldn't be messing with things you don't understand, Lindsey." Tom narrowed his eyes at me as he steamed milk at the espresso machine.

"I carry some of her products in my shop," Christy continued, as if her conversation hadn't been interrupted. She lifted a little white bag as she talked. "Crystal's soaps are a top seller. The scents she uses are quite interesting. They're designed to raise your energy and balance your chakras. Here." Christy handed me the bag. "I brought you some. I thought you could use it, you know, in light of what happened here Halloween night."

I pulled out the soap and smelled it. She was

right. I didn't know what the scent was, but it was both invigorating and calming at the same time. "Thank you," I told her sincerely.

"What are chakras?" Elizabeth asked.

"Ladies, your lattes." Tom placed the drinks on the counter with a smile, then turned back to the high-end machine to clean the milk pitcher and prep for the next drink order.

"I'm not sure," I told Elizabeth. "We should Google it."

"Also," Mom added, holding a mug of black coffee. Mom was like me—we both preferred our coffee black. "Christy came into Ellie and Co. this morning. She has something very interesting to tell you that she remembered after our tea yesterday."

"That's right," Christy said. "It's the other reason I'm here. And, of course, to see Tom," she teased, casting the young man a playful wink. In return, she received a charming grin and a bro-nod. Tom wasn't only a good barista; he was good for business. Ladies of all ages loved him.

"It was shortly after the Pumpkin Pageant," Christy continued. "Leslie and her dog had won the contest, and she was walking through town with Trixie. They were on the opposite side of the street from my store. It was so crowded on Halloween that I almost missed her. But suddenly this tall scarecrow appeared in front of Leslie, blocking her path. Leslie was a short woman, so it caught my attention. The scarecrow must have said something interesting to her. Leslie picked up Trixie and followed the scarecrow into the Village Bar and Grill on the corner. I didn't think anything of it," Christy explained, suddenly looking troubled. "I thought they were friends. I went back into my store shortly after that." Her lips began to tremble. "The scarecrow. I didn't recognize him, but Ellie thinks she knows who he was."

Dread hit me as my eyes shot to my mom's. "Mom?"

"Jordy Tripp, dear," Mom said, confirming the name for me. "Why on earth would Jordy Tripp be talking to a teacher in Beacon Harbor?"

"Never said he knew anybody in this village when I met him," Betty remarked. She'd met the author earlier and had given him a tour of Beacon Harbor. "Nope, he'd never heard of our town before, according to him." Betty took a cautious sip of her latte and shook her head. She looked as glum as Christy did.

"It's not so strange to meet people at a crowded festival," Christy remarked. "However, I got the feeling that he knew who she was, but why? Why Leslie Adams?"

Thanks to Brett Bloom, the intrepid Ghost Guy, I believed I knew why. The pieces of the puzzle were beginning to fit together, but I was sorry to think I still had more questions than answers.

"I'm not sure he knew her," I told them cautiously, "but I believe he knew of her. It's this lighthouse. I recently learned that Leslie Adams had a connection to my lighthouse, and Jordy must have figured it out too. That's why he's here. He even said so himself. He told me he believed there was a secret in this lighthouse worth killing for." Just uttering the words sent a chill down my spine.

"Whoa!" I caught the look Tom exchanged with Elizabeth before he added, "And now Leslie is dead. What if Jordy Tripp—"

I held up my hand to stop him. "We're all thinking the same thing, Tom. However, I'm going to insist we stay quiet about this little piece of information awhile longer. That means no gossiping! Mum's the word, ladies, got it?" They all nodded, and I continued. "Jordy Tripp is here for a reason, but he's unwilling to tell me why he's really here. All I know is that he wants a tour of this lighthouse. When he comes here, which I know he will, I don't want him to know he was seen with Leslie before her murder. I don't want to spook him away. I want to find out exactly what he's looking for."

Mom looked incredibly nervous by this. "But, dear, what if he's the killer? You're virtually defenseless here, and all the smudging in the world won't deter a murderer." For some odd reason, the whole smudging incident had really gotten under her skin. But I could see that Mom wasn't quite finished yet. "Oh, goodness!" she declared with a horrified look. "That man was in my house! He was eating my seven-layer dip!"

"You're a very good hostess, Ellie," Betty soothed with a look of sympathy. "And who could blame the fellow for making a pig of himself eating your delicious dip? The addition of pickled jalapeños was a nice twist." Betty was practically licking her lips at the thought. Tom and Elizabeth shot me looks of tempered impatience. Betty, bless her, had a way of getting off topic.

"Look, I'll be fine," I told them all. "I'll make sure Rory is here with me when Jordy comes for a visit. And Christy," I began, looking at the smartly dressed woman. Christy was not only a competent businesswoman, but she had a warmth about her that was as inviting as her beautiful shop. "Thanks to your sharp observations, we've just discovered our first real suspect in Leslie Adams's murder. Good work, ladies. Now, don't tell Sergeant Murdock. Not yet. First, I want to know what mysterious secret has lured a bestselling author to our sleepy little village."

CHAPTER 27

"**Y**ou have got to be kidding me!" The troubled look that clouded Rory's face was par for the course, as far as I was concerned. I had told him about our most recent discovery regarding one of his favorite authors, and he was having a hard time digesting it. This was partially because Jordy and his assistant, Grant, had paid a visit to Rory's aquatic adventure center, which was still under construction, with the desire to be Rory's first paying customers. Although elated at the offer, which was twice as much as Rory had planned on charging, he had also felt it had been an odd request, being so late in the season. It was November, and nearly all the recreational boats had been dry-docked for the season. The village marina had already closed, and yet Rory, an avid fisherman with search-and-rescue diver credentials, had kept his personal craft in the water. He also had another one moored to the dock beside his warehouse. According to him, there were still beautifully calm days on the lake to be had in November, but they were few and far between. Also, an experienced boater knew just how far they could extend their season and what precautions to take to do so. Therefore, getting wind of his boats, Jordy had asked if Rory would be willing to take Grant and him out on the lake on his boat for research purposes. He hadn't told Rory exactly what research he would be conducting out there, but Rory told him, weather permitting, he'd consider it.

Now he wasn't so certain he would. The fact that Christy Parks had witnessed Jordy Tripp talking to Leslie Adams shortly before she was murdered had made us all question his motives.

Right after I had closed the Beacon for the day, Kennedy had returned from Ellie & Co. with the newly groomed Trixie trotting beside her on a fancy, hot-pink, rhinestone-studded leash. I immediately recognized it and the matching collar from the Ellie & Co. boutique. I couldn't help smiling at the sight. I also had to commend Kennedy's restraint as well. True to her word, she hadn't turned the poor pup into a bedazzled mythical beast, as she'd done to Clara the goat when we had found her. And yet Trixie hadn't totally escaped the eccentricities of the groomer's hand, or a dash of glitter. Along with a good bath, at Peggy's Pet Shop and Pooch Salon, Trixie had been treated to a full manicure. All twenty of her nails had been trimmed and bedazzled with glittering hot-pink dog nail polish. She was also treated to a total brush and blowout of her natural curls, and a trendy teddy bear cut that had turned the rough-and-tumble white poodle into the cutest darn thing I'd ever seen, Wellington excluded. He was still the pinnacle of adorbs in my book. But Trixie was a close

second, looking more like a stuffed teddy bear
with glittering nails than a poodle. I had to hand it
to Peggy, the lady had vision. We decided it would
be best to leave both dogs back at the lighthouse
while we went to chat with the star of the high
school football team, Jake Van Andel.

"You're telling me that mum's the word regarding Jordy and Leslie?" Kennedy questioned from
the back seat. "That's bullocks, Linds! Tucker's
not going to like this one bit."

"We will tell him, Ken, just not yet." I glanced at
her pouty face in the rearview mirror. She was nervously fidgeting with her necklace, the black onyx
protection stone Crystal Henderson had given her
to ward off evil. The thought made me roll my
eyes. I caught a glint of something else on the chain,
likely another new age charm she had added for
good measure. Catching my gaze in the mirror,
Kennedy blushed and quickly shoved the necklace
back beneath her shirt before hitting me with a
smug look.

"Lindsey's right on this one, Kennedy." Rory
squeezed my hand as he said this. "And here's why.
We know that Jordy and Leslie met, but we don't
know what they talked about. We also know there's
something he's looking for in the lighthouse that
he feels, to use his own words, '*is worth killing for.*'
But we don't yet know what that is. We need to
court Jordy a bit to gain his trust. I want to know
what he's hiding and what he's looking for."

"My guess, if his book reviews are to be believed,
is talent, darling. Jordy's last book was a one-star
snooze-fest, according to one colorful reviewer."
She held up her phone to the rearview mirror to
illustrate her point before clicking off her screen.

"All right, Hunts-a-Lot, have it your way. I shall try not to utter a word about Jordy and Leslie to Tucker. Let's hope this young man we're about to visit has some insight on his former teacher and the ghouls who were pranking Lindsey's lighthouse."

The young man we were looking for lived in Pine Bluff Estates, a pricey newer development a mile out of town, albeit one that afforded some truly spectacular long-distance views of Lake Michigan from the bluff after which the neighborhood was named. The moment I turned into the main entrance of the neighborhood, I felt a slight chill travel up my spine. The last time the three of us had paid a visit to Pine Bluff Estates, we had discovered a dead body. I chanced a look at Rory. I could tell he was thinking the same thing I was. At that very same moment, Kennedy leaned over the front seat, seemingly without a care in the world.

"Ooo, I recognize this posh neighborhood. This is where that lighthouse-protesting nutter used to live. I say *used to* because we all know what happened to her." This statement was punctuated with a look of distaste. Kennedy flopped back into her seat, then flew forward once again. "You don't suppose there's any bad juju still lingering here, do you?"

"What the hell are you talking about?" Rory snapped, craning his neck to glare at her.

She glared right back at him. "Juju. That's what I'm talking about, Hunts-a-Lot. The bad kind."

His eyes met mine. "What's she talking about?"

"Ah . . ." I began, nervously guiding my Jeep down the very street where Fiona Dickel had lived. Her house had been at the very end. The dead end. And somewhere deep in my brain, I knew that Betty had resold it. Probably at a reduced rate, due to murder. The kind of rate a growing young family would find attractive. Dangit! Hoping we wouldn't have to revisit that house and all the bad memories attached to it, I took a deep breath and continued driving. "Bad juju is a term used to describe bad luck of a karmic nature. I think Kennedy is just wondering if some of that negative energy from Fiona Dickel's murder might still be lingering here. Isn't that right, Ken?"

"I'll tell you what's still lingering in my head," Kennedy piped up from the back seat. "The thought of finding that woman in her own kitchen! I won't even mention the fact that she was wearing tube socks with Birkenstock sandals."

Rory craned his neck once again to glare at her. "*That's* the vision that haunts you? I would think it would be the neon-colored clown hanging from the oak tree that you bumped into on Halloween night! The *dead* clown!"

"Now you're just being cruel!" She crossed her arms and glared at him.

"All right, kids, we're here." I breathed a sigh of relief as I pulled up the driveway. Not the former home of Fiona Dickel, but the one across the street from hers. Although just as big, the style was different. It was also beautifully landscaped.

Jake's mother answered the door, and we briefly explained to her why we were there.

"Let me handle this," Rory said, as Mrs. Van Andel went to get her son. "I've talked to this kid before. He'll open up to me. You two will just scare him off."

"Mr. Campbell," the young man said as a look of

admiration crossed his face. The look swiftly vanished the moment the teen realized that we were there too. "What's . . . what's this all about? What are they doing here?" It was obvious that our presence was making Jake nervous.

"It's about your former teacher," Rory told him in a gentle voice. I'm not going to lie. The paternal manner with which he addressed the young man made my heart skip a beat. "I'd like to ask you a few questions, and I'd appreciate your honesty in answering them. This is very important, Jake. What you tell us may help us find the person responsible for Mrs. Adams's death. Look, I know you're a good kid. I know you looked up to your teacher. But I also know you're hiding something. It was you and your friends who were harassing Ms. Bakewell's lighthouse, wasn't it? You were the ones hanging those monsters from her tree." Although it was just speculation, the confidence in Rory's voice had worked on the young man's resolve.

I watched as Jake's face drained of all color. He pressed his eyes closed, as if pained, and his jaw began to tremble. "Christ!" Jake blurted, then cast a wary look behind him. He stepped out of the house and gently closed the front door. "Come with me," he said to Rory. "Not them. I want them to stay here." Apparently, Rory had read the situation correctly.

Having no wish to stand on the cold front steps of this kid's house in the growing darkness, I said, "We'll be in the Jeep." As Kennedy and I walked back to the vehicle, Rory followed the young football star into the backyard. The kid wanted privacy, causing me to wonder just what information he'd been hiding.

CHAPTER 28

"Well, you are not going to like this," Rory stated, sliding into the back seat of the Jeep. Kennedy was sitting in the front with me. Rory had talked with the kid a good fifteen minutes before returning.

"What did he say?" I was on pins and needles. "Was he the kid who was pranking my lighthouse?"

"There is that, yes. But he wasn't alone. Jake and four other boys from the football team were responsible for the spooky decorations. They thought it was hilarious. To their way of thinking, by adding a bit of unwanted gore to your lighthouse, they were not only getting a rise out of you, but everyone in town was talking about it. It was a public pranking, and nobody figured it out. Believe me when I say that pulling off a successful prank on that level is pure gold to an adolescent male."

"Utterly juvenile," Kennedy remarked. "That explains so much about you. Go on."

Rory let the comment slide in favor of continuing to relay the details of his conversation with

Jake Van Andel. "Actually, Jake had the feeling that one adult knew what they were up to," Rory said, "and that person was Leslie Adams. The poor kid started tearing up as he told me about it. He said he believed the teacher knew all along that he and his friends were behind the pranking, and yet instead of confronting any of them, or making a big scene about it, which would have gotten all of them suspended from the football team, Leslie chose instead to bring the entire class to the lighthouse. Her plan had involved everyone, and singled out no one, which young Jake greatly appreciated. Leslie wasn't only a great teacher, he told me, but she was also a really decent human being. Jake went on to admit that by meeting you and learning about the lighthouse, he began feeling guilty about what they had done to it. All the boys involved had felt guilty. Jake told me he felt especially bad because you made them all donuts, and they were the best donuts he'd ever tasted. He admitted to eating a half dozen of them. I remember those days," Rory remarked wistfully while patting his hard, trim stomach. That made me smile.

"Did he say if anyone had put them up to the pranks? Perhaps someone with an axe to grind against Leslie?" I asked.

Rory nodded. "I did ask that question, but Jake insisted the idea was all theirs. That's what had him so spooked. Of course, he and his friends had watched the live ghost investigation. To use his own words, they all '*freaked the F out*' when they saw their teacher hanging from the same tree they'd been hanging their Freddy Krueger and Pennywise dummies from all week. I believe the term he used was, 'copycat.' Jake believes the murderer hung Leslie there on purpose, copying their prank in part to get back at them."

"Dear heavens, for what?" I pulled into the parking lot of a lone jerky store a few miles from town and turned off the engine. I couldn't hold such an intense conversation while driving down the country road at dusk. I had already spotted a herd of deer grazing close to the road and didn't want to lose focus in case the animals decided to dash out in front of me. I turned and faced the back seat, where Rory was sitting. He was seldom uncomfortable to the point that he'd rather stare out the window than look me in the eye when he spoke. But something about his conversation with Jake Van Andel had gotten to him, and he was hesitant to tell me why.

"Let me get this straight," Kennedy said from the passenger seat, demanding his attention. "That young man did something that resulted in his teacher's death?"

"No. Not exactly. And this is the part you're not going to like." He looked at both Kennedy and me and let out his breath. "All right, this is high school drama at its best, so I hope you can follow along. Apparently, Jake's girlfriend, Audra, had been growing worried about her best friend, Brittany. This Brittany girl had been acting strange, not at all like a best friend, according to Jake. So, Audra decides to follow Brittany after school one day. She was driving behind Brittany at a prudent distance when she saw her pull into a nearby forest preserve. According to Jake, Brittany is an avid hiker and nature lover, so the forest isn't unusual. But this trail was remote, which had caused Audra to become worried. Naturally, Audra didn't feel it was a smart choice for her friend to be hiking alone. She was about to leave her car and confront her friend, when she saw Brittany leave *her* car and get directly into the only other car in the parking lot. Audra, highly concerned for her friend, gets out of her car, which, according to Jake, was parked down the road. Audra sneaks through the woods to get a better look at who's in this mysterious car with Brittany. It becomes clear to Audra that Brittany is making out with some guy. According to Jake, Audra was a bit miffed that Brittany didn't tell her about her new boyfriend. Figuring that she was hiding something, Audra soon realizes why her friend's been acting so strange. The man Brittany is . . ." Rory, not usually shy about such things, trailed off.

"Boinking?" Kennedy offered, arching a brow at him. "Get on with it, Campbell!"

"Right, well, it turns out to be the high school drama teacher, Mr. Bartlett."

"No!" Kennedy and I both blurted at the same time. I felt like gagging. Kennedy did, too, and cried, "The bloody pervert! He's a teacher at the high school!"

"Yes." Rory gave a pained nod. "Naturally, Audra tells Jake, and they don't know what to do. Finally, Jake suggests that they tell Mrs. Adams . . . Leslie," he corrected. "Audra also tried talking some sense into her friend, but it fell on deaf ears. Brittany apparently warned Audra not to meddle in her affairs."

"Ooo, the bloody scoundrel! I am so angry right now I could strangle this wanker myself!" Kennedy sneered and shivered with disgust.

I was seething too. "Manipulating a high school

girl like that! I can't wait to get my hands on this class-A creeper!"

"Ladies," Rory cautioned. "There's more." Rory, who was obviously better at schooling his emotions than we were, shook his head in dismay. "Leslie often counseled the kids on how best to handle tough situations. Well, as you can imagine, this was one problem Leslie meant to handle herself."

"Oh, Leslie," I breathed and closed my eyes for a moment. I could only imagine how the poor teacher felt learning of such a thing. I remembered then what Leslie had told me the night of my pumpkin-carving party. She had said the kids confided in her, but it was this one remark that had stuck with me. "*They are all good kids, even if some of them don't know it yet.*" Could this remark have been about Brittany? I was sorry to think I didn't even know what the girl looked like.

"According to Jake," Rory continued, "Leslie told Audra not to worry. That she'd handle everything. Then, believing all the students had gone home for the day, Leslie marched down to the drama department and confronted Mr. Bartlett in his office. Jake, who had come from the locker room, saw her and followed her there. He said the argument was extremely intense. Mrs. Adams was yelling at Mr. Bartlett, dressing him down, as he deserved. Jake couldn't hear all of what was said, but he knew Leslie had made some type of threat to the drama teacher. That confrontation had taken place only a few days before the field trip to the lighthouse."

"This Bartlett creature," I began, slightly overwhelmed by the anger coursing through my veins.

"Did he know that Jake and his friends were the ones pranking my lighthouse?"

"Jake suspects that Bartlett knew that his girl-friend, Audra, was the student who'd found them out. After all, Audra was also Brittany's best friend. When Jake saw that Leslie Adams was hanging from the oak tree at the lighthouse, he grew fright-ened. Bartlett knows he's dating Audra. In Jake's mind, Bartlett was sending him and Audra a dire warning. Frankly, the kid is beside himself with fear. He was grateful that school's been canceled, due to Leslie's untimely and very public death. He was also afraid to mention this to anybody until now."

"The poor kid," I said, imagining how sad and scared he must feel. "However, I am very proud of you. You got him to confide this terrible secret to you."

"You know what this means?" Kennedy piped up. "We have another suspect, and this time we have a motive. If word got out about this wanker of a teacher and his affair with his very impression-able female student, the bloke would not only be ruined, but he'd also be facing prison time."

"Bingo!" Rory added with a grim set to his lips. "Bartlett is a teacher at the high school. He'd know where Leslie lived. He might have even gone over to her house under the guise of pleading with her. If she'd kept the damaging information to herself, he might have taken the opportunity to kill her before she took the affair to the authori-ties. Hanging the body in the tree might very well have been a warning to Jake and Audra. I think it's time to call Tuck. Tell him to meet us at Hoot's

Diner." Kennedy nodded and pulled out her phone.

"He won't be pleased by this sordid business we've dug up," she informed us. "The dear man believes in the sanctity of small towns, especially this one." Kennedy pursed her lips as she reflexively ran her fingers through her silky black hair.

Rory leaned over the front seat and looked at her. "That's why we're going to buy him dinner first."

CHAPTER 29

"I'm starving. What a day. Murdock's on the rampage, and we're still waiting on the toxicology report. It's basically come down to that. Doc Riggles has already confirmed that Leslie was dead before she was hung. That was a bold act by the killer, but we don't know why. We're having a hell of a time finding a motive. Everyone I've talked to loved the woman. Leslie didn't have any enemies that we know of. And her daughter, Cali, who, as you can imagine, is devastated by the loss of her mother—her father having died recently too—is basically stating the same thing. Leslie Adams had no enemies. I'm running into walls here. Great call, by the way, meeting at Hoot's." Tuck smiled and picked up his menu. He peered over the top of it, then asked, "What's everyone having?" The fact that we were all unusually quiet had escaped him.

"A burger and fries, the greasier the better." Rory set down his menu and took a swig of his water.

"A patty melt on dark rye for me," I said and set my menu down as well. Like Rory, I was craving comfort food. At times like these in NYC, my go-to meal had been a huge, greasy Reuben sandwich with a side of giant dill pickle from my favorite corner delicatessen. New York City had the best delis in the world. Beacon Harbor had Harbor Hoagies, which was good, but not at all the same thing. However, Hoot's patty melt on dark rye, with plenty of grilled onions and gooey, melted Swiss cheese with a side of their delicious French fries, was to me the small town equivalent of that NYC delicatessen sandwich.

Kennedy set down her menu as well. "I'm having what Lindsey's having, my thighs be damned."

"Cool," Tuck said and snapped his menu shut. "I was afraid you were all going to order salads again and make me feel guilty for ordering the double bacon cheeseburger with a side of cheese fries. Glad we're all on the same page. I'm starving."

Rory cleared his throat and softened his gaze. "Hey, buddy, we might be able to help point you in the direction of a suspect."

"Really?" Tuck looked suspicious. "You guys find something? I thought you were all working today."

"We were," I was quick to add. "But the bakery closes at three. Rory doesn't have set hours yet, and Kennedy had to pick Trixie up from Peggy's pet salon."

"Right," he said. His wary expression morphed into one of adoration as he looked at the beautiful woman beside him. "How did that go, babe?"

"Without a hitch, and with minimal bedazzlement. You'll have to forgive me for indulging my passion for hot-pink and glittery nail polish. Other than that, Trixie is clearly recognizable as a dog."

I tilted my head and gave her a look, mouthing, "*Is she, though?*" Ken conveniently forgot to mention the brush and blowout, and the teddy bear cut that, well, made the little poodle look like the cutest teddy bear you'd ever seen.

"Great," Tuck declared. "I knew you'd get it handled, babe." His faith in her abilities danced in his sky-blue eyes. It was both touching and wildly reckless at once. We were talking about Kennedy here. Tuck then shifted his attention to Rory and me.

"So, you mentioned something about a suspect?"

"We found a person who has a clear issue with Leslie. He's a teacher at the high school by the name of Bartlett."

A blank look crossed Tuck's boyishly handsome face as he shook his head. "I've been at the high school all day. Although school's been canceled for the students, all the teachers were required to show up. I've taken statements from nearly everyone who had contact with Leslie Adams, from the principal to the janitor. But I don't recall talking with a Bartlett."

"He's the drama teacher," Rory explained. "He was having an affair with a student. Leslie found out about it a few days before Halloween."

"Christ!" Officer Tuck McAllister swore under his breath. "I never saw that coming." He looked a bit ill as he contemplated this. He then asked us to tell him what we had found out about the teacher,

Bartlett, and his affair with the student named Brittany. As for our suspicions about Jordy Tripp, those we kept to ourselves, at least for the time being.

"You know something, don't you?"

It was a cold, clear night on the lakefront, with a cloudless sky and a moon so bright I could see my shadow. After dinner at Hoot's Diner, Kennedy had left with Tuck to watch a movie at his place, while Rory and I had come back to the lighthouse to walk Welly and Trixie on the beach.

These were my favorite moments of the day. The quiet moments. Holding hands with the man I was falling in love with as we walked beside the gently lapping waves. Tonight, Rory was unusually quiet as he watched Welly and Trixie trotting in the moonlight ahead of us. He had told Tuck all about his conversation with Jake Van Andel. It was a delicate situation. Jake and Audra might very well be in danger if the drama teacher, Bartlett, had, in fact, killed Leslie Adams to keep his sordid affair quiet. Tuck had made a call to Sergeant Murdock. They were in the process of locating Bartlett. Once they did, Tuck and Murdock would bring him to the station for questioning. I found it unsettling that Bartlett was still on the loose. But it wasn't Bartlett whom Rory was thinking about. He was thinking about Jordy Tripp, and his supposed reason for visiting Beacon Harbor.

I squeezed Rory's hand and asked instead, "What are you thinking?" He looked at me and smiled.

"I'm thinking about treasure."

"Treasure? Do you mean the fake pirate treasure we made Welly pull in a wagon, or real treasure?"

The moonlight illuminated his bright smile. "Real treasure," he whispered. That surprised me. Rory Campbell certainly didn't look like the type of man who chased treasure. "I'm convinced it's the reason Jordy Tripp is here. It must be. Think about it, Linds. Jordy Tripp is a successful author, but the last book in his Matt Malone series was met with criticism and poor sales. He's admitted to trying to revive his career with a titillating work of nonfiction."

"Go on," I said, realizing the proverbial wheels of his mind were spinning, likely from his earlier conversation with the author.

"Whatever nugget of a story he's glommed on to—whatever research he and Grant Fairfield are digging into—has led them both here, to Beacon Harbor. We know Jordy is interested in your lighthouse. He's even asked if you've found anything of interest during your renovation, hinting at possibly an old map. I doubt he's interested in early cartography, or what this town might have looked like in the eighteen hundreds. No, if it's a map he's looking for, it's of a different sort. Jordy's cagey about his research, but he's not above dropping little innuendoes, like there's a secret in this lighthouse '*worth killing for.*' We know that in some way your lighthouse is at the center of this story—"

"We do?" I stopped in the sand and looked up at his moonlit face. My heart stilled for a beat or two, because Rory Campbell looked so handsome in the moonlight. I had to fight the urge to kiss him.

"We do," he confirmed. "Remember what Brett

Bloom told us about the lightkeeper, Arthur Adams? Arthur Adams took over as keeper of your light-house after Captain Willy was murdered. The man, after a career in lighthouse keeping, works here for eight years. Then in the year nineteen hun-dred, Adams makes a sizeable land purchase to the south and west of town and retires from his duties at the lighthouse. Lightkeepers back in the day didn't make much money, at least not enough to make a land purchase like that."

"Right, but he might have inherited the money through a relative," I reasoned.

"Or, perhaps, Lightkeeper Adams witnessed a ship go down, one he knew to be carrying a large sum of money, in short, a treasure."

"But if he saw a shipwreck, there'd be a record of it," I said, jumping to the defense of the long-dead lightkeeper. "That was his job. That was the oath he'd taken. Are you suggesting that a light-keeper saw a ship in peril out there"—I pointed to the dark lake in question—"and did nothing to help the sailors as the ship was going down?"

"I don't know," he replied softly. "When you put it like that, it's doubtful. However, what if he helped the survivors and they told him about a possible treasure that had gone down with the ship?"

"Again, there should be a record of it," I stated. "I suppose I could check the National Archives database again. I've done it before, so I know what to look for."

"That's a great idea. I'll help you."

"Another thought," I said, then paused to call Wellington. He was standing belly-deep in the lake, vigorously chomping at the white-tipped waves as they rolled in. He was as delighted as a child eating cotton candy, but unlike that child, he'd need a serious bout of toweling off. Trixie, thank heavens, wasn't a fan of the water. She was sitting firmly on the beach. Her fluffy, teddy-bear head was tilted as she stared at my big dog, clearly not sure what to make of him. Or maybe the clever girl just didn't wish to visit the groomers again. Welly looked at me as water dripped from his jowls like a sparkling, moonlit stream. He then took one more bite of a wave before trotting out of the lake. I looked up at Rory and continued.

"If there is a sunken treasure out there, I'm sure it would have been the talk of the town. There's likely an article in the paper about it. I'll call Margaret Bingham at the library tomorrow and ask her to do a little digging around for us. If there's any mention of a ship going down with a suspected treasure on it from around the year nineteen hundred, she'd find it."

"Good thinking, Bakewell. Which brings me to my next point. Brett drew the connection between Arthur Adams and the murder victim, Leslie Adams. We know that Leslie's husband had inherited the remaining land from the original land purchase made by his ancestor. Another fact that struck me is that both Leslie and her late husband were avid scuba divers. Leslie made a point of talking with me about scuba diving and her passion for shipwrecks in the Great Lakes. Which, I must admit, is one of my passions too. Is it a coincidence that Jordy wants to charter my boat?"

"What are you thinking?" I studied his pensive face as I asked this.

"I'm thinking that if there was a ship carrying

gold or treasure that went down in any considerable depth of water, recovering it back then would have been virtually impossible. Some valuables might have initially been saved, which might explain Adams's sudden land purchase and retirement. Also, the location of the wreck would have been recorded, but not with the pinpoint accuracy we have today. In short, Linds, I think there might be an unrecorded shipwreck out there somewhere, with a treasure aboard that Arthur Adams knew about and that his ancestors were trying to recover." I could see how the thought of an uncharted shipwreck excited him. If, indeed, there was a treasure, it was beginning to make sense.

"If you're correct about this, Rory, Jordy would have been looking for Leslie Adams."

"Right. She won the Pumpkin Pageant. If Jordy had been there when the winners were announced, he'd have heard her name and made the connection. That could be why he was seen talking with her on Main Street after she'd won best costume in the pageant."

I nodded in agreement. "That clown costume she wore really stood out as well. She'd be hard to miss, even in a crowd."

"And the ransacked house?" Rory remarked, as we made our way back to the lighthouse. "It makes sense, Linds. If Leslie had a map . . . or even a record of the approximate location of the shipwreck in question, and Jordy Tripp knew about it, he'd want to have it."

"He could have followed her home," I said, thinking of the terrible possibility. "She might have even invited him inside . . ." I didn't want to finish that thought.

"Look, Linds, this is just an educated guess. There might not be a shipwreck or a treasure, but given the circumstances, I think this is an angle worth looking into. Let me reach out to Jordy tomorrow and offer him a tour of the lighthouse. Then let's see if we can get him to tell us why he's really here."

"It sounds like a plan," I said, then scooped Trixie up in my arms. I could tell she was still a little unsettled about all that had happened to her and her beloved owner. I pulled her tight against the folds of my coat and snuggled her soft head as she pressed it in the crook of my neck. Wellington, in a rare show of jealousy, began whining as he trotted beside me. He was a wet, sandy mess. He'd need to dry off before I'd let him in the house.

"I'm honestly confused by this whole mess," Rory confided, holding my free hand as we walked up the path from the beach to the lighthouse. "We now have a teacher with a motive to kill, and a writer with a desperate need to uncover a sensational story. I'm not sure which horse to back in this race, but we need to keep an eye on both. Eventually, the truth will come out."

CHAPTER 30

I was in a blissful, dreamless sleep, sprawled across the entire bed when I was suddenly jerked awake by a noise. Welly was emitting a low growl, something he didn't normally do. Trixie was barking. I sat up with a start and tried to make sense of what was happening. I looked beside me and remembered that I was alone. It was a work morning, which meant that I had gone to bed early. Rory, God love him, didn't find a nine o'clock bedtime appealing in general. He'd gone back to his log home, where I imagined he'd stayed up way too late, researching his shipwreck theory.

Was it Kennedy? Was that what the racket was about? Kennedy was a total night owl and abhorred early bedtimes as much as she abhorred early mornings. It was likely why we got along so well, each of us having some quiet moments in the day to ourselves. Had she forgotten her key? I went over to the window to settle the dogs. That's when I heard the bone-chilling sound of breaking glass coming from somewhere on the first floor.

Someone was trying to break into my light-house.

With my heart pounding like the hooves of a spooked horse, I grabbed my iPhone off the night-stand and called Rory. The phone rang. "Pick up! Pick up!" I whispered in full-blown panic mode. Listening to it ring five times felt like an eternity. I hung up and swore under my breath. I then gave a thought to calling the police, when it dawned on me that Tuck might be sleeping just down the hall-way. Like Rory, Tuck was a heavy sleeper.

I was instantly out of bed, frantically looking around my room for something I could use as a weapon. Rory would know what to do. It was part of the reason I loved him. He was always prepared for any situation. I suddenly cursed myself for tak-ing that for granted. Then, as if to add insult to in-jury, Welly rushed my bedroom door, barking like a berserker. That kicked my panic-meter into hy-perdrive. Welly's sudden rise in canine intensity could only mean one thing: Whoever had broken the glass was in the lighthouse with me.

The thought was chilling. There was a murderer on the loose in Beacon Harbor, and a secret in my lighthouse worth killing for. I tried to push the thought from my mind but couldn't. So, instead I grabbed a decorative canoe paddle off my wall. It wasn't even a real canoe paddle, I mused, slightly depressed as I held it. Nope, the paddle in my hand was a replica only two and a half feet long with the phrase *I SURVIVED SHIT'S CREEK* scrawled across it in sloppy, chalk-like print. It was far from fine art. In fact, it wasn't even good wall art. Yet oddly enough, it gave me a ray of hope. The pad-dle had been given to me by a coworker from my

Wall Street days, and at the time I'd thought it was hilarious. Although the proverbial creek I'd "survived" back then was a financial cluster-muck a company I was representing had gotten into. I was hoping I could survive this creek as well. With paddle in hand, I crossed to the bedroom door. I knew my brave dog would make a vicious beeline for whoever was in the house. Trixie, the poor thing, was pacing in anxious circles. If the intruder had a gun, he'd likely shoot Welly, and that wasn't a risk I was willing to take.

With both dogs now barking, I snuck into the dark hallway and firmly shut the door behind me. I then tiptoed down the hallway to Kennedy's room. I gave a quiet knock before loudly whispering my warning, "Cover yourselves, I'm coming in!" That done, I opened the door. To my utter dismay, the dark room was empty, the queen bed expertly made. I had never felt more frightened to be alone in the lighthouse.

I started to dial 911 when I heard footsteps in the hallway below me. Whoever was down there sounded like they were heading to the interior door that led to the light tower.

"Nine-one-one. What's your emergency?"

I stared at my phone a second, then quickly answered, "This is Lindsey Bakewell. I live in the Beacon Point Lighthouse. Somebody's broken in. Please come quickly." I then ended the call and gripped my paddle tighter.

I turned from Kennedy's room and gingerly walked down the stairs, sticking as close to the wall as possible. I was straining to hear the footsteps of the intruder below, but they'd fallen silent. Then, five steps from the bottom, I heard footsteps coming from the hallway above me—the hallway I'd just left. *Dammit!* my mind screamed as every nerve in my body exploded in an uncomfortable prickling. Was it an intruder? How the devil did he get up there? What in the bloody blazes was going on in my lighthouse?

I was about to turn back upstairs when the footsteps below me began again. I made up my mind and went down another step, then suddenly stopped. My heart clenched painfully, and I gasped in fright. Standing at the foot of the stairs was the Grim Reaper himself—a dark figure in a flowing black cloak and hood. The fact that there wasn't a face visible beneath the hood frightened me even more. My intruder was a faceless ghoul in a cloak! The nerve! My Lindsey-tude engaged. New York City Lindsey wouldn't abide it, so why should I? I gripped my paddle like a baseball bat and swung at the reaper's head for all I was worth. But the reaper ducked. My decorative paddle hit the stairwell with a loud *crack*, causing the head of the paddle to shear off completely. The irony of the situation hadn't escaped me. I was, indeed, up that proverbial creek once again, this time with only a nub of a paddle.

"Cheap piece of garbage!" I cried at both the paddle and the reaper. I then jabbed the splintered end at him. He grabbed hold of it and yanked me off the steps with such force that I hit the floor in a painful thud, knocking the wind out of me. Feeling utterly helpless, and gasping for breath, I looked up at the black-cloaked figure and saw he was still focused on the steps. The sweet scent of pipe smoke hit me then. Although I couldn't see him, I believed the captain had returned. Relief filled me, but it was short-lived. The reaper, I realized, was holding the remainder of my broken paddle. His focus was on me as he brought it down on my head. A sickening *clunk* was the last thing I heard.

"Lindsey! Lindsey!" I felt something wet and gooey hit my face. I opened my eyes, but the light hurt, so I pressed them shut again. Rory called my name one more time, and I forced my eyes open, wanting nothing more than to see his handsome face. To my relief, he was there, hovering above me. His forehead was creased with concern. Before I could say a word, Welly's giant head came in for another wet, slobbery kiss, entirely blocking Rory.

"Hey, big guy, she's going to be okay," Rory soothed and gently pushed my big dog away.

"Someone broke in," I told him. "I tried calling you." That was clearly the wrong thing to say. In an instant, remorse, guilt, and concern collided on his handsome face.

"Oh, babe, I know," he said. The whites of his eyes were bloodshot, and his voice was constricted with emotion. I believed he was close to tears. "I'm so sorry. I didn't hear my phone. I was sound asleep. It was the police siren that woke me. I heard them coming here, then looked at my phone. That's when I realized that you'd tried calling me. Oh, Lindsey, I'll never forgive myself for this."

"Don't be ridiculous," I said. "I forgive you." I offered a smile, then tried to sit up, but he stopped me. I was still on the floor, which let me know he had likely beaten the police to my door once he'd heard them coming. I then realized that others were around me, including Sergeant Murdock. She was on my other side.

"Lindsey," Murdock said, using my first name. I couldn't ever remember her calling me anything other than "Bakewell." Like Rory, Sergeant Stacy Murdock looked worried. "We need you to stay put while the paramedics check you out. You've had a fall and were unconscious when we found you."

"I was pulled off the steps and knocked over the head with a canoe paddle," I corrected.

"The Shit's Creek paddle?" A quizzical look crossed her face. "We assumed so. It's right here." She picked up the paddle portion of my impromptu weapon and held it above me so I could read it. I cringed. I might have survived said creek, but just barely. "What I want to know," she continued, "is what idiot breaks into a home using a stupid paddle like this? It's not even real. In what world could a two-foot, shoddily made paddle propel a canoe? Literally, if you were up such a muck-filled creek with this paddle, not gonna lie, Bakewell, you'd be stuck up there. However, looks like our perp made it work. Probably trying to make a statement. A real joker, this one." She shook her head as if it was the sorriest business she'd ever seen. Which convinced me to keep my mouth shut about the paddle.

"The paddle's Lindsey's," Rory offered, obviously thinking he was being helpful. "My guess is, it was the only thing in her bedroom she could think to use. Had she looked in the drawer of the other bedside table she would have found a gun. That would have been a better choice, under the circumstances."

"What?" I said, flinging my body to a sitting position. That was a mistake. Pain shot through my head straight to the back of my eyeballs. I closed my eyes but remained sitting. "You . . . have a gun in my bedroom?" I forced one eye open. I was not only shocked and disturbed by this news, but, if I was being totally honest, I was slightly turned on by it as well. *What in the heck is wrong with me? There's a gun in my bedroom! Why the heck don't I know about it?*

"Relax, Bakewell," Murdock practically soothed. "This is Michigan. Most people have a gun in their bedroom, which makes me think that whoever broke in here either isn't from Michigan or took a gamble on your sensitivities." The brow she lifted as she said this disappeared beneath her wispy blond bangs.

"What about Welly?" I questioned as a paramedic knelt beside me. I briefly answered his questions, then let him flick a penlight in both my eyes before looking at Rory again. "Everyone knows I have a big dog in the house. Wouldn't they be frightened of him?"

"Not if they had a gun too," Murdock stated grimly. "Thankfully, it never came to that."

"Maybe he had a steak?" Rory dipped his chin in apology and shrugged. "No offense, Linds, but if someone had a steak and threw it at this big guy"—he rubbed Welly's fur as he spoke—"he'd eat that first. Wouldn't even have to be a steak. A handful of Beacon Bites would do the trick. Right, Welly? Then he'd save you." As pathetic as that sounded, one look at my big, softhearted dog with his beseeching brown eyes, and I felt that Rory might be on to something there. Then another thought occurred to me.

"They were in my room!" This I blurted, then was instantly grateful for the ice pack the kind paramedic had placed on my head. "The dogs," I clarified. "I kept them in my room, so they'd be safe."

"Sweetheart, when I came through the back door, Welly was lying right beside you, whining and licking your face." His voice was filled with concern.

"What about Trixie?" I asked. "Where was she?" At the mention of the poodle, Rory and Murdock locked eyes.

"We don't know," Murdock finally said, her face looking a bit ashen. "Given the circumstances, we forgot all about her."

Fear shot through me. I was sorry to think it was becoming a familiar feeling. "That's not good," I said to the sergeant. "Not good at all."

CHAPTER 31

The Grim Reaper, who'd broken into my light-house, had banged me up a bit and had given me a mild concussion, but nothing, thankfully, was broken. As I finished up with the paramedics, Murdock and Rory, with Welly's help, searched the lighthouse for Trixie. I was sitting on the couch with an ice pack on my head when they emerged from upstairs. To my relief, Rory was holding the frightened poodle in his arms.

"We found her hiding under your bed," Murdock explained as Rory took a seat on the couch next to me. "Poor little thing is scared. Smart move on her part."

"It was," I agreed and took Trixie into my own arms for a cuddle. "We've got you, sweetie," I cooed, stroking her soft fur. She was the sweetest thing, and like Kennedy, I was growing attached to her too. Welly came over beside us and put his big head in my lap then, slightly jealous of the atten-tion I was showering on the smaller dog. I sup-posed I could relate, being an only child myself.

When one usually got all the attention, sharing it could be difficult. "And you, Welly, are the bravest dog in the world," I cooed, placing a kiss on his head.

"I never asked, but I will now. Did you get a good look at this intruder?" Murdock's intense, deep-set brown eyes were locked on me.

"Sort of," I told her with a shrug. "It was the Grim Reaper."

"Come again?" This time both eyebrows shot beneath her wispy blond bangs, giving her a startled, deer-in-the-headlights look. Not the best look for her.

"You know, the Grim Reaper? The lord of death? The last person you meet before you go to heaven? The ghoul with the long, flowing black cloak, and a hood with no face? It was very unsettling."

"So, what you're, in fact, saying is that this intruder was wearing a costume. Why couldn't you just say that he was wearing a costume, Bakewell?"

My head hurt. I looked at the sergeant and honestly replied, "Well, I wasn't sure at the time. I'd just woken up."

Rory, quietly sitting next to me, suddenly blurted, "You do know there's no such thing as a Grim Reaper, right?"

"Do I? I mean . . . I suppose I do." I had to think about that for a minute. After all, since the paranormal investigation of my lighthouse, I wasn't certain what or who was living here anymore. Noting the concerned look on his face, I added, "Just kidding. Of course, I know. But it's after Halloween now. Who'd wear such a thing?"

"Someone who didn't want to be recognized."

Murdock held me in her scrutinizing gaze a moment longer, then scribbled something down in her notebook. She looked up again. "Do you have any idea why someone would break in here?"

I really didn't, until I exchanged a pointed look with Rory. He looked troubled, and I could tell he was thinking about his wild, mythical treasure theory. But it was just a theory. We had no proof. All we had was a nebulous connection between Leslie, an old lightkeeper, and Jordy Tripp. Jordy Tripp! Holy cow! What if he was the Grim Reaper who had used my own paddle against me? As these thoughts swirled in my mind, I shifted my attention back to Sergeant Murdock.

"Look, all we know for sure is that someone is obviously looking for something. Leslie's house was turned upside down, according to Officer McAllister," I was quick to add. "The only thing I have here of Leslie's is Trixie."

"The dog," Murdock said and turned her focus on the poodle in my arms.

"Do you think the Grim Reaper was looking for her?" The moment I said this, my heart felt as if it dropped into my stomach. *The dog? But why?*

Rory stared at the little poodle in question, too, then ventured, "What if Leslie hid something on Trixie?"

Murdock scrunched her nose. "Really, Campbell?" she chided. "Now you're sounding like her. What would somebody put on a dog that's worth breaking into a house for?"

"He might be right," I added, locking eyes with Rory. We were both thinking the same thing. "It makes sense. After all, it's no secret we have Trixie at the lighthouse. When Teddy found her under the oak tree yesterday, we were so elated that we told everybody who came into to the bakeshop about it. Betty was here that morning, too, and as we all know, she's the next best thing to a town crier. Doesn't take a degree in mathematics to do the math there."

I then ran my fingers over the dog. There was nothing unusual about her, but I unhooked her collar just to be certain. I held it out to the sergeant for inspection. "Here's her collar. Nothing's on it but rhinestones. Don't think someone would be after this. It's from my mom's boutique, so I know those glittering rocks aren't real diamonds. Wait," I said, thinking. "What if Leslie put some critical piece of information on the dog's microchip? I'm sure she's microchipped. Welly is, in case he gets lost. It's a common practice for dog and cat owners. If the person who murdered Leslie was looking for one important thing, maybe Leslie hid it inside of her dog?"

Murdock narrowed her eyes at me. "The murderer is looking for something. The fact that someone broke in here and knocked you on the head the very day you found Trixie has convinced me. Bakewell, that's the single smartest thing you've said since I've been here. I'll make a call to the veterinarian's office when they open. I'll send Officer McAllister for the dog."

"To be fair," I said, smiling at her compliment, "I do have a concussion . . . caused by the Grim Reaper."

When word got out that an intruder had broken into the lighthouse overnight, and that I'd been

hit on the head by a person dressed as the Grim
Reaper, my family and friends swooped into ac-
tion. Mom and Dad had come to the lighthouse
shortly after Murdock left. I allowed Mom to fawn
over me for an hour or so as I lounged on the
couch with my ice pack. Dad, after making sure I
was doing fine, insisted I take the day off from the
bakeshop. Everyone sided with him. I had no say
in the matter. And I was very thankful he went
straight to the bakery kitchen to work beside
Teddy. Dad and Teddy would make sure that the
bakery cases were filled for the morning rush.
Mom was willing to step behind the counter too.
Yet to my surprise, Wendy arrived at the lighthouse, stating that her curiosity and her desire to
bake had overcome her particular empathetic con-
dition.

"Lindsey, I was terrified to hear that some creep
broke in here while you were sleeping." Wendy was
sitting on a chair near the couch, petting Welly as
she talked. "Do you think it was the same person
who murdered Leslie?"

"I'm not sure, but it could be," I told her with a
grimace.

"The fact that he was in here means that you're
getting close to something. Are you getting close?
Do you know who killed Leslie?"

She was so hopeful and had such faith in me
that I hated to disappoint her. "Honestly, I haven't
a clue. But we are turning over stones, so to speak.
We just haven't found the right one yet."

"But you will," she said with confidence. "When
you, Rory, and Kennedy put your heads together,
you turn up things the cops never think of."

"That's because we have a bit more freedom than the cops do. They're required to follow the law to the letter regarding what they can and cannot do. They also wear a badge. They have a tough job."

"Well, we're all behind you. But please stay safe, Lindsey. And don't worry about the Beacon. We've got it covered. Oh, and I was thinking about trying those pumpkin sugar cookies with pumpkin-spice cream cheese frosting that we were talking about the other day. Halloween might be over, but pumpkin is still in season. Besides, the lighthouse looks so festive with all the beautiful fall decorations out front, and those darling jack-o'-lanterns the high school kids carved. Would that be okay with you?" Since working at the Beacon Bakeshop, Wendy had not only become an excellent baker, but everything she made looked beautiful. I knew her cookies would be a hit.

"Pumpkin sugar cookies sound amazing! I'd love nothing more. And I'll even come in later this morning and sample them."

"Good. Then it's a plan!"

Once Mom was satisfied that I was not only going to live, but I was doing quite well, thanks to ice and Tylenol, she decided to head to Ellie & Co. for the day. Shortly after Mom left, Kennedy swooped in.

"Darling, are you sure you're up for this?" Anxious concern wasn't an expression Kennedy often wore, but learning that the lighthouse had been broken into had truly scared her. Like Rory, my dear friend was also feeling a tad guilty that she'd been away for the night. It was a rare occurrence, but she'd fallen asleep at Tuck's place, that place being an apartment above his parents' detached garage.

"I have minor body aches, a headache, and some time off work. In short, I'm ready to party."

"Glad to hear it," she said. "But I insist on driving. No offense, darling, but I don't trust you or that wonky lump on your head."

"Fair enough," I agreed and tossed her the keys.

CHAPTER 32

"Hello, Chadwick."

Kennedy had driven the three blocks to Beacon Harbor's premier hotel, the Harbor Hotel, which was located on the other side of the public beach and marina. The Chadwick she was addressing now managed the hotel restaurant and was a friend of ours. Chad was his preferred name. Kennedy knew it, too, but loved to exercise her Englishness on him. Chad ate it up, being a consummate ladies' man.

"Well, if it isn't Beacon Harbor's dynamic duo. To what do we owe the pleasure, ladies? Tell me, Lindsey, you haven't tired of baked goods already? Are you here to have a real breakfast for a change?"

I glanced into the dining room, admiring the white tablecloths, the nice china, and the tall windows that overlooked the beautiful coastline of Lake Michigan. "It is tempting, Chad," I told him honestly, "but we've come to talk with a young woman staying at the hotel. Her name is Cali Adams."

"As in Cali Adams, the murder victim's daughter?" Filling with intrigue, Chad's eyes flicked from side to side to see if anyone was listening. Determining that we were alone, he lowered his voice and ventured, "I should have known, seeing you two showing up here on a weekday. Tell me, is it guilt," he said, pointing at me, "or conceit," he added, shifting his finger to Kennedy, "that compels you two to play detective? I saw that unfortunate livestream podcast at the lighthouse." His face theatrically contorted into an expression of distaste. "It was all fun and games until someone died. I honestly thought it was all a big put-on, you know, for ratings."

Kennedy leaned an elbow on his kiosk. "Chadwick, you simple, darling little idiot. Conceit? Hardly. Guilt? What a useless emotion. If you must know, it's good, old-fashioned retribution that drives us. No one gets away with murder on our watch."

Chad graced me with a questioning look.

"What she said," I replied. Honestly, there was no need to add more. Kennedy had nailed it. "Now, Chad, we know Cali's here. We'd like to have a word with her."

Chad led us to a booth in the corner of the dining room. Even before we got there, I could tell that the young woman shared an uncanny resemblance with her mother. But Cali Adams wasn't dining alone. A man was sitting across from her, engaging Cali in quiet conversation. At first, I thought he was her boyfriend, but as we got closer, I realized it was Mark Whitcomb, the family friend, and the man we had met outside Leslie's house, who was with her.

As Chad politely interrupted their conversation to introduce us, I couldn't help noticing that Cali had little appetite for the hotel's reputable food. Her plate looked nearly untouched. It was also apparent that she'd been crying. My heart instantly went out to her.

"Lindsey, Kennedy," Mark cautiously greeted us as Chad returned to his managerial duties. Mark turned to Cali and explained. "Lindsey Bakewell is the owner of the Beacon Point Lighthouse, which is now the Beacon Bakeshop." Thankfully he left out the part about her mother being hung from my oak tree. I could tell that behind the chestnut-colored eyes, so like her mother's, that she was making the connection nonetheless. Mark then turned to Kennedy and continued, "This is Kennedy Kapoor—"

"The woman from the podcast," Cali added for him, without enthusiasm. "I recognize you. I . . . um, had to watch part of your livestream investigation at the police station. I'm sorry," Cali said, suddenly breaking down into tears. "It's . . . so hard for me to be here. I . . . um . . ." She was taken by a silent fit of sobbing. When she had control of herself once again, she added, "I still can't believe she's gone, you know?" Her face, undoubtedly pretty, was now red and blotchy with tears.

"We're so sorry as well," I told her, digging in my purse for a tissue. I found an entire little package and handed it to her. "We had just met her during a pumpkin-carving party at the lighthouse held for the high school senior class. Even from our short conversation, I could tell she was a re-markable person."

"She was," Cali said as tears streamed down her cheeks. "I don't know who could have done this to her?"

"That's what the police are trying to figure out," Mark said, placing a hand over the young woman's in a show of sympathy. "Her boyfriend"—Mark pointed at Kennedy—"is, ironically, one of the police officers on the case. I found that out the day after your mom was murdered. We met outside your parents' home. They were snooping around." Mark cast a pointed look at Kennedy.

"We were there looking for your mother's dog," Kennedy informed her. "After realizing the police hadn't found her at the house, we went over to check it out ourselves. It was official business. We were invited to do so. I have no idea why Mark was there at all." She issued a challenge at the man with her piercing brown eyes.

"I didn't know it was a crime scene at the time," he admitted, maintaining his polite manner, al-though I could see that Kennedy was getting under his skin. To be fair, he'd started it. "I thought there was some way I could help."

"So, you were snooping, too, only without per-mission from the authorities." With fists on hips, Kennedy tilted her beautiful head and sneered.

Mark was about to rebut this when Cali sud-denly blurted, "Trixie? She's missing? Oh, my God!" The young woman, struggling with a debili-tating load of grief already, burst into sobs.

"We found her," I quickly added, placing a hand on the girl's trembling shoulders. "Trixie is just fine now. She's just fine. That brave little dog made her way to the lighthouse. We found her sitting under the tree where your mother . . ." I didn't think it best to finish that sentence.

"The dog is at the lighthouse?" Mark questioned. "I didn't think she was at the lighthouse."

"Well, she isn't at the moment,'" Kennedy informed him with narrowed eyes. "The police took her."

"The police!" Cali was seized with fear. "Why? Why do they have her?" This was directed at me.

"Well, we had a break-in at the lighthouse this morning. I have a dog as well. Both my dog and Trixie were shut in my room, but somehow they got out." I didn't feel the need to mention that it had happened while I'd been knocked unconscious. No need to go there just now. "Anyhow," I continued, "the police are just following up on a theory."

"A break-in . . . at the lighthouse? Is this related to my mother's death?" Concern filled her brown eyes.

"What theory?" Mark Whitcomb was intrigued.

"None of your business, Mark." Kennedy flashed him a *tread lightly* glare.

Addressing Cali, I said, "We don't know yet, but we have our suspicions. That's why we'd like to talk with you."

"You're not the police." Mark's cheeks were turning red as he addressed us. "You're not a long-time family friend. Why are you getting in the middle of this?"

"Because we care," I told him sincerely.

Mark slid out of the booth and stood like a sentinel before us. "Look, I get that you want answers. However, Cali is devastated by all this. She lost her father earlier this year, and now her mother. She talked with the police yesterday and had to identify her mother's body. Imagine how traumatic that was. Maybe this isn't the best time, ladies."

New York Lindsey would have screamed, "*Is there ever a good time?*" But the gentler, kinder Baker Lindsey refrained. I wanted to speak with Cali, but not like this. Besides, I could feel the stress of the morning seeping in again. And to make matters worse, the Tylenol was wearing off.

Knowing Kennedy would have fought Mark with the intensity of a pit bull for a seat at the booth and a chance to talk with Cali, I thought better of it.

"I agree," I said, stepping around both Mark and Kennedy to address the young woman. "Cali, I just want you to know that Trixie is healthy and will be returning to the lighthouse shortly. When Kennedy and I learned she was missing after your mother's death, we made it our mission to find her, and we have. Like you, Trixie has been through a lot. I think she'd be a great comfort to you and you to her. Whenever you're ready, just come to the bakeshop. We would be honored to reunite you with your mother's dog."

"Thank you," she uttered, fighting back a new wave of tears.

CHAPTER 33

"Did you get a load of that Mark Whitcomb character? Swooping in like that, playing the protector? He has the reek of an opportunist to me." Kennedy gave a sad shake of her head as she guided the Jeep back to the lighthouse. Bless her, Ken loved to drive my Jeep, but she wasn't the best with a manual transmission. As she accelerated from a four-way stop, she missed a shift. The grinding of the gears, and the *BUMP BUMP BUMP* of the Jeep as Ken scrambled to find second, sent my aching head throbbing again. I took three Tylenol instead of two, hoping the extra one would get me home in one piece. Of course, I knew it didn't work like that, but I was desperate.

"I can't quite figure him out either," I admitted. "Is he a concerned family friend? Or does he have sights on the daughter? After all, she does stand to inherit that lovely home."

"My thoughts exactly. The tabloids are full of such stories. Cute young coed gets wooed by a smarmy middle-aged man." She took a corner too fast, tried to downshift, missed, and hit third instead, nearly stalling the engine. As the Jeep *LUBB-LUBB-LUBBED* back to life, she turned to me without missing a beat. "Usually it's because said smarmy middle-aged man is loaded. This, of course, is the reverse of that."

I scrunched my nose at the thought. "Actually, that doesn't make sense here. Cali is young, beautiful, intelligent, and independent, and she grew up in a financially stable and comfortable environment. Like her mother, she appears confident as well. Young women like that are more apt to blaze their own trails instead of hitching their wagons, so to speak, to a middle-aged man. I think we're just jaded. I think our anger for that Bartlett teacher seducing his student has seeped into our better judgment."

Kennedy shrugged. "Agreed. It was just a thought. But you must admit, we don't really know much about Mark Whitcomb other than that he's a teacher at the high school as well as a family friend."

"True, but Tuck told you they've questioned him. He said they can't find any holes in his story at this point. The guy checks out. In fact, except for that Bartlett creep, the police have interviewed all the teachers at the high school," I reminded her. "Regarding Mark, he drove to Leslie's house the morning after learning of her murder to see if he could be of any help to the authorities." Kennedy pursed her lips at this.

"Lurking's more like it," she offered. "What if he was trying to get in there too? What if he was looking for something as well? Maybe he thought he could lift some valuables before anyone noticed."

"A petty criminal envious of his friend's wealth? That's dark, Ken." I started to smile, but the impulse faded as I began thinking about Mark and his sudden appearance at Leslie's house. "He was there for a reason," I agreed. "But instead of theft, what if he was hoping to remove some incriminating evidence?"

"Ooo," she began as her eyes grew wide with intrigue, "like sappy love letters he'd written to Leslie? Remember, he was friends with the husband. Leslie was an attractive, rich widow. Not too far out of the realm of possibilities." Obviously, Kennedy was still on the theory that Mark was a player of some type. "Or what if there was other evidence Mark didn't want the crime scene investigators stumbling upon?" Kennedy wiggled her eyebrows suggestively as she pulled up the lighthouse driveway. The bakeshop parking lot was nearly full, indicating that it was a busy morning. After parking the Jeep in my boathouse-slash-garage, Kennedy suddenly looked at me. "What if Mark Whitcomb had come to Leslie's house looking for Trixie too?"

It was a moment before I realized what she was implying. I inhaled sharply. "If Mark and Leslie were such good friends, she might have confided a secret to him. She might have even told him she had hidden some valuable piece of information on her dog. Mark could either be trying to protect this secret from Leslie's killer, being a family friend, or he could be the killer himself." A chill ran down my spine just mentioning it. I shook my head and reminded her, "Remember, this is all just speculation, but it wouldn't hurt to write it down in our suspect logbook."

"Good idea," she said with a nod. "So, our

Markie-Mark has a motive to protect the family, due to friendship, of course. What's his motive to kill Leslie?"

I met her probing dark gaze and shrugged. "Knowing the motive would make this so much easier." I lifted my palms to the heavens in frustration. Because I was frustrated, and she was too. It felt like we were spinning our wheels.

"As it now stands, only that wanker of a drama teacher, Bartlett, has a motive."

"Don't forget about Jordy Tripp," I reminded her. "I'm not sure he has a motive to murder Leslie, but he didn't come to town for a vacation. He's looking for something he claims is worth killing for. I find his mere timing to be suspicious."

"Me too," she said. "There are two possibilities as I see it. He's either being dramatic and trying to drum up a little interest in the story he claims to be working on—it is Halloween, after all—or he's here because of Leslie." I looked at her.

"I never thought about that. But maybe you're right. After all, he was seen talking with her hours before she was murdered. It could be mere coincidence, or it could indicate that he knew her and knew about her connection to my lighthouse."

"That's what I'm thinking," she admitted. "But again, I ask the question, why murder her?" Kennedy's perfectly shaped brows were nearly touching on her forehead as she thought hard over this. "Unless Leslie *was* the secret, and he killed her?" I shook my head at this. That didn't make sense.

"Or she knew the secret," I offered. "But you'd think he'd be happy about that. Secret found. Problem solved!" I declared regarding Jordy and his mysterious hunt.

"By the way, darling, what is this *secret?*"

"I wish I knew. Rory has a theory, though."

"Do tell! If Hunts-a-Lot has a theory, I'm sure it's entertaining."

"I mean, it's out there," I told her honestly. "But it does make sense . . . in an abstract sort of way. However, we have no proof. Maybe we can get Jordy to confirm Rory's theory this afternoon, when Rory brings him to the lighthouse for a tour."

"Well, that would be just great, darling, *IF I KNEW WHAT THE BLOODY HELL YOU WERE TALKING ABOUT!*" I cringed from the loudness of her voice.

"Treasure." I flung the word at her like a hot potato, hoping she'd catch it, then drop it. End of story.

However, looking at her now, as she sat in the driver's seat with a white-knuckled grip on the steering wheel and eyes closed so tightly her eyelids were fluttering like the reluctant wings of a newly emerged butterfly—I had the feeling that this little nugget of a theory had lodged itself into her brain and was burrowing deep. I gingerly cleared my throat and pressed on.

"Rory thinks that treasure is the only thing worth killing for that could possibly link both Jordy Tripp and Leslie Adams to my lighthouse, and he believes this mythical treasure might be somewhere out there." Although Ken's eyes were still closed, I pointed in the direction of the lake nonetheless.

Her eyes popped open with the same terrorizing surprise as a jack-in-the-box. "Treasure?" she cried, doubling down on my frayed nerves. "That's his theory? Bloody hell, Lindsey! Do you realize how ridiculous that sounds? Least of all because the lot of you were dressed as pirates for Halloween! Welly was toting around a fake treasure chest in a cart, and now you're telling me you actually think there's treasure in the lake? I think you've all gone mental!"

That was one way to put it.

CHAPTER 34

I took Welly for a walk down the beach while Kennedy, stewing over Rory's treasure theory, went to the police station to pick up Trixie. Getting the poodle scanned for a microchip had been a good idea, especially since I believed the intruder, Mr. Grim Reaper, had been after the dog in the first place. After all, nothing else in the lighthouse had been taken. Granted, the moment my bedroom door had been opened, Welly would have burst out in hot pursuit of the creeper. I believed he'd done just that. However, I'd never know for sure what had happened after I'd been knocked unconscious. Who had opened my bedroom door? Was it the intruder, or was it Captain Willy Riggs, the protector of the Beacon Point Lighthouse—and possibly its secrets? The only thing we knew for sure was that I had been hit on the head, and the Reaper was gone by the time Rory and the police had gotten to me. Welly had been right beside me, while Trixie had hidden under the bed, terrorized, no doubt, by the ordeal. Poor dog.

Anxious for an answer regarding Trixie's microchip, I had called Sergeant Murdock.

"Your instincts were correct, Bakewell, Trixie has a microchip," she'd told me. That got my hopes up. However, in true Murdock style, they were dashed by her next sentence. "But all we found out was the name of her owner and how to contact her. Leslie Adams," she proclaimed with a pinch of sarcasm. "No surprises there. According to Dr. Townsend, the veterinarian, aside from the unconventional grooming Ms. Kapoor instigated, there's nothing out of the ordinary about this dog. Any other great suggestions?" Honestly, I was kind of flattered she'd even asked me. Unfortunately, I was fresh out of them.

After my talk with the sergeant, I told Kennedy she could pick up Trixie. She was only too happy to comply.

Maybe Kennedy was right. Maybe we were just so desperate to find a motive and make a connection to Leslie's horrific murder that even something as ridiculous as treasure seemed to fit the bill. It was the twenty-first century, after all. Rational human beings didn't chase after lost treasure. Besides, what would a treasure be doing at the bottom of Lake Michigan? No, I thought we were getting too distracted by all the loose ends and weird coincidences. I believed it was time to turn our focus on hard evidence, like the only person with a real motive to cause Leslie harm, namely the drama teacher, Mr. Bartlett.

"What do you think, Welly?" I asked my happy dog. The reason he was so happy was because he'd been chasing seagulls down the beach, ultimately following them into the water. "Could there be treasure somewhere out there in the lake?" I asked him. I might as well have asked him how he'd gotten out of the bedroom this morning. Words sailed like seagulls over my dog's fluffy black head. Besides, I knew the only treasure Welly cared about was the kind he could eat.

After toweling off Welly, I gave him a treat and put him back in the lighthouse to wait for Kennedy and Trixie. I then thought I'd pop into the bakery and help bake. Sure, there was still a lump on my head, but the Tylenol was working its magic, and I felt pretty darn good, all things considered. Unfortunately, the moment I appeared in my own bakery kitchen, I was treated like an invalid.

"Darling!" Dad exclaimed, dusting his hands off on his apron and rushing over to me. "What are you doing here?" Honestly, did he even need to ask?

"I thought I'd lend a hand, gentlemen. I'm feeling much better."

"Nope," Teddy said, oozing concern. "No baking for you today, young lady. James and I have it all handled. Wendy's been helping out as well. Lindsey," he reprimanded, shaking his head at me. "I can't believe the lighthouse was broken into! And I can't believe you were foolish enough to engage this lunatic."

"With a canoe paddle!" Dad added, casting me a look that let me know just how he felt about that. Not my smartest moment, I'd admit.

"*A canoe paddle!*" Teddy emphasized, trying to look as stern as Dad, only he was failing miserably.

He was well aware of the ridiculous weapon I had used. Teddy, embracing his role as the bakeshop comedian, couldn't stop himself from adding, "Most people find themselves without a paddle when they're up that creek, but I hear you had one on your wall. Badass, Lindsey Bakewell. But you're still not baking today." He gave me a wink and a big Teddy bear hug.

I hugged him back. "It was a miniature, brittle paddle, but I obviously survived again, Teddy." That had them both laughing.

"We'll have to get you a new one," he said. Then, with a theatrical wave of his arm, he proclaimed, "*I survived Stink Pickle Creek and the Grim Reaper.* 'Stink pickle' is my euphemism for you-know-what," he explained with a grin. Referring to the paddle, he added, "It'll have to be at least four feet long to handle all that."

As I laughed, Dad placed a hot mug of coffee in my hand and shooed me out the door.

Wendy, Alaina, and Tom were working behind the busy bakery counter. They were remarkable, and I felt a welling of near-maternal pride as I realized they had it all under control. After another round of hugs, and a plate of Wendy's freshly baked pumpkin-sugar cookies, I was shooed from the bakery counter and into the café, where I was instructed to enjoy my cookies.

I certainly did enjoy them! The pumpkin-sugar cookies were scrumptious and just the thing I needed to ease my nerves. Although not as crisp and buttery as a traditional sugar cookie, Wendy's pumpkin-sugar cookies were softer, fluffier, and filled with a burst of delicious pumpkin flavor that was hard to beat. The spiced cream-cheese frosting on top with a sprinkle of cinnamon was the perfect complement to the cookie. I congratulated Wendy and was thankful she had made a large enough batch of them. The pumpkin-sugar cookies would be a hit with the afternoon crowd.

I was in the middle of a sip of delicious and much-needed coffee when I spied Betty Vanhoosen marching up my pumpkin-lined walkway to the bakeshop door. Her lips were pursed, her face pensive, and her arms pumping vigorously as her long, wool coat fluttered in the wind behind her. She reminded me of a middle-aged superhero preparing to face an insurmountable task, like trying to figure out what baked good to order today. The thought made me smile. I set my coffee mug down and turned to the bakery counter. "Hey, guys, do any of you know if Betty was in this morning?"

"Not yet, boss," Tom answered, spying the plucky Realtor on the other side of the bakeshop door. "I'll get her latte started."

"Excellent idea. But let's make it a pumpkin-spice latte today. On the house." I turned once again to the door. Betty heaved it open, letting in a burst of autumn wind and a sprinkling of leaves with her.

"Lindsey! I'm so glad you're here," she began, rushing over to my table. "I heard what happened at the lighthouse this morning." She paused long enough to take off her coat and drape it over the back of an empty chair. "I saw Ellie. She told me all about it. Terrible, just terrible! We're all glad you're okay. She also told me you were having breakfast at the hotel. I drove over there but didn't see you. Probably too late. I had a showing on Water's Edge Road this morning." She took the seat across from me and continued without missing a beat. "I try to be patient, but sometimes prospective home buyers really rattle my shingles. Anyway, we need to talk." Her round blue eyes shot to mine as she loudly whispered, "Death angel."

My jaw dropped, but I took control of it a heartbeat later when I believed I knew what she was referring to. "Um, actually, Betty, I believe the term is 'angel of death'."

"No, no, I'm pretty sure it's 'death angel'."

"I mean, we're just arguing semantics now. Let's just call it the Grim Reaper, shall we?" I offered a smile. Betty shook her head.

"That's a good name, but that's not it. I'm pretty sure it's 'death angel' . . . No, wait. 'Destroying angel'?" She quirked a brow, as if she wasn't sure of the name herself.

"Honestly, let's just leave the word 'angel' out of it. The guy was a creep."

"What guy?"

"The guy who broke into my lighthouse dressed as the Grim Reaper. I thought we were discussing him?"

"Are we?"

My head started to throb again. It was too early to take more Tylenol, so I took a swig of coffee instead. I set the mug down, looked at her, and asked, "Are we not? What, then, Betty, are we talking about?"

"Why, the murder weapon, of course," she said. Again, she was trying to whisper, but Wendy, Alaina, and Tom were staring at us from behind the bakery counter, hanging on her every word, no doubt. "I told you I'd tell you the moment I got word of it from Bob. Well, I got word this morning."

"I don't understand," I said. "What is this 'destroying angel'? Is it some type of drug?"

"Wait! I remember. It's death cap. The death cap mushroom. It has a Latin name, but I'd have to ask Bob what it is again. Leslie Adams died from eating the most poisonous mushroom in Michigan."

"But that's ridiculous," I countered. "Leslie wouldn't eat poisonous mushrooms. A woman like Leslie would know better." Although I'd just met Leslie, I was fairly certain she wasn't the type of person to eat things that could kill her.

"Well, that's just the thing, isn't it?" Betty said. "She obviously didn't realize that what she was eating was poisonous. According to Bob, she ate enough to kill an entire family."

My hand flew over my mouth as my heart clenched painfully. Poisonous mushrooms! Leslie had eaten poisonous mushrooms! The mere thought was unnerving. As my mind raced in circles, trying to make sense of what Betty was telling me, another thought hit me. I gasped and stared at Betty.

"The kids," I said. "Dear heavens, I've been focusing on the wrong group of kids."

CHAPTER 35

We had surmised Leslie Adams had likely been poisoned before she was found hanging from my oak tree, but the actual murder weapon came as a shock. Something as innocuous as a mushroom had done the deed, and that thought hit me with the same force as a punch to the gut. I didn't know much about poisonous mushrooms, but I assumed, as with any poisoning, it had been a painful death. I offered up a little prayer for the soul of Leslie Adams before looking up the death cap mushroom on my phone.

I felt all the blood drain from my face as I read about the deadly mushroom's toxic effects. It was the deadliest of all fungi, with a lethal dose being only half a mushroom cap. The Latin name was *amanita phalloides*. I didn't pretend to know what that meant, but what shook me most about this mushroom was that it looked so similar to a common button mushroom. How easy it would be to mistake this deadly mushroom for an edible one. Another jarring fact was that the death cap mushroom was commonly found in Michigan, growing under birch and oak trees, of which we had plenty. The article also said that foragers sometimes confused the death cap with a small puffball mushroom, a local favorite and one Leslie had even mentioned to me. As I read further about the mushroom, it became apparent why it had taken so long to identify the cause of death. It took between six and twenty-four hours after ingesting the mushrooms before any symptoms would occur. Once they did, treatment was ineffective. That's why the mushroom was so deadly. The symptoms were excruciating—vomiting, diarrhea, and abdominal cramping. As the toxin destroyed the internal organs, a reprieve could set in, making the victim feel well again for the span of a day. The toxins were then recycled throughout the body, leading to kidney and liver failure. It was this lag time between ingestion and the appearance of the first symptoms that made tracing the source of the poison nearly impossible. No wonder Doc Riggles had had such a difficult time with it.

Poor Leslie. When did she eat the mushrooms? She'd appeared fine the night of my pumpkin-carving party, but she wasn't looking too well Sunday morning at the bakeshop. I thought about that morning. Leslie had come in with a few of her students. She looked a bit green, admitted to having had a rough morning, but she had kept up appearances in front of her students. I also remembered she was acting nervous about something. She'd wanted to tell me something, hadn't she? What was it? Had she known then that she'd been poisoned? I knew she hadn't eaten the mushrooms willingly, which meant she was either forced to eat them or didn't realize she was eating them. That thought terrified me. Maybe Doc Riggles had figured out a timeline.

I turned my mind again to the events of Halloween morning. However, as much as I wanted to delve into this new piece of evidence, I had to refrain. Dad and Teddy, having finished the day's baking, had left just before noon. Since the lunch rush was now on us, I couldn't sit still. I jumped behind the bakery counter and filled orders. Honestly, I was grateful to be working. It kept my mind from spinning out of control over murder suspects and poisonous mushrooms. It also helped me think. At the pumpkin-carving party, Leslie had told me that some of her kids, the ones dressed in woodsy clothing and who referred to themselves as goblincore, were in a foraging club. She told me how they picked mushrooms and sold them to some of the local restaurants. I wasn't about to jump to any conclusions, but I needed to talk with one of those kids.

We were getting ready to close for the day when I spied Rory out the bakeshop window. All my pent-up tension seemed to melt at the sight of him. I wanted to pull him up the light tower stairs with me and discuss the latest finding, the murder weapon that had killed Leslie Adams. Maybe Rory already knew about it, but that conversation would have to wait. Rory wasn't alone. Following our plan, he was coming up the pumpkin-lined walkway with Jordy Tripp and Grant Fairfield. Jordy desperately wanted a tour of the lighthouse, and we would give it to him, in exchange for information. Somebody had broken into my lighthouse looking for something, and I wanted answers.

The sight of the tall, lanky author entering my bakeshop sparked a memory. I suddenly recalled speaking with Leslie Adams for the last time. She'd come to the Beacon on Halloween morning. She had wanted to talk with me about something, but she had lost her train of thought, and I couldn't remember why. I remembered that Trixie had barked. That had caused Leslie to look toward the door. It had been a busy morning, but it hit me now. There'd been something about Jordy Tripp that had set her on edge. She'd left the bakeshop before Jordy had spotted her. But he did eventually find her. Thanks to Christy Parks, we knew that Jordy and Leslie had met on the crowded sidewalk across the street from Christy's shop. The two then disappeared into the Village Bar and Grill. Only Jordy knew what was said, and thanks to the internet, I was now sure Leslie hadn't eaten a deadly dose of mushrooms there. Nope, she'd been poisoned before that meeting, but by whom? The wheels of my mind were spinning. There were so many pieces of this puzzle, but I didn't yet know how they all fit together. However, thanks to Rory, Jordy Tripp and Grant Fairfield were now entering the Beacon. For the life of me, I was going to twist the screw until I had answers.

"Lindsey," Jordy began in a conversational tone as he crossed to the bakery counter, where I was cleaning the cases. I set down my cleaning rag and gave him my full attention. "We heard about the break-in this morning. We didn't think a visit would be possible so soon after so much tragedy, but we're very grateful you're allowing us to visit." This contrite Jordy Tripp was quite a contrast to the brash, overbearing man of a few days ago. I believed this had something to do with the death of Leslie Adams. The moment Leslie's body had been discovered hanging from my gnarled old oak tree, Jordy had made himself scarce. I'd like to think it was out of respect, but I knew better. There was a reason the author didn't want to be connected to the murder victim, namely bad publicity.

Although my curious staff were still lingering behind the counter with me, I gave them the signal that it was time to leave. Of course, they were hesitant. Elizabeth, with her bright blue eyes, shot me her best *Please! Please let us stay* look. But they knew it was time for them to go. Just as they knew I would fill them in on all the little details later. As my young employees marched out the back door, I locked the café door, turned the *OPEN* sign to *CLOSED*, and ushered the men into my living quarters on the other side of the bakeshop door.

"Where's Welly?" Rory asked. I could tell he was a little disappointed that his best buddy hadn't met him at the door with happy tail wags and a slobbery kiss.

"The dogs will be back shortly. They're on a photo shoot with Kennedy." He was about to ask a question when I held up my hand to stop him. "There are still plenty of pumpkins around Beacon Harbor. There's something about photographing dogs and pumpkins that really excites Kennedy. Also, word on the street is that Mom's modeling some gorgeous fall coat they're pushing at the boutique."

"Ellie's modeling?" Grant Fairfield's eyes were nearly popping out of his head at the news. "That's awesome. She still looks amazing for her age."

"*Well,*" I began slowly, trying hard to keep any note of mockery out of my voice, "I'll let her know you said so. Now, gentlemen, if you'll take a seat." I brought them to the dining room table, where the now-infamous oak tree was visible through the undamaged panes of the dining room window. Thanks to Rory and Anders Jorgenson, the broken panes had been covered with cardboard until new glass could be installed.

"This is the original dining room, where the keeper and his family, if he had one, would take their meals. The original kitchen over there"—I pointed to the room in question on the other side of the cased opening—"has been totally remodeled. The original wall that once separated the two rooms has largely been removed and reinforced by the cased opening to allow better flow between the rooms. The only remodeling in this room was basic wall repair, fresh paint of an agreeable color on both the wainscoting and the walls, and the sanding and refinishing of the hardwood floors. But I highly doubt you've come all this way to inspect the keeper's house and my improvements."

"They are remarkable," Jordy said. "But you are correct. We're looking for an artifact, or the mention of an artifact that might still be on the lighthouse grounds."

"What time period are we talking about?" Rory asked. It was a good question. We knew Leslie's husband's ancestor had left his duties at the lighthouse in the year 1900. If the object Grant and Jordy were looking for was from that time period, there was a good chance that what they were looking for was connected to Arthur Adams. The two men looked at each other before Grant answered.

"It would be from the turn of the last century."

Bingo! Rory and I exchanged a look. I then asked, "Would it be an object that was in the possession of the second lightkeeper, Arthur Adams?"

Again with the covert looks. Jordy took the lead this time. "We believe so."

My heart was pounding in my ears, causing me to leap in with both feet. "Leslie Adams, the teacher found hanging from that tree on Halloween night"—I pointed out the window to said tree— "knew about it, too, didn't she?"

Jordy, without flinching, nodded. "We believe so. I had tried contacting her by phone several times. We were trying to set up a meeting with her, but she wasn't interested. And now she's . . ." A troubled expression crossed his face as he dropped his gaze to his hands. "Imagine our horror! The one person in this town connected to the story we're working on was found dead—before we ever got the chance to speak with her."

"But you *did* speak with her," I countered, narrowing my eyes at him. "You were seen going into the Village Bar and Grill together." I noticed that Rory's normally gentle gaze was now laser-focused on the author.

Grant, sitting quietly, looked to Jordy for an answer. "I spotted Leslie after she won the Ellie and Company Pumpkin Pageant. I thought that if we happened to bump into each other on the street, I could get her to talk with me. She humored me for a bit, listened to what I had to say, but before I could get her to agree to a meeting, a friend of hers showed up and pulled her away. He wasn't too happy to see me."

"This friend, did he have a name?" Rory asked. Jordy grinned.

"I'm sure he had one, but he didn't tell me what it was. He was awfully quick to intervene, almost like a husband would, but he wasn't her husband. We know Leslie's a widow. Anyhow, the moment he showed up, the meeting was over. I was hoping to get another chance to convince her, but that's not going to happen." There was no doubt he was glum about this. I couldn't blame him. I was also curious about this friend of Leslie's who had intervened.

"So, you killed her." I flung the question at him like a war hammer, hoping to catch him off guard. It had the impact I thought it might. Both men looked stunned and horrified.

"What? Of course not! Leslie was the only living link we had to this story!" Jordy defended. "We needed her. We needed her cooperation. Because without her, all we have is . . . is . . . ." Whatever the author was going to say, he either lost the heart or the words to convey his meaning. Instead, he threw his hands helplessly in the air.

"Did you believe she would cooperate?" Rory asked.

Jordy shrugged. "I believe she was considering it. But I could tell she wasn't feeling too well at the restaurant. All she had was a glass of water with a slice of lemon in it, and I'd offered to buy." Apparently, from his pointed look, we were to take it as a generous offer. Then the author deflated and leaned back in his chair. "I did press her," he admitted with a hint of guilt. "I can be relentless when I'm working on a project. That's when her friend showed up and rescued her." He hung his head in disappointment.

Noting the author seemed truly remorseful, Rory, bless him, doubled down and went on the attack.

"The two of you came to Beacon Harbor on Halloween and told us there was something in Lindsey's lighthouse 'worth killing for.' A woman is now dead, and Lindsey was attacked this very morning at the lighthouse! Gentlemen, I have to be honest. This isn't looking too good for either of you. The time has come to address the elephant in the room—namely, what in God's name are you looking for?"

"Don't say 'treasure'," I warned, giving them a stern finger-pointing. I didn't know why I said that. Maybe it was to spite Rory, who believed it had to be about treasure? Maybe it was to spite Kennedy, who believed the notion of treasure to be ridiculous? And maybe it was to alleviate my own fears that somehow my beloved lighthouse had been involved in illicit dealings—spurred on by the promise of treasure.

Taking my warning to heart, Jordy swallowed, then peeped, "A map."

"To a treasure," Grant added, driving his point home with a smirk.

CHAPTER 36

I wanted nothing more than to knock that condescending little grin right off Grant's face, but I refrained. Mostly because he was across the table from me, and I couldn't reach him. I was gobsmacked nonetheless. Rory had been correct when he'd told me he believed the only thing worth killing for involving my lighthouse would be treasure. Treasure helped explain why Leslie's husband's ancestor, Arthur Adams, had suddenly made a large land purchase and retired from his duties as lightkeeper, passing this wealth in land down through the generations. And if that was the case, a person could logically assume that this mysterious treasure had been found. Hurrah! End of story. However, Grant surprised us all when he told us otherwise.

"I'm a professor of Great Lakes history with a specialty in underwater archaeology." I hadn't known that, but it was now making sense. Grant continued, "I recently stumbled across a nugget of a story that piqued my interest. I did a little research and soon realized I had found something that, while not the holy grail of all Great Lakes shipwrecks, might be just as profound."

"*Le Griffon?*" Rory blurted, positively oozing intrigue. I was sorry to think I had no idea what he was referring to.

"How I would love to find *Le Griffon*," Grant admitted. "But that illustrious ship, wherever she may lie, shall keep her secrets yet."

"Excuse me, but am I the only one in this room who doesn't know what you're talking about?" From the looks on the men's faces, apparently I was.

"*Le Griffon*, Lindsey," Rory began, "was the ship the famous French explorer La Salle built for his explorations of the Great Lakes. It was a seventeenth-century barque, and the first large sailing vessel to sail across the Great Lakes at that time. Up until that point, fur trading and exploration was conducted in canoes. Anyhow, in the early fall of the year sixteen hundred seventy-nine, La Salle disembarked on what is thought to be Washington Island, off the Door County peninsula in Wisconsin. He and most of his men set off in canoes to explore the western shore of Lake Michigan."

"Or as the Ojibwa called it, *mishigami*, or 'great water'," Grant added.

"Right." Rory bent his head to the scholar in acknowledgment. "Back to *Le Griffon*. La Salle sent the ship back, loaded with furs, to Niagara. But the ship and the six men aboard her disappeared, never to be seen again. To this date, no one has found her, making *Le Griffon* the holy grail of the Great Lakes."

"I bet you'd love to find it," I said, knowing a little something about what drove the man I had fallen in love with. Rory had the heart of an explorer. Maybe someday he'd be the one to discover that ship, but today we were discussing another.

"*Le Griffon* aside," Grant continued, "the shipwreck I've stumbled upon would create quite the stir if it could be located. I'm a huge fan of Jordy's books, and that's why I contacted him with the idea."

"Out of the blue," Jordy admitted with a grin. "And Grant's timing couldn't have been better. As I've told you before, my last Matt Malone novel didn't go over too well. I was looking for another project—one that would put me back on the bestseller lists. Grant, I believe, has given me that. If we can find what we're looking for, I can turn this into a spectacular work of nonfiction."

"He can," Grant averred with near–hero worship. "What makes this story so compelling is that, other than an obscure record of the ship's name and the date it left port on the Canadian side of Lake Superior, there's no other record or account of this ship or the treasure it was carrying. It just vanished."

"Excuse me," I said, breaking the glittering spell of treasure that had come over the men. *Treasure!* I rolled my eyes at the thought. "You just said there's no record that this ship you're looking for was even carrying treasure. How do you even know this treasure exists?"

Grant hit me once again with his smirk. "Would you trust the word of a lightkeeper, Lindsey?"

"I would," I said, having a profound respect for

the keepers who had illuminated the rugged coasts of the world for seafarers. "But if you are referring to my lighthouse, I have to be honest, Grant. There haven't been any lightkeepers here in a very long time."

"True. But one of the old lightkeepers who worked at this lighthouse made a very compelling deathbed confession."

The hair on my neck stood on end at this, causing me to look at Rory. If I was spooked by the thought of a deathbed confession from a lightkeeper at the very lighthouse I lived in, Rory was enlivened by it. His broad shoulders rose and fell from the deep, measured breaths he was taking. His face was calm, but the intensity in his vibrant blue eyes gave him away. Scuba diving was his passion, and he had made it his new career. If there was such a shipwreck in the lake with treasure aboard it, he'd be the first to jump at the chance to discover it. Jordy and Grant had obviously known that when they had contacted him about a boat. But it was November, and November was not the time for such a discovery. I looked at Grant and offered a challenge. "Deathbed confession, you say? Then, how is it you know about it? I assume the keeper in question has been gone a long time."

"Let's just say, I stumbled across it quite by accident. It is the deathbed confession of a lightkeeper by the name of—"

"Arthur Adams," Rory finished for him.

Jordy lifted a brow. "You've heard the legend too?"

"No. Amazingly, our information comes from one of the Ghost Guys," Rory confessed with a grin. "It was Brett Bloom who did some background investigation on the possible spirits of past lightkeepers who might still be lingering in this old lighthouse. It's what they do. After Leslie was murdered, Brett focused on a lightkeeper with the same last name as the murder victim. He not only found a family connection, but he dug up information at the library regarding a large land purchase made by Arthur Adams in the year nineteen hundred, right before he suddenly retired."

Grant rubbed his stubble-covered chin. "That is interesting. I wasn't aware of any land purchase. We weren't focusing on the old lightkeeper. According to my source, this confession was made by Arthur Adams to his son. Not another word was said about it again until two years ago. That's when this original deathbed confession resurfaced in the form of a letter passed to one Douglas Adams upon the death of his grandmother."

"And how would you know about that?" I questioned, finding it suspicious.

Grant shrugged. "I heard a rumor and followed up on it. What I uncovered made me a believer. Apparently, in the late spring of nineteen hundred, lightkeeper Arthur Adams, from this very lighthouse, spotted a small lifeboat in peril a mile down the coast. It was just after midnight when Arthur packed up his gear, saddled his horse, and rode down the beach. Arthur then rescued the two men from the boat. They had claimed to be the only survivors of a ship that had gone down in a storm. These men had in their possession three bars of gold. They told Arthur the ship was carrying a fortune in Yukon gold, and the two survivors knew the exact location where the ship went down. They told Adams they planned to recover the fortune in gold and urged him to keep quiet about it. In exchange for his silence, Adams was given one of the gold bars as payment, with the promise of more should they succeed. The two men then drew a map of the wreck site for Adams and told him their plan. Once the weather cleared, Adams would help them sneak out under the cover of darkness to recover the gold. However, the men were never seen again. Three months later, Adams received word that two unidentified bodies had washed up on a beach near Leland. Curious, Adams made the trip to Leland. There, he supposedly recognized the deceased men as the two he'd rescued at his lighthouse. Due to their untimely deaths, Adams knew the treasure had never been recovered. Since he'd never recorded the rescue of the men, nor the name of the ship they'd supposedly sailed on, he knew he was the only person who knew about the ship and the gold. But Adams never tried to recover the treasure. He believed it was cursed. Instead, he retired from his post at the lighthouse. Thanks to you, we now know he used his bar of gold to purchase land here in Beacon Harbor."

"This map of the wreck site," Rory began. "Was it in the letter given to Douglas Adams?"

Jordy and Grant exchanged a look before Jordy nodded. "We believe that it was. And if it was,

Leslie Adams had it in her possession. But we couldn't get her to admit it. She wasn't about to give away the location of the shipwreck. It was her husband's legacy, she told us. She wouldn't say if they had found it either. I'm afraid Leslie took her secrets to the grave. However, we believe the original drawing of the map might still be here. We'd like to see if we can find it."

CHAPTER 37

While Rory took the men on a tour of the lighthouse in search of the mysterious treasure map, I went to the kitchen to brew a pot of coffee. At least that was my excuse. I really wanted to check in with Kennedy and see where she was. She and the dogs should have been back to the lighthouse by now. It was getting dark, and I really wanted to tell her that Jordy and Grant were on a treasure hunt. Their wild tale of a treasure ship had ignited Rory's imagination as well. That would get under her skin. I also wanted to tell her about the "friend" who had pulled Leslie away while she'd been talking with Jordy in the Corner Bar and Grill. Could that have been Mark Whitcomb? If so, the man was popping up everywhere. Very suspicious. I didn't quite know what to make of any of it yet, but I felt we were getting close to the truth. Kennedy would help me sort out the details.

I had just shot Ken a text and had a pot of coffee brewing when a knock came at the front door. Normally Wellington, the official lighthouse greeter, would bound to the door ahead of me with a series of excited barks. But Welly wasn't here, and Rory had taken the men to the lightroom. Why was I so nervous about answering the door? Probably because it was getting dark outside, and somebody had broken into the lighthouse last night and knocked me unconscious. The knocking came again, and this time I decided to answer it.

"Lindsey?"

To my great relief, it was Cali Adams. I had told the young woman to come to the lighthouse to pick up her mother's dog. However, Trixie was still out with Kennedy, which made a rather convenient excuse to pull the girl into the kitchen with me for a private talk.

"I've just made some coffee, and I always have baked goods on hand. It's one of the perks of my job." I cast her a smile as she sat at the kitchen table. "How about a warm pumpkin scone and a mug of coffee?"

"That sounds great, but please don't go out of your way. I've just come to get Trixie. By the way, where is she?" Her eyes nervously darted around the room.

"She's out for a walk with my friend Kennedy." It wasn't quite the truth, but it was better than telling her my friend was using her dog's adorableness for personal gain. "They should be back in a few minutes." I kept my fingers crossed on that one. Kennedy had yet to respond to my text. I poured a mug of coffee and set it before Cali. I then went to the refrigerator and took out a plate of pumpkin scones. I plated one up, popped it in the microwave for twenty seconds to give it that fresh-baked feel once again, and brought it to the table.

"It smells delicious. My mother loved anything pumpkin," she said, but at the mention of her mother, her eyes began to tear up. "I bet she would have loved these."

"If it's any comfort to you, I gave her one in the bakeshop on Halloween morning. She came in with a few of the girls from her class. They had a bouquet of flowers for me. It was the sweetest thing. Unfortunately, I don't think your mom was feeling too well that day."

Cali dropped her gaze to her plate. "She wasn't. The police told me that Mom had eaten poisonous mushrooms." Her eyes met mine. "She would have known better."

"I believe so too," I told her with a nod. I took a sip of my own coffee, then set the mug down again. "I'm sure the police have asked you this already, but do you know who might have given her deadly mushrooms?"

"If someone gave them to her, she would have thrown them away. I think someone put them in a dish. Mom was trusting to a fault, and she wasn't the best cook. If someone made her food, she'd eat it." It was a good point, and one I had already entertained. The most likely scenario was that Leslie had eaten a dish that had been made with the deadly mushrooms. She'd never suspect someone of trying to poison her. "I have to ask you something else. We believe your mom had knowledge of a shipwreck that was rumored to be carrying gold."

The chestnut-colored eyes, so like her mother's, were now shooting daggers at me. "How would you know about that!"

"It's true?" Yet before she could reply, Kennedy

came bursting through the kitchen door with the dogs.

"Yoo-hoo! I'm home. Oh, hello there." Kennedy smiled at Cali. Trixie, looking more like a fluffy white teddy bear than a dog, strained at the end of her leash, barking at the girl with excitement.

"Trixie?" Cali was clearly confused.

Welly, smelling scones, ran straight to me. Kennedy, wisely, had let go of his leash. Then, as if there wasn't enough commotion, shouting rang out from the vicinity of the lightroom, followed swiftly by the sound of racing feet pounding down metal stairs.

Both dogs started barking. Welly, abandoning me and my scone, ran straight to the light tower door. I couldn't tell whether he was nervous or excited. A moment later, the door burst open, revealing two very frightened men, and Rory. Welly jumped up on Jordy, knocking him on his keister. Rory took hold of his leash and brought my giant dog under control. He helped Jordy up, but the author wasn't smiling.

"What happened?" I asked as the men came into the kitchen.

"All the lights came on!" Jordy cried. "They just popped on!"

"We smelled smoke. Pipe smoke," Grant added.

With a sinking feeling, I asked Rory, "Ghost lights?"

He shook his head. "No, the Edison lights. The decorative lights. They turned on without notice. Shocking, but not deadly. My guess is that someone has angered the captain."

"What captain?" Jordy asked. Rory ignored him.

"I'll try to make amends," I told him with a grin.

Poor Captain Willy. Suffering a ghost hunt, a murder, and now a couple of men hunting for treasure and bent on defaming the second lightkeeper of the Beacon Point Lighthouse. Not the best week for a ghost. However, my thoughts soon shifted from the ghostly captain to the young lady sitting across from me. Clutching the poodle in her lap, she had turned to the source of the noise. The men might have been frightened by a ghost, but Cali looked as if she was staring at one. Her face blanched as her mouth stood agape.

"Professor Fairfield?" she uttered in disbelief. "What on earth are you doing here, in Beacon Harbor?"

Grant Fairfield, professor of Great Lakes history and underwater archaeology, looked like a child caught with his hand in the cookie jar. For once, the smug man was speechless.

"Oh, my God!" Cali cried, filling with anger. "Oh, my God! You've ruined everything!"

CHAPTER 38

"I won't admit to much, darling, but I will admit to this. There's seldom a dull moment at the lighthouse." Kennedy punctuated her statement with a wicked grin.

I looked at my friend over the rim of my wineglass. "I'm not sure how to take that. Is it a compliment or a dig?"

"I'm crushed you even have to ask." In a highly theatrical gesture, Kennedy brought a hand over her heart. That same hand then reached out for her own wineglass, and she took a much-needed sip. She tilted her head back, her eyes closed in pleasure, and she eventually swallowed. She then brought her attention back to me. "It's a compliment, of course. I give the proverbial finger to the man who once told me that all the best drama in the world occurred on the stages of the West End. What a load of hooey. That bloke hasn't been to the Beacon Bakeshop! We have the ghost lights. We find a body that has been murdered twice, first by poisonous mushrooms, then by hanging, and all while dressed as a psychedelic clown. That costume alone could commit murder." She gave herself a toast for that one. "We had a missing poodle, and we met kids who think they're witches, and boys who delight in hanging vile monsters in trees. There are hot girls, and goblin girls, and a creeper of a teacher trying to seduce his student, for shame. But that's not all. A famous author comes to town, and we find ourselves in the midst of a treasure hunt. That's right. Crazy, stupid treasure! And how do they know about this mysterious treasure? That's easy. The sleazy professor, acting as a mentor and friend, betrayed his grad student's trust by exploiting her private account of her ancestor's deathbed confession. The poor student was grief-stricken after the loss of her father, and possibly drunk as well! I needn't mention an epic ghost hunt, an unfortunate viral video, and a whole lighthouse smudging that went horribly wrong. Am I wrong to say that it went wrong? And I nearly forgot! Lindsey was knocked on the head with her own paddle. What a memorable Halloween, everyone! Bottoms up." She raised her glass again, then emptied it.

"Karen," Rory said, flagging our waitress. "Another bottle of wine, if you please."

Karen, a trim, blond, frazzled, no-nonsense woman in her late forties, was our favorite waitress at our favorite local restaurant, the Moose. The walls of the Moose were knotty pine, like an up-north cabin, and decorated with the heads of the majestic animals that once roamed the surrounding woodland. Truth be told, the taxidermized heads were a tad off-putting, but the food and the close-knit community the Moose catered to more than made up for it. Besides, I'd had my first date with Rory at the Moose. Karen marched right over to our table.

"Well, if that ain't a record, I don't know what is!" She stared at the empty wine bottle with awe. "I just set that bottle down. Don't say that I blame ya, Kennedy, after that viral video." Of course, she had watched it. "Creepy stuff. I'll tell ya what I'll do. This next bottle's on me, hon."

"Oh, Karen." Kennedy was genuinely touched.

The waitress then glanced at the hopeful faces of Rory and Tuck, both men enjoying a Scotch on the rocks. "You two," she said, wiggling her finger between them, "you're on your own."

"You're the best, Karen," Tuck remarked with a touch of sarcasm.

"Don't flatter me, Officer. I'll be back with your rolls and butter because that's my job."

"She's angling for a big tip tonight," Tuck teased as the waitress disappeared in the crowded restaurant. He took a cautious sip of his Scotch, then looked at the woman with whom he was infatuated. "Now, back to what you were saying, babe. You're not wrong. There's a lot going on right now. But this new revelation by Cali Adams needs to be considered. I interviewed her Tuesday afternoon, as well, when she arrived. She's devastated by the loss of her mother. But interviewing her again this evening, I could see that the betrayal of her professor from the University of Michigan is hitting her hard."

After Cali had spotted her professor in the lighthouse kitchen, the last place she'd expected to see him, a heated confrontation had taken place, and the police were called in. Sergeant Murdock insisted that everybody head to the police station for questioning. I had planned to make dinner at the lighthouse. The Ghost Guys and Teddy and his wife were going to join us, but I had to cancel. This new revelation had thrown a wrench in my plans. Tuck continued.

"Cali explained that after her father received the strange letter from his grandmother's estate regarding the deathbed confession of their light-keeper ancestor, she was inspired to take Grant's underwater archaeology class. She said her parents didn't quite believe the story in the old letter, but they were determined to check it out. Both were experienced divers and had grown up on the shores of Lake Michigan. Cali believed she was doing her part by taking that class. She enjoyed it so much, she told me, that she began working for Fairfield, helping him with his research. Her goal was to use what she had learned in the hunt for the *Eldorado*, for that was the ship's name."

"The *Eldorado*?" Rory remarked. "That's the name of the ship they're looking for? Grant never told us what it was. Maybe we can do a little research on it ourselves?"

"Good idea," I told him. The wheels of my mind were already spinning. If there was information on the ship out there, Rory and I would find it.

"Anyhow," Tuck continued, "Cali decided to tell Fairfield about the deathbed confession, swearing him to secrecy. She was hoping he'd give her some pointers or help her with the research. Instead, Fairfield made it his own search and hired a famous author to tell the tale."

"He's suspect number one in my book," Kennedy stated. "He wants the story, he wants the gold, and he needs the map to find it. We know Jordy talked with Leslie before she died. He was obviously trying to bribe her for the map. My bet is, Grant was so desperate to find it that he poisoned Leslie so he could break into her house to look for it."

Kennedy's comment got me thinking. "That's a good point. Grant must have known of Leslie long before coming here. He was teaching her daughter, and he was also a Great Lakes historian. Do we know if there was any foul play regarding Leslie's husband's death?"

Tuck shrugged. "Douglas Adams's death was ruled an accident. I read the report. He was ice fishing alone in his shanty, which wasn't unusual. At some point, he left the shanty and was walking back to the shore when he went through the ice. It was determined the thin ice was over a natural spring."

"I would think an experienced ice fisherman would be aware of such spots," Rory commented.

"Obviously, not all ice fishermen are as thorough as you are." I graced him with a smile before turning back to the matter at hand. "Grant Fairfield had motive and opportunity. When Cali saw him in the lighthouse, she connected the dots. She knew in an instant he was looking for the shipwreck she'd told him about. And I think she suspects him in her mother's death as well. Remember, Grant and Jordy have been in Beacon Harbor for at least a week. Also, Grant learned of the shipwreck and its treasure even before the death of Cali's father."

"I was thinking the same thing." Rory swirled the glass of Scotch in his hand, watching the amber liquid swirl around the ice. He took a sip, then said, "Although it was ruled an accident, it's not out of the question that Grant Fairfield could have found Doug Adams fishing in his shanty and confronted him there."

"It's the old 'what happens in the shanty stays in the shanty' scenario," Kennedy quipped. "The other ice-loving blokes would be so preoccupied with their own poles they'd never know if Grant had confronted Doug. He could have bumped him off without anyone knowing, making it look like an accident."

"Grant's a professor down in Ann Arbor," Tuck reminded us. "It's a long drive from there to here. Also, ice fishing can be dangerous. Accidents do happen."

"It's just a suggestion. But think of it." I leaned in and lowered my voice. "With Doug gone, Grant might have believed his grieving widow, Leslie, would be easier to crack. Obviously, he was wrong. Even Jordy said Leslie had no interest in telling him anything about the deathbed confession or helping them in the search for the shipwreck."

"This is all good, Lindsey, but what about the murder weapon?" Tuck asked. "Leslie was poisoned by the death cap mushroom."

"Grant could have bought them," I suggested.

"I don't think you can just 'buy them'," Rory said, adding a slightly admonishing twist of his lips. "Not legally, anyway. But he could have picked them."

"He could have," Tuck agreed. "However, as I'm discovering, using mushrooms as a murder weapon takes planning. It's not a quick death. And what about the hanging? Why would Grant hang Leslie in the tree after she'd already died?"

"Because he's a wanker," Kennedy added with a sneer.

"Because he wanted to throw suspicion off his trail in the case he was found out," I offered, although I wholeheartedly agreed with Kennedy's comment as well. "The terrible hanging had thrown us off, and maybe that was the point."

"This is all well and good," Tuck said, "but here's something else to consider. We have nothing physical connecting Grant to the murder victim. We now know he's on a quest to find a shipwreck. He's looking for this mysterious map, but we haven't found one. It might not even exist. The entire story might be just that, a story. And while breaking the trust of one of his students makes him an epic dirtbag, it doesn't make him a criminal. But we will be questioning him again. Then there's the matter of Jace Bartlett."

"The drama teacher?" Rory narrowed his eyes at the young police officer. We'd almost forgotten about him.

"Rrrr, Mr. Bartlett." I sneered, and Kennedy and I exchanged a disgusted look at the mention of the teacher.

"Why, I'd sure hate to be Mr. Bartlett right now," Karen remarked, plopping a basket of hot rolls on the table. The waitress had a way of sneaking up on a table without warning. It was almost spooky. "What's he done?" she asked, taking Kennedy's empty wineglass and filling it again. She refilled mine, as well, then set the bottle on the table.

"Nothing respectable," I told her. She raised a brow at this.

"Is he a murder suspect?"

As Tuck shook his head, Kennedy blurted, "Yes, he is." She received a chiding look for that.

"Well, I hope our legendary league of super-friends is getting close to catching the killer, because that murder at your lighthouse, Lindsey, has us all on edge. Your fried perch dinners will be out shortly." With that, Karen left us again.

Tuck wisely waited until she was out of earshot. "Murdock interviewed the student whom Bartlett was dating, Brittany Weaver. Brittany is also the president of the foraging club. According to Murdock, she was frightened by the death of her teacher and the implications. She was pretty quick to give up the location where Bartlett was hiding. We were finally able to locate him this afternoon," he told us. "He was on the lam, but I have to say, he's not the craftiest actor on the stage. The guy rented an Airbnb at Torch Lake under his own name. We found him in the outdoor sauna, drinking kombucha and wearing a towel. Nothing else. Just a towel. Not quite the actions of a man on the run." Tuck raised an eyebrow before raking his fingers through his smartly cut blond hair. "I honestly thought we'd made a mistake, but it was him, alright."

"Eww!" Kennedy remarked, crinkling her nose. "The mere thought of that creepy old man makes my skin crawl. Did he admit to the affair?"

Tuck nodded. "Yes, he did. But he's not quite what you think. Here." Tuck paused to pull out his cell phone. He found what he was looking for and handed it to Kennedy.

She was speechless as she gawked at the picture on the phone, letting her jaw dangle a bit. Kennedy looked back at Tuck. "Are you serious? *This* is Bartlett?"

Curiosity got the best of me. I plucked the phone from her hand. "Oh, my," I said, looking at the picture of the sweaty man wearing a towel around his waist. "He doesn't look much older than a high school student, and he's . . . how shall I put it?"

"'Smoking hot' is the term I'd use. No offense, darling."

Tuck made a *whatever* face and shrugged.

The phone was then passed to Rory while Tuck continued with his story.

"That's the problem. Jace Bartlett is twenty-six and looks like a hipster movie star. The young ladies in his class were relentless, he told us. They passed him notes, left him gifts, and waited for him after school by his car. It was his misfortune that he took the bait with one of them. His affair with Brittany had been going on for two months before Leslie found out. The moment she confronted him in his office, he knew his job was in jeopardy."

"Do you think he murdered Leslie?"

"I think there's a fair possibility," Tuck told us. "Jace Bartlett is also the teacher sponsor of the foraging club. According to him, he spends a lot of time in the woods communing with trees and collecting mushrooms. Coincidentally, the young lady with whom he was having an affair was the club president."

"Ooo, she's the goblincore girl Leslie pointed out to us at the pumpkin-carving party—one of the young ladies with green-tinted hair. The plot thickens," Kennedy said with a heavy dose of scandal in her voice. Kennedy loved a good scandal.

"I agree," I said. "I didn't see that coming. The philandering drama teacher is also an expert forager. He'd know where to find death cap mushrooms."

Rory's dark eyebrows furrowed in contemplation as he leaned back in his chair. "My money had been on Grant Fairfield. But Bartlett has means, motive, and access to the murder weapon. Is he in custody?"

"For now," Tuck said. "But we can't keep him long. His home was searched, but no death cap mushrooms were found. Jace Bartlett is swearing he had nothing to do with Leslie's murder. Worst of all, due to the nature of the murder weapon, we can't link him to the crime scene. We're not even certain when Leslie ingested the mushrooms. According to Doc Riggles, her stomach was empty when she died, meaning she hadn't eaten anything or kept anything down in the last four to six hours of her life. As we now know, that's due to the toxic effects of the mushrooms. Hopefully, something will show up, and we'll get a break in this case."

Our dinners arrived, and silence engulfed the table. Truthfully, I was starving, and the delicately fried perch, with a slice of lemon and homemade tartar sauce, was ambrosia. As I was eating my dinner, though, a terrible thought struck me. I dropped my fork and looked at my dinner companions. "Trixie. We're forgetting about Trixie."

"No, we're not," Tuck said, looking annoyed. He shoved the rest of a piece of perch in his mouth, chewed, then swallowed. "She's fine. She's with Cali."

"And she was at my house last night when it was broken into. She was at Leslie's house Halloween night when it was broken into. It might be just a coincidence, but what if Cali is in danger?"

"I don't understand what that dog has to do with any of this," he admitted.

"I don't either. But I have a gut feeling. We need to call Cali."

CHAPTER 39

"She's checked out of the hotel," Tuck said, ending his call. "I think Cali went back to her mother's house."

"Do you have her phone number?" Rory asked, looking at Tuck in the back seat of his pickup truck. Rory had driven us to dinner.

"Not on me, but I have the address. Mind taking us there?"

Rory pulled out of the Moose parking lot and followed the directions on Tuck's phone. Although it felt like midnight, having been dark for hours, it was only nine thirty. Hopefully Cali would still be awake when we arrived.

As we drove down the dark, heavily wooded road, I was surprised to see lights peeking through the bare forest branches in the distance. As we drove closer to the house in question, it became clear that the lights I had spotted lined the long, winding, stamped-cement driveway of the Adamses' home. The low lights running along both sides of the driveway underlit the tunneled branches of the trees above, giving it an enchanted feeling.

"Nice touch," Kennedy remarked as we drove up to the house.

"I'll say," Rory quipped, having never visited the large, modern-rustic home before. I believed it was the style of architecture he liked best. After all, he lived in a lovely log home himself, even if it was only a third of the size of the stately dwelling before us. He cast me a grin. "This place is impressive. Very cool. If old lightkeeper Arthur Adams really did receive a gold bar in exchange for his silence, I have to give him credit. He invested it well. Land was so cheap back then, but land like this is worth a fortune today, especially with a home like that sitting on it."

I returned his grin. "As Betty always says, you can never go wrong investing in real estate."

Kennedy leaned over the front seat. "That's because she's trying to sell you something, darling."

According to Tuck, the Adamses' house was no longer an active crime scene. The crime scene unit had collected what evidence they could find and were still in the midst of processing it. Aside from the ransacked rooms, the house had been very clean.

"It's even better on the inside," Tuck told Rory, knowing that Kennedy and I had been dying to get a peek at the interior. "Judging from all the lights, it looks like she's home."

Cali *was* home. I could hear Trixie barking the moment I knocked on the door, which gave me a measure of relief. However, the moment the door was opened, panic took hold.

Standing in the doorway, blocking our view of the interior, was Mark Whitcomb. "It's an odd time for a visit, don't you think?" he remarked, raking the four of us with a wary gaze.

Kennedy, mustering a mama bear attitude, stepped forward. "What are you doing here, Mark?"

"Cali's asked me to be here. The better question is, why are all of you here? I think you've all traumatized the poor girl enough with your lighthouse charade tonight."

"It was an unfortunate, yet necessary turn of events," I said, standing beside Kennedy. "We now know why those two men are here."

"We're concerned for Cali's safety," Tuck told the man plainly. "This is important. We need to talk with her. May we come in?"

Still blocking the doorway, Mark considered this. "You're one of the cops on the case," he said, recognizing Tuck, who was dressed in a quilted down jacket and jeans. "What's this all about?"

"You'll see in a minute. Move aside, Mark," I warned him, right before pushing my way through the door. Kennedy was right behind me.

"Lindsey, Kennedy," Cali remarked upon seeing us. She was ensconced in a large, stately leather chair in the great room, wrapped in a blanket with Trixie curled in a ball on her lap. The dog's poofy white tail wagged excitedly at the sight of us. Although we had come to speak with the girl, I couldn't help myself from soaking in the beautiful room. A stunning, ornate crystal chandelier hung from the beams of the soaring cathedral ceiling. There was a wall of windows overlooking the back deck and the forest beyond. But the two-story fieldstone fireplace with a live edge oak mantel took my breath away. With all the décor and tasteful little touches, it was even more beautiful than I had imagined.

"We just wanted to make sure you were okay," I told the girl. "It recently dawned on me that whoever is behind the murder of your mother might be after Trixie as well."

"What?" she cried as an expression of both disbelief and fright seized her pretty face. The men had entered the room and were now standing beside us.

"Look," Mark began with the intensity of an angry parent, "I don't know what's going on here, but Cali's had a tough day. She's just told me about what occurred at your lighthouse, about that professor of hers who suddenly showed up, bent on finding the old shipwreck that only her family is supposed to know about."

"Did *you* know about it?" Rory asked, giving the man a hard stare.

Mark didn't answer that. Instead, he offered, "I'm a concerned family friend, and I don't like what's going on in this town one bit."

Cali set the excited dog on the floor. To my surprise, Trixie ran straight into Kennedy's arms. Ken swept the little poodle up and gave her a cuddle as Cali explained, "I asked Mark to be here tonight. I didn't want to stay at the hotel any longer, not with Professor Fairfield and that author staying there too. I wanted to come home, but I didn't want to be here alone. It's a bit remote out here, and it's my first night in the house since Mom passed. It's so sad being here, and Mark's been such a wonderful friend to the family. And . . . and," she continued, "I'm still so angry and so shaken at seeing

Grant Fairfield at your lighthouse! I can't believe that creep had the audacity to do this to me! I trusted him with that story. It was a confession from Dad's great-great-grandfather, who was a lightkeeper at your lighthouse, Lindsey! I found it so intriguing and so amazing that I just had to share it. I thought adults could be trusted. Mark can be trusted, but the ones who get paid to teach you should know better! I didn't even know if it was true, but it was a great story. Mom and Dad delighted in trying to prove the shipwreck existed. It was meant for them—for us, and that despicable little man betrayed me!" Tears streamed down her face as she spoke. "And . . . and the worst part is I . . . I think I'm the one to blame for Mom's death!" At that, the heartbroken young woman burst into a fit of soul-rending sobs.

"Cali, Cali, my dear." Mark was at her side in a moment, wrapping the girl in his arms. The sight of him comforting Cali made me feel ashamed for thinking he was trying to seduce her for her inheritance. He appeared genuinely concerned for the young lady. Maybe Mark Whitcomb was exactly what he claimed to be, a concerned family friend.

When Cali had calmed down, I tried to explain to her why we were there. "The reason we're here at such a late hour is because I believe you might still be in danger. I'm glad you and Grant Fairfield came face-to-face." I didn't dare suggest we might have had some help in that due to Captain Willy. The truth was, if the men hadn't been scared out of the lightroom, Cali might have left the lighthouse without ever having seen them. But she *had* seen them, and now more of the story was coming together.

"We now know that Grant Fairfield was trying to locate a map to the shipwreck of the *Eldorado*," I continued. "We learned that was the name of the ship supposedly carrying a fortune in gold. He told us he believed the map was in the letter given to your late father upon his grandmother's death. Do you know if there really was a map to this shipwreck?"

All eyes were on the girl as I asked this. After thinking a moment, Cali nodded. "There was."

"Is it still in this house?" Rory asked.

Cali shook her head. "I don't think so. After Dad died, Mom burned the letter. There's a rumor that the treasure was cursed, and Mom was beginning to believe it."

That made sense to me, for I was beginning to believe the treasure was cursed as well. Addressing Cali, I said, "I have another question. Do you know if there is any reason someone would want Trixie? I ask this because the night your mother was killed, Trixie was missing from this house. She showed up a day later at my lighthouse. We were so happy to find Trixie that I let everyone in the bakeshop know she'd been found. Then that night someone broke into my lighthouse. I think they were looking for Trixie."

"Your lighthouse was broken into?" Mark looked at me with concern. "Obviously, Trixie's okay, but was anything taken?"

"Lindsey was attacked and knocked out cold," Rory told him. "We believe her attacker was scared away before he could find what he was looking for."

"Did you get a good look at this person?" Mark asked with a probing gaze.

"I did. It was the Grim Reaper." He was either surprised by this or intrigued, it was hard to tell which.

"He didn't stick around long," Rory added. "We think Wellington somehow got out of Lindsey's bedroom and went after the intruder." Again, in my mind, Captain Willy had something to do with that, too, but I kept my thoughts to myself as Rory continued. "We're not sure how that happened, but Trixie was found hiding under Lindsey's bed. That incident got us thinking."

"I'm fine now," I assured them all, in case anyone was wondering. "But again, we want to know whether someone would be after Trixie—and why."

"Well," Cali began, looking at the dog in Kennedy's arms, "she's a purebred, and adorable. Other than that, I don't know. Maybe Mom put something on her collar? Trixie was always with her, except when she was teaching. She was like Mom's shadow."

Kennedy then unhooked Trixie's collar and held it up for us to inspect. "Good guess, except there's nothing on here." Kennedy handed the collar to Cali.

"This collar's adorable," she commented, looking at Kennedy, "but this isn't her usual collar."

"That's right," Kennedy said. "The poor thing was a mess after traipsing through the woods all the way to the lighthouse. I took her to Peggy's Pet Salon, had her washed and groomed, and then I bought her a new collar. It matches her new leash, which is still back at the lighthouse." She offered a look of apology.

"Thanks, but where's her old collar?"

"Her old collar?" Kennedy repeated the question as if she hadn't heard it correctly. Realizing she had, her nose wrinkled in distaste. "That old strap? I threw it away!"

"Wasn't there a tag on it?" Cali asked. "I think she has an identification tag and the one that's required by the village for proof of her rabies vaccination. Wasn't that on the old collar?"

Guilt wasn't an expression Kennedy was familiar with, as she usually claimed that guilt was a useless emotion. Unlike some of her more outlandish mottos, her thoughts on guilt had served her well. But now that distasteful emotion had seized my dear friend's face. I had to admit, it wasn't her best look.

"There might have been tags on it?" Kennedy offered breezily, trying to make light of the fact that she'd thrown away the dog's collar, which just might hold the piece of the puzzle everyone was looking for. After a sharp look from Rory and one of disappointment from Tuck, she offered, "I suppose I should check the bin at Ellie and Company tomorrow. That's where her adorable collar came from, and that's where her old collar was put out of its misery. Keep your fingers crossed that Ellie hasn't emptied the trash."

CHAPTER 40

After this new and disturbing revelation, of which Kennedy was the perpetrator, we left Cali and Mark with explicit instructions to lock up the house and stay on their toes. The Adamses' house had quite the security system, Tuck had told us. That security system had been turned off the night of Leslie's murder, making the police believe that whoever killed the teacher had been invited inside.

With a sinking feeling of doom in the pit of my stomach, we had driven straight back to the lighthouse. After giving Welly a big hug as he met us at the door, Rory took him outside to the back lawn to do his business. Tuck and Kennedy, in the midst of an argument, headed right up the light tower stairs, where we'd meet them shortly. It was late, and dark, and the bitter wind coming off the lake was howling terribly. However, there was a murderer still loose in Beacon Harbor, and Kennedy had quite possibly thrown away something important. We didn't know for sure. It was only a hunch, but the fact that Kennedy had been stricken with such a terrible bout of guilt suggested there was more to the story than she was letting on. It would all come out in the lightroom.

This time Kennedy's careless, fashionista attitude had really irked Rory. While he was out with Welly, trying to subdue his barely contained anger, I went straight to the kitchen. Tensions were running high since we'd left the Adamses' house, and we needed something special to calm our nerves and bring our focus back on the problem at hand, namely finding Leslie's murderer. I had just the thing for it too. While I set a kettle of water on to boil for a pot of soothing tea, I took out the beautiful cheesecake I had made the day before. I had planned on serving it for tonight's dessert. Due to Jordy Tripp, Grant Fairfield, and their surprise meeting with Cali Adams, any plans I'd had for dinner at the lighthouse had gone off the rails. Well, there was no better time for dessert than now.

Teddy and I had come up with the cheesecake idea in late September, thinking it might be nice to offer in the colder months. We'd been making this cheesecake most of October and sold it by the slice in the bakeshop. It had been a big hit with the lunch and after-lunch crowd. The cheesecake was a delicious pumpkin spice with a layer of gooey caramel on top and a sprinkling of toasted pecans. In a phrase, it was pumpkin-cheesecake heaven.

I had just put four slices of the cheesecake on the tray with the pot of brewed tea when Rory came back inside the kitchen with Welly.

"Is that cheesecake?" he asked. A smile crept on

his sullen face. "Is that pumpkin-spice cheesecake? You're bribing me, Bakewell, aren't you?"

"Look, we just need to calm down and figure out what Kennedy did with Trixie's old collar. I'm sure we'll be able to find it. In the meantime, this will help us all get along."

"You dessert-making angel," he breathed huskily, and gave me a kiss. "Because you made my favorite cheesecake, I won't wring your friend's neck now, although she deserves it. I mean, what bonehead takes someone else's dog to get groomed, then throws away the old collar, dog tags and all?"

"You know very well what bonehead does that. She has an eye for fashion and a knack for teasing out beauty in dirty animals, Tuck included. Did you get a load of that sweater he was wearing tonight?"

Rory grinned. "Patterned-navy-and-orange cardigan over a light-blue crewneck shirt. He definitely didn't pick that one out himself."

"Right? And in her defense, Kennedy's never owned an animal herself."

Rory picked up the tray, and we both headed for the light tower stairs. "Well, thank heavens for that!"

"Look," Kennedy began, addressing us from the comfort of her wicker chair. She was wrapped in a fleece blanket, which I kept in a basket in the light-room for that very reason, and was clutching a steaming mug of tea. "I didn't want to say anything back there, because, well, I don't trust Mark Whitcomb one bit, and I certainly didn't expect to see him with Cali tonight. But here's the thing, darlings, I didn't throw everything on that dog collar away."

Rory narrowed his eyes at her and leaned forward in his chair. His generous slice of pumpkin cheesecake, I noticed, was nearly gone. "What do you mean? Do you still have the old collar?" He looked almost hopeful.

However, Rory's hopes were dashed when she told him, "No. That collar was rubbish. It was caked in mud, so I threw it in the bin. But I didn't throw away Trixie's dog tag. She only had one, and it didn't have anything on it. It was purely decorative, and quite lovely."

"Babe!" Disbelief seized Tuck's adorable, boyish face as he looked at his girlfriend. "Are you telling us you still have that dog tag?"

"Uh-huh," she replied, then took another sip of her steaming tea as she stared out the window to the dark lake beyond.

We were all waiting for her to say more about the dog tag. "Kennedy, where is it?" I finally demanded.

Startled, she set down her mug of tea and looked at us again. "Okay, don't get mad. I have it. I'll show you." And with that, to our utter amazement, Kennedy unzipped her coat a few inches, reached beneath the collar of her shirt, and withdrew her amulet necklace. Dangling at the end of the silver chain was the black onyx crystal given to her by the psychic medium, Crystal Henderson. I knew she was wearing that, only now there was another charm dangling beside the black crystal.

Tuck looked shocked. "What the heck is that?" Missing the point, he jabbed a finger at the shiny black rock. To be fair, it did look a bit pagan.

"That's my black onyx crystal," she told him proudly. "It's protecting me from evil. After smacking into Leslie's very dead, very stiff body, I thought I'd give it a try. Then, when I found this apple dog tag, I decided to wear it too." She took hold of the dog tag so we could get a better look at it. Sure enough, the small round tag was in the shape of a shiny red apple. "After all, apples are good luck too." Kennedy punctuated this with a knowing grin.

"Are they?" Rory challenged, staring at the apple dog tag with narrowed eyes.

"Of course, they are, Hunts-a-Lot. Haven't you ever heard the saying, *an apple a day keeps the doctor away*? That's because apples are full of good luck. I figured that with a charm for luck and one for protection, I'm covered, and I have been. Point in fact, I should have been here last night when the Grim Reaper broke into the lighthouse and knocked Lindsey on the head, but I wasn't. I was otherwise engaged."

"That saying is in regard to eating the apple, not wearing one around your neck," Rory told her in no uncertain terms. "I can't believe you didn't know that! Didn't they teach you about nutrition in the Shire?"

"I turn a deaf ear to your sarcasm, sir," she declared with an upheld hand. "Apples are good luck to me."

"Hey!" I cried, knowing Rory and Kennedy could fire insults at each other all day. I now had their attention. "Kennedy has the dog tag. Maybe this is what the killer was looking for?"

"An apple? Doubtful," she said, but she took it off nonetheless.

"Leslie was a teacher," I reminded them. "The apple is a symbol of the teacher, and not because apples were good luck either. It was all about pay. In the early days of education, especially in the rural areas of the country, people wanted to educate their children but didn't have the money to pay for a teacher, so they bartered bushels of produce for education. Apples were a favorite. It's a fruit that stores well, can be eaten whole, can be baked into a delicious pie or made into hard cider. Hence, the apple stuck as the symbolic pay for a teacher."

"Well, thank you for the history lesson, Lindsey darling. But I still think apples are lucky."

"Fair enough," I said as Rory inspected the dog tag.

"I don't get it," he said. "It's just an apple. It doesn't look like a treasure map to me. Wait. It's not a clear print. I think it's made up of lines. Do any of you have a magnifying glass?"

"There's one in the guest room," I said and ran down the light tower stairs to get the old artifact that had come with the lighthouse. When I came back, I took the dog tag from Rory and held it under the old magnifying glass.

"Oh, my goodness!" I exclaimed, studying the apple. "I can't believe it! Do you remember Teddy's cupcake of irony?" I looked at Kennedy as I said this. She nodded. "This apple is exactly like the cupcake on the back of Teddy's résumé! I had overlooked that, too, until it was brought to my attention."

"What are you talking about?" Rory and Tuck looked at me, but Kennedy knew what I meant. Teddy had made a word-art graphic on the back of his résumé in the shape of a cupcake. The tiny type, looking more like a thin line, denoted all Teddy's experience in the film industry. He was proud of his former achievements, yet they weren't relevant to his current career anymore. Hence his "cupcake of irony" placed on the back of his résumé. Leslie Adams had done the very same thing with the dog tag.

"This apple is made up of a series of dots, small type, and numbers," I told them, studying the little apple. "This type is even smaller than the type on Teddy's résumé. *Dot-dot-dot-dot*," I read, scanning down the apple stem to the meat of the fruit. "*October eighteen-hundred-ninety-nine, the schooner Eldorado set sail from Thunder Bay, Canada, heading south across Lake Superior, through the locks of Sault Sainte Marie, downriver into Lake Huron, through the Mackinaw Straits, into Lake Michigan, heading to the port of Muskegon, Michigan, carrying the personal belongings and fortune of Klondike speculator Adam McDonald and crew. On the tenth of November, during raging storms and heavy winds, the schooner went down in the lake. Two survivors rescued at Beacon Point Lighthouse at one-twenty-two in the morning. The survivors had in their possession three bars of gold. They gave a description of the schooner and the approximate coordinates where she foundered, N44-53.58.W86-15.58.155. Survivors, refusing to give their names, were never seen from again. Dot-dot-dot.* It repeats itself. I think we've found Arthur Adams's account of the wreck of the *Eldorado*!"

"And the treasure map!" A proud grin animated Kennedy's face as she added, "All thanks to me and my love of good luck apples!"

CHAPTER 41

A s we marveled over the clever dog tag and our good fortune that Kennedy had an affinity for shiny red things, the question became, Who? Who had figured out that Leslie Adams had hidden the family legend of the *Eldorado* shipwreck on her dog? When I'd met her at my pumpkin-carving party, she had struck me as a lively, intelligent woman. Now, with the discovery of the apple dog tag, I felt a welling of newfound respect for her as well. Leslie had embraced the symbol of her calling and had hidden the coveted information in plain sight on the collar of her dog. Yet whoever had been after Trixie hadn't counted on the dog's loyalty or her bravery. I was now more determined than ever to find her killer and end the terror that had descended on our little village during Halloween.

"Leslie was a teacher, and so is Mark Whitcomb," Kennedy pointed out, voicing her suspicion of the man. "They worked at the same high school and knew the same kids."

I hastily scribbled her remarks in the logbook, trying to keep track of our suspects and their connection to Leslie. We had four main suspects to date, each with a possible reason to kill. Mark Whitcomb, Kennedy's prime suspect, was currently at the top of the list. Then there was Grant Fairfield, the professor from the University of Michigan. He had betrayed the trust of Cali Adams, his student, and knew about the map. Grant was after the treasure. The man was slimy for sure, but was he a killer? There was also Jordy Tripp, the author who was trying to write a bestseller. We didn't believe he was after the treasure as much as he was after a compelling story. He'd wanted Leslie's cooperation, and she hadn't been interested. Would he have killed her for that? Then there was Jace Bartlett, the philandering teacher, who ticked all the boxes as a suspect, having means, an obvious motive, and likely the best knowledge of the murder weapon and where to find it. His underage girlfriend, Brittany, was also on the list as a possible accomplice. None of us believed she had the gumption to pull off the poisoning and hanging of her beloved teacher on her own. It was a puzzling mystery for sure.

Although it was late and I would be up in a few hours to start baking, I wasn't about to go to sleep, and neither were the others. We had found the last piece of the puzzle, and now it was time to put our heads together and try to sniff out the murderer. Kennedy continued talking about Mark Whitcomb.

"I don't think it was a mere coincidence that Lindsey and I met him the morning after Leslie's murder," she stated. "He was lingering outside her big house. They say the murderer always returns to the scene of the crime. Well, Mark was there. He hasn't denied knowing about the treasure, either, or the connection the Adams family had to it. What if he was after the treasure as well? He might have killed Leslie, then searched her house, trying to find the hidden map, not knowing it was hidden on Trixie. Maybe he figured that out too? He might have been the one who broke into the lighthouse last night."

"While that's an interesting take on it, babe, we don't have anything concrete linking Mark Whitcomb to the crime scene. For that matter, we don't have anything concrete linking *anyone* to the crime scene." Tuck pursed his lips and shook his head in frustration. "Mark was Leslie's coworker and a close family friend. It's not a crime, and he's sticking to his story."

"Wait," I said, searching the internet on my phone. It had been such a busy day I hadn't had time to poke around for information. But the internet is an amazing thing. I found what I was looking for in only a few moments and scanned the article. "According to this article in the local newspaper from last January, regarding the accidental death of Doug Adams, Mark Whitcomb was the person who found the body." I looked up from my phone. "What if he killed Doug Adams too?"

Tuck raked his fingers through his hair in frustration. "I didn't know that. I never thought to read the old article. How did I miss that?" He berated himself a moment longer, then took a deep breath. "While finding the body of a friend is not exactly a smoking gun, so to speak, it is suspicious. I need to question him again."

"If Mark Whitcomb knew about the family legend, he might be the murderer," Rory agreed. "We know he's a single male, a teacher, and maybe he had his sights set on finding the gold at the bottom of the lake too. Leslie might have confided in him after Doug's death. She might have told Mark about the shipwreck. Just as she might have told him about her discovery regarding the drama teacher, Bartlett, and his affair with his student. Mark would have known Bartlett was also the teacher sponsor of the foraging club. He could have easily used the poisonous mushrooms on Leslie in an attempt to frame Bartlett for the deed. Bartlett had motive, means, and, if not direct access, a pretty good working knowledge of the murder weapon. After Leslie was found murdered, Bartlett skipped town and rented an Airbnb an hour away. He's an idiot, but I'm not sure he's the killer. He is, however, the perfect fall guy."

"I agree," Tuck said. "He looked more interested in sweating out his impurities than seeking revenge."

"Mark Whitcomb, being a teacher, would also have a good idea of what students were harassing the lighthouse," I reasoned. "Leslie, and most of the kids, knew that Jake Van Andel, the quarterback of the high school football team, was one of the boys behind the pranking. My guess is that Mark would have known it too. And he certainly knew about the livestream ghost hunt at the lighthouse. I think he hung Leslie's body on the oak tree as a distraction."

"I agree," Kennedy piped up. "Hanging the body also helped cover up the true cause of her death, ingesting poisonous mushrooms. Cali said her mom wasn't the best cook. But I'll bet Leslie would have eaten a meal made by Markie-Mark Whitcomb without question."

"And the moment Cali arrived," I added, thinking of our visit to the Harbor Hotel, where Mark had been sitting with Cali, "Mark swooped right in, using his 'family friend' status to manipulate her into believing he was her protector, when in reality he's probably after the treasure himself!"

"Okay, again," Tuck began, tempering our careening suspicions of Mark Whitcomb, "these are all great points, but we don't have concrete evidence that he's behind the murder."

"He's with her now in that big house!" Kennedy reminded us, looking terrified by the thought. "What if he kills Cali too?"

"We need to do something, Tuck!" I cried.

"Maybe we already have," Rory mused. He pulled his gaze back from the lightroom windows and looked at the young police officer. "While I'd love to drive out to the Adamses' house and check on Cali, it's late. However, Kennedy told Mark she threw the old dog collar away at Ellie and Company. We could get in the truck and stake out the boutique. If anyone comes along and tries to break in tonight, we make our move and catch our killer."

While the men headed out for their predawn stakeout at the boutique, they insisted that Kennedy and I stay in the lighthouse and get some sleep. Fat chance of that happening. While we were up in the lightroom, Welly had fallen asleep on the couch. I sat with him for a while, then took him outside for a walk around the backyard. It was a cold, dark night, with fog so thick it was hard to see anything. Once Welly had done his business, I urged him back inside for a treat. My poor pooch was tired and confused. *Why aren't we sleeping in the bedroom?* his sleepy eyes seemed to ask me. But I was too keyed up to sleep. Instead, I decided to head to the bakery kitchen and start the day's baking.

"I'm going with you," Kennedy said, jumping off the couch. The moment she vacated her spot, Welly was back on the puffy red leather cushions, nearly taking up the entire couch.

"No need to thank me for keeping it warm for you, sweetie," she teased him, giving Welly a pat on the head. Still wrapped in her blanket, Kennedy then padded along with me to the bakery kitchen.

Since neither of us could sleep, and since Kennedy could barely *cook up a pot of coffee*, as she often said, I pulled a stool over to the butcher-block counter for her to sit on. We then chatted about Mark Whitcomb and our suspicions of him as I walked around the kitchen, taking out the ingredients I needed to start making the sweet roll dough. I had no sooner put the flour in the giant mixer when my phone rang. It was Rory.

"It looks like you and Kennedy were right," he said. "We were sitting on the street by the boutique, watching for another car, when I decided to walk around to the back of the building. Someone's broken in. Tuck has called for backup, and I've alerted Ellie. We're heading out to the Adamses' house now."

"Promise me you'll be careful," I said, panic seizing me.

"You know I will, babe. Love you," he said and ended the call. My heart was racing as I turned to Kennedy. "They're going after Mark Whitcomb."

"May that ruddy, murdering villain get what he deserves!"

It wasn't long after I'd ended the call with Rory that my phone rang again. This time it was Dad.

"Honey, I heard you were still awake," Dad began. "We're on our way to Ellie and Company to meet with Sergeant Murdock. Someone's broken in."

"I know, Dad. Are you and Mom okay?"

"Shaken, but that's all. However, there's another matter that's put me on edge. I was reading and came across something that struck me. I think I know who killed—"

Yet before Dad got a chance to tell me, the bakery door burst open with a loud *bang*. There, framed in the doorway with a gun trained on me, was the Grim Reaper. I screamed and dropped my phone.

CHAPTER 42

It's hard to think rationally with a gun pointed at your head, especially when that gun is held in the hand of the Grim Reaper. Of course, it was just a costume, but its implication was frightening. The Angel of Death was pointing a gun at me. But he was no angel. Kennedy and I were both tired and mentally exhausted. I gave a thought to running for the café door but knew that one of us would likely be shot in the process. Whomever was in the Grim Reaper costume was obviously demented. In a matter of seconds, Kennedy and I were shoved out the door and into the foggy darkness, heading toward the lake. Kennedy had a blanket; I didn't have time to grab my coat. I was in a sweatshirt and jeans.

Thanks to the cold wind, the fog wasn't as thick as it could have been. I could see about ten feet in front of me, but that was all. Sound, however, carried, and Wellington's frantic barking was breaking my heart. I started screaming then. Kennedy did the same, but the Reaper just laughed and poked me in the ribs with his gun. In a deep, obviously disguised voice, he said, "Go ahead. No one will hear you."

We got to the shore and were made to wade through the water to a boat that had been anchored just off the beach. The waves were high, and the cold water was just slightly warmer than the air as it drenched my thighs. While I was thinking on how to get away, Kennedy was shouting insults at the costumed man.

"Idiot! I know who you are. Stop this charade, Mark, and let us go!"

"If you want to live, I suggest you shut up," Death told us, then indicated with his gun that we should climb aboard the awaiting motorboat.

As I took hold of the ladder, I realized the boat we were getting on was one of Rory's. He still had a couple in the water this late in the season, but only one was docked at the marina. With a sinking heart, I realized that Mr. Grim had obviously stolen it.

"Bloody hell!" Kennedy cried, stepping into the boat and falling headlong onto a giant inflatable unicorn float that filled up the entire back deck. It seemed ridiculous and totally out of place. I knew for a fact that it didn't belong to Rory.

As I was trying to make sense of the incongruous sight, avoiding the same mistake as Kennedy, I looked back at the lighthouse, now hidden in the fog. I could still hear the forlorn sound of Welly's earth-shattering bark. Then something even more terrifying happened. Like the flash of a bolt of lightning, an eerie green light pierced the darkness and the fog.

"What the—" The Reaper didn't know what to make of it.

"It's the ghost lights," I told him. Both Kennedy and I knew what they meant. Someone was going to die.

"Sit right here," he demanded, pointing at the ridiculous unicorn raft. "If you move, I'll kill you." As Kennedy and I huddled together in her blanket on the raft, the Reaper raised the anchor, then ran to the wheelhouse. A moment later, the motor kicked on and the boat took off at speed, crashing headlong into the waves as we went. I was petrified with fear. Sitting on the ridiculous raft made it even worse. Cold, wet spume hit our faces as we were tossed around like a couple of toddlers in a bounce house. Had that been this lunatic's plan?

"We . . . need-need-need . . . to . . . take-ake-ake . . . him!" Kennedy hollered as we flopped on the raft clinging to our blanket.

"Right-right!" I replied. I steeled my nerves and let go of the blanket. The moment I did, I rolled off the inflatable unicorn and crashed on the deck with a thud. Kennedy followed my lead and landed on top of me, all 140 soaking-wet pounds of her. "Roll off me!" I hiss-whispered, trying to raise my drenched head. My heart sank when I noticed that the green light from the lighthouse had faded in the fog. It was gone. It was still early in the morning and very dark. But I knew, due to the speed of the boat, that we were far out on the cold, choppy waters of Lake Michigan.

We had just gotten to our feet and were making our way to the covered wheelhouse when the Reaper suddenly cut the engine. The boat whooshed to a sudden stop as it hit an on oncoming wave. Kennedy and I both lost our footing again. The Reaper spun around on us and laughed. His laughter sounded unhinged.

"You two are pathetic!" He stood towering over us.

"At least we aren't in costume," Kennedy lashed out. "I'll take pathetic over deranged any day."

I flashed Kennedy a *let's not irritate him* look. The man had a gun, after all. And as we'd firmly determined, he *was* deranged. I got to my feet and helped Kennedy. "Why are we here?" I demanded of the Reaper. "In my boyfriend's stolen boat?"

"It was on hand," he said, regarding the boat. "The raft is for you two. We are here on the lake because I'm making you a deal. It's nearly the same deal I made to that stubborn, foolish woman. Your life for the map. I know you have it."

"How do you know we have it?" Kennedy asked. We both knew there was only one way he could have figured it out, and that was from Cali Adams. We were both stunned when the Grim Reaper reached into the pocket of his flowing black robe and pulled out a dirty little dog collar. He shook it. He was the one who'd broken into Ellie & Co.!

"Because it's not on this," he said. "That made me realize that you"—he pointed at Kennedy—"must have taken it when you found the dog."

Kennedy and I exchanged a look, both of us knowing we were facing Mark Whitcomb. My stomach gave a painful lurch as I thought about poor Cali.

"You horrible man! What have you done with Cali?"

"She and her friends are suffering the same affliction as her mother."

"You monster!" Kennedy cried.

"What 'friends'?" I asked.

The Grim Reaper stilled and looked at me. "You don't know who I am?" A sinister chuckle escaped him.

"We do," Kennedy told him in no uncertain terms. "Bloody Mark Whitcomb!"

"Oh, dear," the Reaper said and shook his head. Then he did something surprising. He pulled off his mask.

I inhaled sharply. Kennedy gasped. We were so shocked we nearly forgot he was still holding the gun.

"Jordy Tripp!?"

"Bloody hell!" Kennedy cried, slightly disappointed she'd guessed wrong. Honestly, I was surprised too.

"Spare me your astonishment. I'm the only one with my career on the line here."

"But why?" I asked, dumbfounded. "Why did you kill Leslie Adams?"

"You want to know why? I'll tell you why! At first, I was intrigued when Grant Fairfield contacted me with the request to cowrite a nonfiction book with him about an old shipwreck and a mythical treasure. Neither his source, nor his research, were very sound regarding this treasure. But he did have passion. I had the name, being a bestselling author. I needed a project that paid. It wasn't a bad proposition, considering the pickle I was in. Plummeting book sales. No contract. And the soul-crushing reviews!" He jerked his head at us and demanded, "Have either of you gotten bad reviews?"

What an odd question, but I felt inclined to answer. "Umm, I sell quality baked goods out of a refurbished old lighthouse that overlooks Lake Michigan. I have a solid five-star rating on Yelp." Jordy snarled at me, then pointed the gun at Kennedy.

"Unlike Lindsey, I'm not a people pleaser. I don't give a fig what people say about me . . . unless it's a glowing review. I mostly get glowing reviews," my friend declared. "I didn't know if that was true. Her podcast was popular, but controversial as well. However, true or not, we'd clearly irked Jordy Tripp with our failure to understand his pain.

"I . . . I was pub . . . publicly excoriated for my last Matt Malone novel!" he spat, foaming at the mouth. "It . . . was unlucky number thirteen! I was having a hard time thinking up a new way to murder somebody. It's hard, you know," he practically shouted, as if thinking of an unusual way to murder somebody was normal. It wasn't. He was bonkers!

To illustrate his dilemma, Jordy counted on the fingers of his gun-less hand. "Stabbing, strangling, gunshot, machete, ice pick, a hammer to the head, asphyxiation, ice bullet, pufferfish, flesh-eating bacteria, and a poisoning by the death cap mushroom. I was tired of thinking up new ways to kill bad guys. I hit a wall! I had writer's block! And the only thing that kept popping into my head was oleander."

"Like the flowers?" I asked.

"YES-LIKE-THE-FLOWERS!" he screamed. "I write a high-octane series, and all I could think of was a little white flower. I took a gamble and wrote a flop! Stupid oleander!" he yelled in our faces once again, as if it was the end of the world.

"You should have tried eating one first," Kennedy said. "It might have helped."

I was still stuck on the fact he'd mentioned the death cap mushroom. "Wait." I narrowed my eyes at him. "Back up a step. You killed somebody in one of your novels by using the death cap mushroom?" I remembered then that Dad had called me. Could he have stumbled upon this fact after reading a Matt Malone novel? With a new wave of horror, I looked at the writer.

Jordy nodded with a sneer as his head gave a little jerk. He had a nervous tic. The fact that he was still holding a gun wasn't sitting too well with me. "Poisonous mushrooms are diabolical, excruciating, and hard to trace. Leslie also confessed to liking mushrooms. When I began to realize there might be an old shipwreck in the lake with a treasure on it, my plan kicked in. I created Matt Malone; therefore, I must be him. Right?" he asked us. All I could do was sit in silence and stare. Jordy continued. "But readers don't like him anymore." This thought obviously made him both angry and sad. "I needed something new. I needed a blockbuster, and I had uncovered a remarkable true story that no one knew about. Don't you see? I had it in the palm of my hand. A fortune in gold only made it more desirable and sensational. This shipwreck is my story. MY STORY! And that insufferable woman wouldn't cooperate with me!"

"You're a nutter," Kennedy told him. Jordy ignored her.

"I lied when I told you that Leslie didn't talk with me. Of course, she did. I'm the famous author, Jordy Tripp!" In that moment, I felt his big ego was quite possibly more offensive than the gun in his hand.

"She agreed to meet with me for dinner the night before Halloween," he admitted. "We went to that tacky diner outside town." He was referring to Hoot's Diner. I loved that diner! "It was all fun and games until I confronted her about the death-bed confession of her ancestor. She couldn't fathom how I knew about it and didn't want to talk about it either. I had come prepared for that!" he said with a knowing look. "Leslie had ordered a salad and a cup of clam chowder. When she excused herself to use the ladies' room, I sprinkled the mushroom powder into her soup. I had dried the mushrooms and powdered them. They're more potent that way," he added before his head jerked again.

"You went back to her house after the parade," I surmised. Jordy nodded.

"It was late. All the festivities in town were over except for the ghost hunt at your lighthouse. Leslie was in a bad way when I found her there. She was in so much pain that she never bothered to remove her ridiculous costume. I told her that if she gave me the map to the treasure ship, I'd call an ambulance."

"She didn't tell you," I said, thinking of the poor woman and how much pain she must have been in.

"No. But she did confirm for me that one existed. I was sure it was in her house. But then, when I couldn't find it anywhere, I went to talk with her again. But I was too late. Yet as I watched her take her last breath, I noticed she was staring at her little dog. Stupid little thing in a matching clown costume! I thought nothing of it until it was too late. I had already hung her body from your oak tree."

"Why did you do that?" I cried, filling with fury.

"Because she was dressed as a clown. It was a twist, a touch of drama, and I thought it would put the blame on you, Lindsey. After all, Leslie had been carving pumpkins at your lighthouse. She'd eaten your baked goods. I thought it was a brilliant stroke of irony, hanging her in that tree during that disgraceful ghost hunt. I never expected the body would be found so soon."

"You bloody villain!" Kennedy cried, excoriating him with her eyes. "I ran into her dead body . . . on a livestream feed!" She couldn't help herself. She kicked him in the shin. Unfortunately, due to his billowing robe, she kicked a bit wide of her mark.

"Enough!" he cried. "Give me the map, or I'll shoot you both!" I believed him. After all, I had seen the ghost lights.

"Give it to him," I told Kennedy. "It's not worth it." Besides, we didn't need it. Each one of us had taken a photo of the dog tag with our phones.

Kennedy knew this too. I watched as she removed the dog tag from her necklace. She wasn't about to remove her black protective crystal, and I didn't blame her. We would need a stroke of good luck to get out of this one.

Jordy took the dog tag. "It's on here?"

"It is. You have to figure out how to read it."

Apparently, he was up for the challenge. With a grunt, he crossed to the back deck. Once there, he threw the giant unicorn raft overboard. "That is your lifeline, ladies," he told us. "You have one minute to get yourselves on that raft."

Filling with relief, Kennedy and I raced to the back of the boat and climbed aboard the ridiculous unicorn raft. It would be a cold, wet ride, but anything was better than being on a boat with a madman. Besides, the fact that the unicorn head jutted above the waves would make it easier for us to spot a rescue craft. I prayed one would come soon.

I clung to that thought as I huddled beside Kennedy on the unicorn raft. This time we didn't have so much as a blanket for warmth. It was cold.

Jordy cut the rope and sent us adrift. He started the boat engine once again. And then the psycho shot our raft.

CHAPTER 43

The head of the unicorn had been shot. Kennedy and I both scrambled to grab it to stop the air from escaping as Jordy sped away into the fog. But the more we moved, the more air we were losing. The waves would overcome us.

"Lie down flat!" I told her as a wave crashed over the sides, filling the soft bottom of the raft with freezing lake water.

"It's cold!" she cried, shivering. Yet Ken valiantly fought her instincts to scramble.

The water was too cold. I knew that if the raft went down, we wouldn't last long. We were already freezing from our boat ride, but our anger had kept us from feeling it. Even worse was the betrayal. This had been Jordy's plan all along. He couldn't let us escape on the raft. We had seen his face; we knew what he had done. This was his way of dealing with us—giving us hope, then dashing it away. He was a devil. A stupid, greedy, flipping mad devil! As I wrangled the shot unicorn head, I twisted it hard, imagining it Jordy's neck. I tucked the wilted head and neck under my arm, pinning it hard against my body. I prayed it would slow the escaping air.

"Got it!" I told Kennedy as I joined her in the bottom of the raft. "We're going to be fine," I assured her as the freezing water drenched my clothes. I tried to smile, but Kennedy saw through me. She was crying.

"We're going to die!" she exclaimed with a violent sob. "We're going to die, Lindsey! In this bloody lake! How will they find us in this fog?" It was a good question, and one I was pondering as well. But I couldn't let Kennedy down. She was my best friend.

"We're not going to die, Ken."

"Don't bloody lie to me!" Her teeth were chattering as she held me in her wide-eyed, frightened gaze.

"I'm not lying," I told her, praying it was true. I tried to smile as I reasoned, "I have faith enough for the two of us, and you're wearing a crystal that's supposed to protect you. We're covered. Just in case, though," I added as tears and cold water tumbled down my face, "I . . . I want you to know that if . . . if I had a sister, I couldn't love her more than I do you. I love you, Ken."

"I lo . . . love you, too, Linds. More than any sister. And . . . I have . . . a sister!" We both smiled through a sob at that.

"We are not going to die," I said again. "But we should call out. We need to call for help!" I prayed that Rory was already on the water. He was our only hope. And if he was coming, he'd need to know where we were. I didn't know how he was going to manage that. But I knew that if he was on his way, he'd want me to make a racket. "We need them to hear us!"

Once we started our cries for help, we couldn't stop, because we were nearly underwater. Only the rim of the unicorn was keeping us afloat now. And we were freezing. I knew hypothermia was setting in, and if any more air escaped . . .

"Take off your shoes," I screamed.

"What?" she squawked.

"They'll weigh you down if we go in. We might need to tread water. Kick them off."

"Go in?" Horror seized her face. "They're Italian leather!"

"Nothing is more precious than your life, Ken. Kick them off." I did the same. My body was already numb. What little protection my shoes and socks provided me was negligible.

We were trying to scream, but our voices were nearly hoarse, and we were very close to treading water. My hope of a rescue was draining with every wisp of escaped air. Then, right after being drenched by yet another ice-cold wave, I heard a sound that gave me hope.

Welly was barking. My dog was on a boat! And that boat was getting closer.

"Hang on, Kennedy! They're coming!" I cried for all I was worth, knowing that the moment Rory realized we were missing he'd come to find us.

Just as the boat cleared the fog, Welly spotted us and jumped into the lake. Rory couldn't stop him. My powerful dog swam right for us, oblivious to the cold water and fog.

"Wellington!" I nearly sobbed as my dog greeted me in the water. It was a short greeting. Welly's instincts had kicked in. He wanted nothing more than to pull me to the boat. It was what he was bred to do, and there was no arguing with him. "It's going to be cold, Ken," I warned my friend, but to my horror, Kennedy wasn't responding. She was unconscious. Without thinking, I grabbed hold of her, placed her on her back, and wrapped my other hand in Welly's fur.

"Go, Welly!" I commanded. As Welly swam for the boat, I kicked free of the waterlogged raft. The next wave that swept over us sank it completely.

We didn't have far to go. The boat was in front of us. Rory, Dad, Tuck, and Teddy were all there, ready to pull us aboard.

"Kennedy's passed out!" I alerted them as Rory grabbed my arm. With seemingly little effort, he lifted me out of the water. Dad was already there with a blanket.

Tuck and Teddy had Kennedy out in a flash and immediately went to work, stripping off her wet clothing and wrapping her in warm blankets. As Dad held me, Rory pulled Wellington aboard before running to the wheelhouse. After a good shake, Welly sat at my feet, where he then lavished me with a series of frantic, welcoming licks. I believed it was his way of telling me he was happy to see me safely aboard. I gave him a big hug. With everyone safely on the boat, Rory then turned the bow of the craft around and took off at speed for the lighthouse.

"It was Jordy Tripp!" I told them, standing in the wheelhouse by the captain's chair.

"We know," Dad said. "It hit me when I was reading his twelfth novel. He used death cap mushrooms as the murder weapon. Everything clicked then. Rory happened to call us at that moment, too, alerting us of the break-in at Ellie and Company. He thought the murderer was Mark Whitcomb. He and Tuck were on their way out to the Adamses' house when I called you. The moment I heard you scream, I called Rory again. I didn't know what was going on, but I knew you were in trouble. Hearing that scream sent the fear of God in me, sweetheart." Dad was holding me tightly, afraid to let me go. I knew I was getting him wet, but I reveled in the warmth of his embrace.

"What about Jordy?" I asked Rory. "He's going to get away."

"Coast Guard's on it, babe," he informed me without missing a beat. "I called them the moment James called me. An ambulance is waiting for us the lighthouse. We also called Murdock. She and Officer Bain went out to the Adamses' house."

"Grant and Jordy had made a visit there last night, right after we left," Tuck added, sitting on the bench while holding Kennedy tightly against him. She was still unconscious but breathing. We were moving as fast as we could. I prayed we'd make it in time. "Murdock found Cali, Mark Whitcomb, and Grant Fairfield there," he told me. "They'd been tied up and poisoned by Jordy Tripp. Thank the good Lord that Murdock got to them in time."

Bless Sergeant Murdock.

"Lindsey!" Teddy took over for Dad in the hugging department. He then stepped back and explained. "I arrived at the bakery right before they did. That damn green light was on again, and Welly was throwing a fit when I got there. I then realized that all the lights were on in the bakery and the dough had been started, but you weren't there. That scared the devil out of me! I had no idea what was going on, but I knew it wasn't good. I called the cops. Tuck and Rory showed up a minute later. It was Welly who ran to the beach, barking all the way. That's when we saw all the tracks in the sand. We figured you'd been taken. By the way, congrats on finding the hidden treasure map. You can thank me later for the lesson in creative word graphs." He winked.

"Welly was going to swim all the way out to you," Rory added, stepping away from the wheel. Dad took over for him. A moment later, I was in Rory's arms, and this time I was being held so tightly that I could barely breathe. But I didn't mind. "You gave me the fright of my life, Lindsey Bakewell." His eyes teared up then, because he knew that if he'd been a minute later, Kennedy and I wouldn't be there. I held him back just as tightly.

"I knew you'd find me. I just knew it."

"I will always find you," he whispered in my ear. "But for the love of God, Lindsey, don't ever get into another one of my boats with a stranger again."

CHAPTER 44

"You should have seen the look on Tuck's face," I told Kennedy, sitting in the chair beside her hospital bed. Kennedy was at Memorial Hospital, being treated for hypothermia. They let me bring Trixie in to visit her, making me promise that I'd keep the pup from getting into trouble. She was hardly trouble. Trixie had curled up beside Kennedy in the bed, resting her head on Ken's leg. For some reason, the dog loved her. As for Kennedy, she'd given us all a good scare, no one more so than poor Tuck McAllister. "He was beside himself with worry," I continued. "The moment the boat hit sand at the lighthouse, he single-handedly ran you to the awaiting ambulance. It was so heroic."

"My sweet Westley," she said with a soft smile on her lips, referencing their Halloween couple's costume. She stroked Trixie's head. "I don't deserve that sweet boy," she admitted with a flash of guilt. "He should be with some young, apple-cheeked farm girl who'll make him fortifying suppers and fresh-baked apple pies. Instead, he puts up with me. My own mother had a hard time doing that." That made me smile.

"He puts up with you because he's either still super-infatuated with you, being an exotic beauty with a snarky attitude, or, Ken, he loves you." I thought she'd be happy to hear that, but her beautiful face clouded over with worry.

"I'm not sure that's healthy. I'm not sure I belong here."

"What do you mean, you don't belong here?" I studied her through narrowed eyes, thinking she'd possibly gotten hit on the head as well.

"You're thriving here. Everything you love is right here, Lindsey darling, including your hunky, Sir Hunts-a-Lot. I never imagined it, but he seems to suit you. Me, however? I'm not sure Beacon Harbor is the place for me. I really screwed up on that livestream ghost hunt, Linds. Other than my role at Ellie and Company, my professional life is in a quagmire. I recorded bumping into the dead body of a beloved teacher on a live video feed. I stole a valuable treasure map from this dear poodle's collar. And I nearly died! Add to that the fact that I'm a thirty-seven-year-old woman dating a twenty-nine-year-old man, and I'm bumming a room off my bestie. The truth is, I'm afraid to put down roots here. I'm afraid because I don't think I'm cut out for this life."

"What . . . are you saying?" I was trying to remain calm, even though my stomach was doing flip-flops. It ached. It was the ache of loss. I loved having Kennedy in Beacon Harbor with me. I wanted to beg her to stay—to point out how wrong she was—but being a good friend meant supporting your best friend's decisions, no matter how much it hurt to do so. Nearly two years ago, I had moved out of New York City to follow a dream of my own. I knew how hard that had been on Kennedy. I had the feeling it was going to be my turn now.

I watched as she took a sip of tea before resting on her pillows. "I've committed to spending the holidays with the Kapoors of London," she informed me, adding an ironic twist of her lips. Kennedy was going back to England to visit her family, something she'd been avoiding for a while. Nearly drowning in the freezing lake had shaken her to her core. I didn't blame her. I was shaken too.

"I might even take a drive to the Cotswolds to visit my gran," she added. "I miss her. She might be a bit batty, believing in the fairy folk and all, but Gran has a way of setting me on my feet." She then pulled out the black crystal she wore around her neck and held it out to me. "Speaking of batty. The apple doesn't fall far from the tree, I'm afraid."

I took the crystal and held it in my hand. It got me thinking. The young witchtok girl, Kylie Henderson, had admitted to thinking Kennedy was in danger. It was Kennedy, not her teacher, whom she was afraid for. Was it mere coincidence, or was there something to premonitions and seeing the future? I'd never know for sure, but visiting the psychic medium had been an interesting adventure. As for the crystal? If Kennedy believed it had mystical powers, so be it. To me it was just a rock. A pretty black rock.

"Well, if you're the apple you're referring to," I began, handing the crystal back to her, "I'd say you are very far from the tree. I don't blame you for wanting to go back to England for a while. You're going to break a heart, though, and I'm going to miss the heck out of you. But I also respect whatever decision you make. You know that."

"I do. This isn't good-bye, darling. This is me trying to figure it all out. I shall plague you with phone calls and video chats."

"I'm counting on it."

With a heavy heart, I picked up Trixie and left Kennedy's room. I then went to visit another patient at the hospital. Rory and Doc Riggles were already there.

"Cali," I said to the girl and placed the little poodle in her arms. She was delighted to see Trixie and gave the dog a hug. Cali, along with Mark Whitcomb and Grant Fairfield, who were in yet another room at the hospital, were all being treated for poisoning. Jordy Tripp, after tying them up, had forced them to drink a tea he had brewed that contained a hefty dose of the death cap mushroom powder.

Doc Riggles greeted me with a smile. "This case really tested me, my dear," he said. He was a kind man with a bald head, bushy white eyebrows, and intelligent brown eyes behind his wire glasses. After losing his wife to cancer a few years ago, he had started dating Betty. We liked to joke that they were Beacon Harbor's power couple. "We're just finishing up here. Since I was made familiar with this poison, I've been asked to consult on the treatment of dear Cali and the others. If the four of you hadn't put your heads together on this one"—he wiggled his finger at Rory and me to illustrate his point—"we might not be so lucky. But Cali is lucky. By the way, I told that very same thing to Sergeant Murdock. The sergeant bristled a bit, not liking the sound of that, but she had to admit that you two and Kennedy have a knack for solving crimes." He grinned before writing something in Cali's medical chart. When he was done, he hung the chart back on the foot of her bed.

"See you at the Beacon, my dears." Doc Riggles shook Rory's hand and gave me a hug before leaving the room.

As I sat beside Rory, Cali offered a wan smile. "Rory was just telling me that the map to the treasure . . . or more like the coordinates, really . . . will be returned to me. I'm so glad to hear that creep, Jordy Tripp, is behind bars."

"I honestly thought he was going to die." I looked at Rory and explained. "We saw the ghost lights. They came on when we were taken. For a while, I thought Kennedy and I were going to be the victims. But thanks to you, we're still here." Rory squeezed my hand at this.

"I'm not sure what the ghost lights mean," he remarked. "I don't think anyone can get inside the head of a ghost. But I think it's safe to say they don't always mean death, Lindsey. I'm beginning to believe Captain Willy is looking out for you."

"Who's Captain Willy?" Cali asked.

"The lighthouse ghost," Rory and I replied in unison, as if having a ghost around was normal. Poor Cali looked confused.

Rory wisely changed the subject. "Regarding the dog tag treasure map, Cali, you should probably know that Lindsey and I took a picture of it with our phones. We did that for safety reasons. We're sending the pictures to you and will wipe them off our phones. We weren't about to let that man, or anyone else, rob you of your family heritage. By the way, now that all this is coming to light, what are you planning to do about the shipwreck?"

Cali shrugged. "Truthfully, Mr. Campbell, I haven't thought that far yet. Mom believed the treasure was cursed. I think it is too. For me, it's not about the supposed treasure. I'd like to prove that the shipwreck exists."

"Even with the coordinates, it's going to be hard to find. Storms and shifting sand will have affected it."

"You know a lot about diving, I hear." She looked at Rory as she said this. "My mom told me someone was building out a dive shop and aquatic center in Beacon Harbor. She was so excited by that news. My parents loved scuba diving. They weren't treasure hunters, but I believe they were trying to find the fabled wreck of the *Eldorado*. They didn't have much luck. I would really like it if you and your dive shop would help me on this."

Rory couldn't have been more excited with the proposition. He grinned from ear to ear, and I couldn't have been happier for him. "By the way," he said, looking at her, "do you know the story of the *Eldorado*?" Cali shook her head. After learning of the shipwreck, I knew Rory wasn't going to sit still. While I had spent the last few days in bed, sipping hot tea and cuddling Welly and Trixie, he had done some poking around on the internet.

"I found some information," Rory told her. "It does suggest that the ship was carrying gold when it went down. In the late eighteen hundreds, a poor, young man named Donald McIver fell in love with a young woman from Muskegon, Michigan. This young lady was from a wealthy family, and her father refused to let his daughter marry a man without a penny to his name. Donald vowed to this young woman that he'd make a name for himself. He decided to make his fortune in the Alaskan gold rush. It was a risky venture at best, and yet Donald, against all the odds, decided to stay in the Klondike and stake his claim at a little creek named Eldorado."

Cali's face brightened. "That's where the name of the ship comes from."

"It is." Rory grinned. "And the story gets better. Donald started mining, and his claim on Eldorado Creek turned out to be one of the most lucrative claims in the entire Klondike gold rush. By eighteen ninety-nine, Donald had amassed a fortune. He had done what he'd set out to do, and he decided to sell his claim for a large sum of money. His wealth was spread around a bit in various investments, but a good deal of his gold was carted to Thunder Bay. There he purchased a ship. You already know what he named it."

"*Eldorado*," she whispered, hugging Trixie.

"Donald, now a millionaire, was ready to ask for his sweetheart's hand in marriage. Unfortunately, his incredible luck ran out on the Great Lakes."

"Oh," I said, placing a hand over my heart. "What a tragic tale of unrequited love." I could see that Cali was touched by it too.

"That man risked the November Witch for love," Cali said, using the term mariners did for the unpredictable and dangerous storms of November. "Maybe someday, Mr. Campbell, we might be able to tell the rest of the story."

Rory smiled at the young lady. "I would like that very much."

CHAPTER 45

"Lindsey! Rory!" Brett Bloom exclaimed the moment we came through my kitchen door. Welly and Trixie pushed their way through, greeting our friends with tail-wagging delight. Brett, looking a bit out of his element standing in my kitchen, was wearing an apron. Teddy, working intently over a large, steaming pot on my stove, was wearing one too. The place smelled heavenly. "Have you ever experienced what we in the ghost-hunting community call the 'Glorious Feast'?" This was said with a mischievous grin.

"Also known as Teddy's famous spaghetti and meatballs," Jessie, Teddy's wife, informed us, popping into the kitchen with a grin. She and Ghost Guy Mike were setting the dining room table for a crowd.

"Not yet, but I'm excited!" I told them sincerely. Rory, echoing my enthusiasm, held up four loaves of Italian bread.

"Good man, Campbell." Teddy grinned at him

from the stove. "You got my bread. Can't have the Glorious Feast without garlic bread."

"Lindsey and I picked it up on our way home from the hospital. Before you ask, everyone's doing fine." This was true, but Rory and I exchanged a look nonetheless. I had told him about Kennedy and her decision to leave Beacon Harbor on the drive home, but there was no need to mention any of that at our good-bye feast for the Ghost Guys. Tonight was a celebration, and celebrate we would.

"Thank you all again for getting here early and helping with this farewell dinner. As promised, I have desserts," I said. "I have two whole pumpkin caramel cheesecakes, along with plenty of pumpkin-sugar cookies for those striving for a proper sugar coma. My parents are bringing a Caesar salad; Betty and Doc are bringing the wine, and Sergeant Murdock and her man, Brian, are bringing themselves. I insisted."

"Lindsey's just trying to score brownie points with the sergeant." Teddy turned from the stove with a teasing grin. "And speaking of cops, will Tuck be joining us this evening?"

Rory remained quiet. I offered, "He's having dinner at the hospital with Kennedy."

"Figured," Teddy said. "That boy won't leave her side for anything, including the Glorious Feast. He's like a love-struck puppy, that one."

"Lucky girl," Jessie teased, casting her husband a wink.

It was, indeed, a glorious feast. The only thing better than Teddy's delicious spaghetti and meatballs was the company. There was something truly special about sharing a great meal with old friends and new. Halloween had been traumatizing for us all, and yet with the help of family and friends, we had made it through to the other side, although not without paying a price. The loss of a beloved teacher would weigh heavily on the hearts of the community for a long time to come. Kennedy's shocking news was more personal, although it was a loss I would be sharing with Tuck. I thought of the unlikely couple and said a silent prayer for them both. They were each so dear to me. But we would all get through this, too, in time. Embracing the fact that a feast was meant to be enjoyed in the moment, I pushed aside all my worries and laughed, talked, and ate more than I should have.

It wasn't until the coffee had been poured and the pumpkin cheesecake was being served (along with a platter of pumpkin-sugar cookies!) that Sergeant Murdock, dressed in casual fall clothing, addressed me.

"Delicious! Just delicious. But I must say, Bakewell, that you and Kapoor really gave us a good scare this time. I hate to admit this, but the thought of you two out in that freezing cold lake, treading water for your lives, really got to me. You're a newcomer to this village, but if anything were to happen to you, we'd all suffer. Your baked goods and coffee are what get me up in the morning. I look forward to coming to this lighthouse, seeing you and your hardworking staff behind the counter, and hearing the latest gossip circulating in the village. It's become part of my routine, and I'd hate to have it disrupted. What I'm trying to say is that you've created a real gem here, Bakewell. I know you have a propensity for courting trouble, but if and when trouble should ever come calling again, I must insist that you contact the Beacon Harbor Police immediately. Got that? No sniffing around, no sleuthing on your own, and certainly don't bring Kapoor and Campbell into it. Just call me. Got that? Good, now, pass me some of that heavenly cheesecake!"

"I wholeheartedly agree," Mom said, squeezing my hand. Mom was helping me serve the coffee and cheesecake. Although Mom was always up for a little sleuthing, as well, both my parents had been beside themselves with worry when Kennedy and I had been kidnapped by Jordy Tripp and left in the lake to drown.

"I heard you talked with Jordy Tripp." Rory turned to the sergeant just as she took a bite of her cheesecake. Murdock nodded, swallowed, then set down her fork.

"As you know, Campbell, the Coast Guard caught him just beyond the Manitou Islands before returning your boat. I had a chance to interview him before they took him away. Although at first look, Tripp comes across as rather normal, once you get him talking about his career, a sort of manic desperation coupled with an incredible ego takes hold of him. I found it an insufferable combination. More importantly, Tripp also failed to understand that any shipwreck found in these waters wouldn't belong to him. It would belong to the state. Although, as you well know, Campbell, any person is free to look for a wreck or artifacts on the lake bed, but the moment anything is found, it must be reported. Then there are a series of permits required. Jordy was going to skip all that, take the gold, and write a blockbuster book about his discovery. All those years behind a keyboard writing fiction obviously skewed his sense of reality. Authors!" she proclaimed with an eye roll. "Jordy Tripp is insane."

Everyone agreed. Demented as Jordy Tripp was, he wasn't going to ruin dessert for us.

"We have some news as well." Brett Bloom offered a grin before refilling his coffee. It was nine o'clock at night. Obviously drinking coffee so late was part of the ghosthunter's code. How else would one stay awake until dawn? The Ghost Guy took a sip before addressing me.

"This, Lindsey, is what we call *the wrap-up* in our business," he told me with a professional tone in his voice. "After conducting a thorough investigation of your lighthouse . . . on Halloween night . . . and after going through all the footage more times than we cared to, we not only helped to catch a murderer, but we've also come to a conclusion regarding our investigation of this property. Lindsey Bakewell, we, the Ghost Guys, would like to inform you that your lighthouse is not only extraordinary, but it is also most definitely haunted."

Although some homeowners would obviously have been upset by this news, I couldn't help it. I laughed.

Our guests had all left, and Welly and Trixie had been fed, walked, and were sleeping peacefully by the fireplace in the parlor. It was the perfect time for Rory and me to escape to our favorite place in the lightroom for a quiet moment. After the Halloween we'd had, we needed it.

We'd been sitting side by side in the cushioned

wicker chairs, holding hands while staring out across the dark lake, when Rory turned to me.

"We haven't had much time to talk about it, but are you going to be okay? You know, with Kennedy leaving?"

It was sweet of him to ask. I gave his hand a gentle squeeze. "I'm going to be just fine. I have you. But I am worried about Tuck."

Rory kept his eyes focused on the lake as he shrugged. "He'll be fine. Tuck's young, attractive, and let's face it, he can do better. A lot better."

"*WHAT*?" I turned to him with a look of incredulity. "What do you mean by '*he can do better*'? We're talking about *Kennedy*!"

"Right," he muttered, as if shocked by my sudden outburst. "What I meant to say was, he's young. He shouldn't be tied down to a demanding older woman with a handful of screws loose. He should be with somebody younger, nicer. For instance, he should be with someone without an addiction to Instagram." As Rory talked, he finally noticed the look on my face. "What? Am I wrong?"

"Kennedy's *my* age, or did you forget? You're basically saying that I'm an old lady."

"No. No, I mean, *you're not young* . . . but you're not old either. You're just—"

I held up my hand. "You should probably stop talking."

"Right. Right, but let me just say one more thing." He offered a conciliatory smile. "What I was going to say was that you are just perfect. To me."

And with those few words, he entirely redeemed himself.

We had been kissing for only a few moments when the soft Edison lights started flickering.

Rory looked up with a grimace. "I think the captain is trying to tell us to take it downstairs."

"You're undoubtedly correct."

As Rory headed down the circular stairs, I lingered a bit longer in the lightroom.

"Thank you, Captain Willy," I whispered to the room at large. "Thank you for helping my friends and me. I'm truly sorry for the disruption, and the smudging." At this last word, I sheepishly glanced at the ceiling. "But I'm glad you stayed," I told him sincerely. "The Beacon Point Lighthouse is your home too."

As if in answer, the lights flickered again. I turned them off and ran down the stairs after Rory.

RECIPES FROM MURDER AT
THE PUMPKIN PAGEANT

Nothing quite says fall (including Halloween!) like the taste of spiced pumpkin. I hope you're in the mood for some delectable pumpkin treats, because the Beacon Bakeshop has got you covered. Here are some of Lindsey Bakewell's favorite fall recipes to try at home. Your friends and family will be happy that you did!

Easy Pumpkin-Spiced Latte

Prep time: 5 minutes. Cook time: 2 minutes. Makes one latte.

Ingredients:

1 cup milk (any type of milk you prefer is fine)
2 tablespoons pumpkin purée
4 teaspoons pure maple syrup (may add more for taste)
½ teaspoon vanilla extract
½ teaspoon pumpkin pie spice (plus more for sprinkling)
Pinch sea salt
¼ cup espresso or strong brewed coffee
Whipped cream, sweetened, for garnish

Directions:

In a microwave-safe bowl, combine the milk, pumpkin purée, maple syrup, vanilla extract, pumpkin pie spice, and the pinch of sea salt. Cover with plastic wrap and vent by cutting a small hole in the top. Microwave on high for two minutes or until the mixture is hot. Whisk vigorously until foamy. If using an immersion blender, which works great, use with caution due to the hot temperature of the milk.

Add the shot of espresso to the coffee mug, then pour the hot, foamy latte mixture on top. Garnish with a dollop of whipped cream and a sprinkle of pumpkin pie spice. Enjoy!

Pumpkin-Pie Martini

Prep time: 5 minutes. Makes 1 martini.

Equipment:
  Cocktail shaker
  Martini glass

Ingredients:
2 ounces vodka
1 ounce spiced rum
½ ounce half-and-half
2 tablespoons pumpkin purée
1 ounce pure maple syrup
¼ teaspoon vanilla extract
¼ teaspoon pumpkin pie spice
4 ice cubes

Rim of glass:
Maple syrup
Crushed gingersnap cookies

Garnish:
Sweetened whipped cream, cinnamon

Directions:
   In a food processor or zip-lock bag, crush ginger-snap cookies until they resemble fine crumbs. Place the crumbs on a small plate. Drizzle maple syrup on another small plate. Dip rim of glass in the maple syrup, then roll in the ginger crumbs until rim of glass is covered. Set aside.

In a cocktail shaker, combine the cocktail ingredients and the ice cubes. Shake vigorously until shaker is cold to the touch. Strain into prepared martini glass and garnish with a dollop of whipped cream and a sprinkle of cinnamon. Enjoy!

Pumpkin Scones with Maple Glaze

Prep time: 15 minutes. Bake time: 20–25 minutes. Makes 8 servings.

Ingredients:
2 cups all-purpose flour, plus more for dusting
1 tablespoon baking powder
2 teaspoons ground cinnamon
1 teaspoon pumpkin pie spice
½ teaspoon salt
½ cup (one stick) cold butter, cubed
½ cup brown sugar
½ cup pumpkin purée
1 large egg
1 teaspoon vanilla extract
⅓ cup heavy cream
½ cup chopped pecans (optional)

Maple glaze:
1 cup powdered sugar
2 tablespoons heavy cream
1 teaspoon maple extract

Directions:
Preheat oven to 350°F. Line a baking sheet with parchment paper and set aside. In a large bowl, mix the flour, baking powder, cinnamon, pumpkin pie spice, and salt. Using a pastry blender or a fork, cut in the cold butter until small pea-sized crumbs form.

In a smaller bowl, whisk together the brown sugar, pumpkin purée, egg, vanilla extract, and heavy cream. Pour the wet ingredients over the dry ingredients and mix until the dough is moist, adding pecans if desired. (If the dough is too sticky, add more flour one tablespoon at a time.)

Transfer dough to a lightly floured work surface. Shape the dough into a 9-inch circle that is approximately 1-inch thick. Using a floured knife, cut the dough into 8 even pieces. Transfer the scones to the prepared baking sheet, spacing them 2 inches apart. Cook for 20–25 minutes or until done. Scones should be crispy on the outside and soft in the middle. Remove to a cooling rack.

In a small bowl, whisk the glaze ingredients together. Once the scones have cooled, top each scone with the maple glaze. Let the glaze set, then enjoy!

Pumpkin Chocolate-Chip Muffins

Prep time: 15 minutes. Bake time: 20–25 minutes. Makes 12 regular-size muffins.

Ingredients:

1⅔ cup all-purpose flour
1 cup granulated sugar, and more for sprinkling
1 tablespoon pumpkin pie spice
1 teaspoon baking soda
¼ teaspoon baking powder
¼ teaspoon salt
1 cup pumpkin purée
2 large eggs
½ cup (1 stick) butter, melted and cooled
1 cup semi-sweet chocolate chips

Directions:

Heat oven to 350°F. Grease or line muffin pan. In a large mixing bowl, combine flour, sugar, pumpkin pie spice, baking soda, baking powder, and salt. In a smaller bowl, add pumpkin purée, eggs, and melted butter. Whisk until blended. Stir the chocolate chips into the wet ingredients. Pour the wet ingredients over the dry ingredients and gently fold in with a rubber spatula just until all the batter is combined. Do not overmix.

Place about ¼ cup of batter in each muffin cup. Sprinkle a little sugar on the top of each one, then bake in preheated oven for 20–25 minutes, or until done. Cool and serve.

Savory Roast Chicken and Vegetables

Prep time: 20 minutes. Cook time: 1 hour, 30 minutes. Serves 6.

Hint: I always double this recipe for hearty eaters and/or leftovers!

Ingredients:

1 (5–6 pound) roasting chicken
3 tablespoons of butter, melted and divided
Kosher salt
Black pepper
1 clove garlic, cut in half lengthwise
5 sprigs or more fresh sage (dry sage will do in a
    pinch)
5 sprigs or more fresh thyme (dry thyme will do in
    a pinch)
1 lemon, cut in half
1 large yellow onion, cut in thick wedges
5 carrots, peeled and cut into 2-inch chunks
1 pound fingerling or small red potatoes, washed
Olive oil

Directions:

Preheat oven to 425°F. Clean chicken and remove giblets. Wash chicken inside and out and pat dry with paper towel. Drizzle a tablespoon of melted butter inside the chicken cavity. Liberally salt and pepper the inside of the chicken. Place the lemon, garlic, and the sprigs of both herbs inside the chicken as well. Brush the outside of the chicken with the rest of the melted butter. Liberally sprinkle with salt, pepper, and sage. Tie the chicken legs together with kitchen twine.

Place the onion, carrots, and potatoes in the bottom of a large roasting pan. Sprinkle with olive oil, toss to coat, then add salt and pepper to taste. Place prepared chicken in the middle of the roasting pan and spread the vegetables around the chicken. Roast the chicken for 1½ hours or until the juices run clear when you cut between the leg and the thigh. The internal temperature of the chicken should be 165°. Remove the chicken and vegetables to a large platter and cover with tinfoil. Let chicken rest for 15 minutes before cutting. Serve with vegetables and Savory Apple Stuffing.

Savory Apple Stuffing

Prep time: 20 minutes. Cook time: 30 minutes. Makes 8 servings.

Ingredients:
1 loaf white or wheat bread, cut into 1-inch bread cubes, about 12–16 cups
¼ cup butter
1 cup onion, diced
1 cup celery, diced
1 cup tart apple (Granny Smith or your favorite variety), peeled, cored, and diced
1 tablespoon dried parsley
1 teaspoon poultry seasoning
1 teaspoon kosher salt (or more to taste)
½ teaspoon black pepper
1 cup chicken stock

Directions:
Preheat oven to 350°F. Butter the bottom and sides of a large baking dish.

Put the cubed bread in a large bowl and set aside. In a large sauté pan, melt the butter, then add the onion, celery, apple, parsley, poultry seasoning, salt, and pepper. Sauté until the vegetables and apple are soft, about 10 minutes. Pour the warm vegetable mixture over the bread cubes and toss to mix. Drizzle with the chicken stock until moist. Place stuffing in the buttered baking dish and bake for 30–40 minutes, until bread cubes on top are crispy. Serve warm.

Delicious Pumpkin Cheesecake

Prep time: 15 minutes. Bake time: 1 hour, 15 minutes. Serves 10 to 12.

Equipment:
   10-inch springform pan
   Aluminum foil
   Roasting pan for water bath

Ingredients:

For the crust:
¾ cup graham cracker crumbs
¾ cup gingersnap cookie crumbs
½ cup (one stick) butter, melted

For the filling:
4 8-oz. packages cream cheese, softened
1¼ cup sugar
4 eggs
2 tablespoons vanilla extract
1 teaspoon grated lemon peel (lemon zest)
1 15-oz. can pumpkin purée
¼ cup heavy cream
1½ teaspoon ground cinnamon
1 teaspoon ground nutmeg
½ teaspoon ground ginger

Garnish:
Your favorite store-bought caramel sauce, warmed
1 cup toasted pecans, roughly chopped
Sweetened whipped cream

Directions:

Preheat oven to 350°F. Line bottom of springform pan with parchment and spray the sides with cooking spray.

In a large bowl, mix graham cracker crumbs, gingersnap crumbs, and butter together. Press in bottom of prepared springform pan.

In bowl of an electric mixer, beat cream cheese on high until fluffy. Beat in sugar, eggs, and vanilla. Add the lemon peel, pumpkin purée, cream, and spices. Mix well and pour on top of the crust in the springform pan. Double-wrap the outside of the pan in aluminum foil, making sure the bottom of the pan is covered. Place the springform pan in large roasting pan or baking dish and pour enough boiling water into the pan to reach halfway up the side of the springform pan. Place in oven and bake until cheesecake is done, about 1 hour, 20 minutes, or until cheesecake is only slightly jiggly in the center. Remove from heat and cool completely. Place in refrigerator for at least 4 hours or overnight.

Hint: It's always best to make any cheesecake the day before serving it.

To serve, garnish with a layer of warm caramel sauce, chopped pecans, and a dollop of whipped cream. Enjoy!

Fabulous Frosted Pumpkin-Sugar Cookies

Prep time: 10 minutes. Bake time: 10–12 minutes a batch. Makes 3 dozen cookies.

Ingredients:

For the cookies:
2¼ cup all-purpose flour
1 teaspoon baking soda
1 teaspoon pumpkin pie spice
½ teaspoon kosher salt
1 cup (2 sticks) butter, softened
1¼ cup granulated sugar, plus more for rolling
½ cup pumpkin purée
1 large egg
2 teaspoons vanilla extract

For the frosting:
6 tablespoons butter, softened
4 cups powdered sugar
3 or more tablespoons whole milk
1 teaspoon vanilla extract
2 teaspoons ground cinnamon

Directions:
Preheat oven to 350°F. Line two baking sheets with parchment paper.

In a medium bowl, combine flour, baking soda, pumpkin pie spice, and salt. Set aside.

In bowl of electric mixer, beat butter until fluffy.

Add sugar, pumpkin purée, egg, and vanilla extract. Add dry ingredients and stir until combined.

Place half cup of sugar in a small dish. Form a tablespoon of cookie dough into a round ball, then roll in sugar. Place cookie on baking sheet, spacing each cookie 2 inches apart. Bake cookies for 10–12 minutes or until lightly golden in color. Cool, then remove cookies to a cooling rack.

To make the frosting, beat the softened butter until fluffy. Gradually add the powdered sugar, milk, vanilla extract, and cinnamon. Beat until frosting is a nice spreading consistency. Spread frosting on top of each cookie. Enjoy!